Friends Don't

BOOKS BY LEAH DOBRINSKA

The Mapleton Novels
Love at On Deck Café
Good To Be Home
Together With You
Choosing Love

The Larkspur Library Mysteries
Death Checked Out
Mayhem In Circulation

The Fall In Love Series
Friends Don't

Friends Don't

LEAH DOBRINSKA

1

FALL
IN
LOVE
SERIES

Editing: Jenn Lockwood

Cover Design: Melody Jeffries

Library of Congress Control Number: 2023909239

ISBN: 978-1-7374483-8-9 (paperback) | 978-1-7374483-9-6 (ebook)

For Nick.

1

THe Downer

Poppy

It's my first day in a new town, and I'm naked.

I blink my eyes firmly shut before batting them back open and glancing around, hoping this is a dream. But I'm on the same rickety deck behind my half of the duplex I just moved into. The air conditioning unit I came outside to check is still coughing and wheezing as if it were limping to the end of a marathon with minimal training. It's rattling, and the entire unit is shaking—which, subsequently, is causing my entire bathroom to vibrate, hence the naked check-up.

In other news, the birds are chirping. The sun is blinding. I can faintly hear the trickle of the creek that runs along the lot line of the backyard.

So no, I'm not dreaming.

I'm nightmaring in real life.

I should clarify that the only bright spot in my current circumstances—and I'm only seeing it because I'm mentally squinting really, really hard and cocking my head to one side to make it out—is that I'm not actually naked. Well, not *fully* naked.

I'm in a towel.

A skimpy, threadbare towel that's barely covering my unmentionable regions and might be a bit see-through.

Like I said, I'm really working to see the silver lining here—or in the case of my towel, the lack of any lining whatsoever.

I blow out a breath, trying to quell the sweat that's beading on every inch of my body. My shower was basically pointless at this point, and I wanted to look my best before I saw Holland off. It's not even eight a.m. and already the day is a scorcher. I thought I was leaving these sorts of heat indexes behind when I moved away from Florida, but apparently Cashmere Cove, Wisconsin didn't get the memo.

That, or the little peninsula town I now call home is immune to the climate norms of this part of the country.

Anyway, that's not the point. I've got bigger fish to fry. I'm naked.

And afraid.

I roll my eyes. Sometimes my inner monologue is ridiculous. I'm not *afraid* afraid—at least not yet. But this situation has the potential to spiral into full-fledged terrifying in a fast hurry, so I need to think.

Good thing problem-solving mode is my thing. I can figure this out.

Let's assess the facts.

One. The back door to my duplex seems to have locked automatically when it snapped shut behind me.

Two. I'm in my mostly private backyard. There's a wooden wall that goes up to my chin separating my half of the deck from my neighbor's.

Three. My sister is inside the duplex.

Four. I've got about thirty minutes before Holland gets here, which means I've got thirty minutes to get ready and make myself into something that he'll miss while he's out on tour.

The sassy side of my brain says I should stay like this, walk around to the front of the duplex, and wait for him on the porch in the towel. Should do the trick right quick.

The focused part of my brain just punched the sassy part of my brain in the face.

Holland and I do *not* have that type of a relationship—not yet, anyway. We've only been dating for two months.

A queasy feeling wells up in my stomach at the thought of my circumstances. And I'm not talking about my half-naked-and-locked-out predicament.

No. Every time I remember that I moved across the country to the hometown of a guy who I've been dating for less time than it takes Starbucks to cycle through a seasonal drink menu, I feel a little sick.

I blink again and go through my mental spiel. I didn't move *just* for Holland. Sure, the fact that this is his home base and I'll have the chance to see him when he's off tour is a bonus. His roots here are a major perk. They're the reason I was able to land my dream job.

That's my main motivation—the job I was offered and gladly accepted.

There is nothing wrong with moving for an amazing career opportunity.

There, see. I'm a problem solver. I talked myself down from the metaphorical ledge like a boss.

If only I could mentally make myself into a locksmith.

I tug on my aforementioned towel, wedging the flimsy material firmly underneath one arm and clamping my opposite arm across my chest. When I survive this, I'm going to purchase plush linens. This'll be the last go-round for this towel.

The final thread.

Literally.

I roll my eyes at myself. "Focus, Poppy."

Glancing over my shoulder, I confirm that the other half of the duplex is quiet. No signs of life. Maybe the person who lives there isn't home. Or maybe he or she isn't awake. Either way, I'm counting my lucky stars. But I need to work fast. Circumstances could change in a second. Best to stay on my toes.

I glance down at my bare feet and cringe at the layer of grime coating them. The deck has seen better days. There appears to be some sort of algae or fungi coating the worn planks, and now it's coating the soles of my feet.

Never mind that. I've never been one to complain about getting my hands dirty—or feet, as it were. I need to focus on what's in front of me. Namely, this self-locking door.

I jiggle the handle, and it turns. *Thank goodness.* My heart rises in my chest. I was panicking prematurely. I push against the door, expecting it to open, but instead, I get a bruised shoulder, and the resounding thud from my contact sends some birds squawking.

Then again, maybe the panicking was warranted.

But wait a minute. If the handle turns, then the door isn't locked. It's...stuck?

Stuck closed.

I grit my teeth. I wish I could say I'm surprised, but honestly, since last night when my sister, Rose, and I got to this place Holland set up for us, I've been having minor heart palpitations about the state of things. Sure, we're getting to stay here for a steal. Two hundred bucks a month for rent? That's unheard of. For that price, I can overlook almost anything. And I'm going to have to.

There's a slow drip from the kitchen sink. The wallpaper in the bathroom has seen better days. Rose stepped through one of the front porch steps. We've already been over the air conditioner situation and the fungi deck. And now this. Some sort of trick door.

I prefer my tricks on Halloween and only Halloween, *thankyouverymuch.*

Holland warned me the place was a fixer-upper, but I still didn't expect it to be such a *downer*. That's what Rose and I have taken to calling our humble abode.

The Downer.

I think it has some gravitas, yeah?

We're used to making the best of things, so it'll be fine. Everything will be fine. I just need to get back inside.

I ram myself into the door again. "Come on. Come on. Open!"

It's not listening to my whispered pleas. It's not budging. I'm still sweating, and my half-wet, half-dry hair is plastered to my forehead and my bare back. Time is dwindling as the front-porch-in-a-towel rendezvous becomes less of a sassy, bad idea and more of a reality.

"Rose," I hiss, pressing my full weight into the door and trying to get my sister's attention. She was sound asleep while I was showering, and she doesn't rise before the hour of ten, so I'm not holding out much hope here, but I've got to at least try to wake her up.

"Rose. Open the door."

I'm walking a fine line here. I want to get Rose to wake up, but I certainly do not want to draw the attention of my new neighbor. Can you imagine what kind of first impression *that* would make?

"Rose. Can you hear me?" I pitch my voice a little higher. I'm like a mom in the library who is trying to scold her kids but also trying not to make a scene. I'm getting screechy and clearly don't have the mom cred required to pull this off. I've never been a mom...just a pseudo-mom, so I guess that tracks.

"I'm naked out here, Rosie. I could use a hand. The door is stuck."

I start kicking the base of it at this point because nothing else is working. My algae-covered toes are going to pay for this, but what's my other option? I know for a fact the front door is locked. I triple-checked it last night before I went to bed. Part of my pseudo-mom duties.

"Rose, if you *are* awake and you're hearing this and not rescuing me, I swear on our last name that I will—"

The sound of a clearing throat behind me stops me mid-threat.

I freeze, but not before landing one last firm kick to the bottom of the door. The shock of the impact reverberates up my spine, and I wince, my grip on the towel slipping.

I frantically use both hands to claw at the top of the measly piece of cotton that's the only thing standing between me and this stranger.

I peek over my shoulder to find a man standing on the opposite side of the privacy wall separating my deck from my neighbor's. He's tall enough that I can see his shoulders, neck, and head. He's got a five o'clock shadow of stubble lining a hard-edged jaw. His eyes are shielded by a baseball cap, so I can't tell where he's looking, and that's almost worse because I can't defend his gaze.

I chronicle my options in a millisecond. Either I stand here with my back to him, not entirely sure how much of my rear end is covered. Or I turn and give him a full-frontal view of me in my towel, but at least I know what I'm working with.

I always like to know what I'm working with.

"Oh, hello," I say, spinning to face him. My face feels like the surface of the sun, but my grip on the towel doesn't waver. I beam my best smile in my neighbor's direction and refuse to shrink back.

That's one of the lessons Gram instilled in me—never cower. She always used to say that no one would believe in me unless I believed in myself.

So, I'm going to fake like I'm perfectly unperturbed. Standing here with my lady bits nearly hanging out and a door that should work but doesn't? Water off a duck's back. Water off *my* back. It's all evaporated, anyway—I'm sure of it. I am a picture of nonchalance and grace.

Ironically, it's in this moment that Gram's other bit of wisdom flies straight to mind. That is, never leave the house in an ugly pair of underwear. She said it helped with confidence. She would also give wild examples of why nice undergarments were essential. *What if you croak?* Gram would ask. *You want someone at the morgue undressing you and seeing ugly panties? No, you don't!* Or she would go on when she was on a roll. *What if you meet someone? You never know when you want to be dressed to impress.*

I don't know what kind of social calendar Gram thought I was keeping while she was still alive, but fancy underpants have never been my priority.

Present circumstances have me thinking that maybe I should have taken her advice to heart. Honestly, at this point, I wouldn't be picky. I'd take underwear of any variety—fancy, ratty, clean, dirty, *granny*. This woman just wants some clothing!

I straighten, and the towel slips a fraction of an inch. I gulp and press it more firmly into place, and with it, my perma-smile. "I'm your new neighbor—well, one of them. My sister sleeps like the dead. I've been trying to get her attention." I gesture to the door with my non-towel-clenching hand. "I seem to have locked myself out, though I never locked the door. It's the darndest thing."

All this time I'm babbling, the stranger next door is standing there. He hasn't said a word, hasn't moved a muscle. I don't know if he's blinking because, again, I can't see his eyes. It's like he's a statue. Maybe he is. That would be a relief of epic proportions.

"I'm so sorry if I woke you up. I only wanted to check the air conditioning unit. It seems like it's about to take off on me." I chuckle, but my laughter sounds hollow in my ear. Let's all hope I don't have to cross paths with this guy around town too often. It's bad enough I have to live with the knowledge that he's going to be right next door. We share a wall, for heaven's sake. The mortification is going to follow me around like a tail, and you better believe it'll be between my legs for the foreseeable future. I may be channeling Gram right now, but my fake confidence is already doing a walk of shame.

"Anyway, I'll let you go. I'm sure my sister is almost up and can help me out of this conundrum." I pound on the door with my full fist for effect.

Statue man clears his throat again.

It's *alive*, my sassy brain says in my best Frankenstein voice.

Good to know near nakedness and supreme humiliation doesn't stop my mind from making its cultural references.

"May I?" He motions toward the door, and I glance at it—and at him—confused.

"Oh!" I realize he's asking for permission to join me on my side of the deck to try to help me. "Of course. Be my guest."

Be my guest? Who am I? Lumiere the candlestick? I do feel a bit like I'm melting, so maybe?

He turns and skirts the length of the privacy wall, walking out into the grass that our backyards share and then back alongside the wall toward me. He's bigger up close. His shoulders are broad underneath a white V-neck shirt. He's wearing worn blue jeans that are so faded they nearly match the white of his shirt. His hat is black with the letters M-E across the front in white-threaded script.

I've changed my mind, and I'm thankful for his hat. I don't want to see what his eyes are doing. Is he judging me? Is he laughing at me? Is he disgusted with my all-too-on-display body? Worse, is he attracted to me?

I debate the merits of announcing that I have a boyfriend, but I stop short. Chances are he's not looking at me greedily. Hungrily. That sort of things only happens in romance novels, and let's face it, this is the worst meet-cute in the history of meet-cutes.

I'm not cute right now, nor am I looking for a man. Because I have Holland, and this guy is...who knows what he is. Thank goodness I have a filter, because had I blurted out something that would have made it sound like I thought he was coming on to me only to have him shut me down, my humiliation levels would have sailed straight off the charts. As it is, I'm wishing my towel would magically turn into a turtle shell that I could tuck into.

My neighbor smells like spearmint, and I take a step back to give him full access to the door. His hand, which is twice the size of mine, wraps around the door handle. He pulls up, then out, while at the same time angling his shoulder into the center of the door. It springs open, and I'm so relieved I could hug him.

But I'm not going to do that because I'm still in a towel, and I don't know this man at all.

"Thank you so much," I rush to say, blowing past him in my hurry to get inside and clothed. "You're a life saver. I'll be on my way. I'm sure I'll see you around." I say the last words as I'm shutting the door behind myself. When it clicks shut, I sink down to the ground, letting the towel pool around me.

Rose chooses that very moment to walk out of her bedroom. Her hair is mussed, and she's yawning, but when she spots me, she freezes comically, holds up her hand to block the sight of me, and pretends to fall against the wall in horror. "My eyes. My EYES!"

"That's enough out of you." I hoist myself up and hurry to my room. I've got a boyfriend to send off and a new town to charm.

I better find myself some nice underwear.

2
A Disagreeable Agreement

Mack

Leave it to me to stumble upon my brother's new girlfriend half naked.

In my defense, she'd been making a racket to end all rackets, and I was afraid something might have been seriously wrong.

Turned out nothing was wrong...except for, you know, the half-naked woman walking around in my backyard.

I guess some people might not consider that wrong.

But contrary to what most of this town believes, I'm a gentleman.

Truthfully, I felt sort of bad. Her predicament was my fault. I own the duplex. I'm well aware of all the...*quirks* of the property. Frankly, Poppy's side is nowhere near ready to be lived in. That didn't stop Holland from offering it up for her and her sister to use—which, let's be clear, is *totally* like Holland. Things just work out for him, so he expects things to work out for other people. Newsflash, little bro, it's going to take more than a positive attitude to make that half of the house livable.

I tried to warn him, but he insisted they would be fine there. Said they were happy to have a place to live. Said Poppy was the type of woman who made the best of things.

Let's hope her resume includes making the best of leaks in the roof, because I can't guarantee that our next summer storm won't end up happening *in* her kitchen.

I glance at Holland and Poppy from where I'm leaning against my work truck, waiting for them to say their goodbyes. Holland is dressed in joggers and a white V-neck t-shirt. He's got his sunglasses perched on top of his head. He looks like the superstar that I'm pretty sure he's about to become.

Poppy has the total girl-next-door look going on. Her feet are bare. She's wearing cut-off jean shorts and a flowy floral top that shows about an inch of skin above her waistline. Her dark-brown hair is tied up in a messy knot on the top of her head, and her skin is all dewy in the morning sun.

Either that, or she's still sweating from her earlier battle with the back door.

I know I am.

The two of them are lingering, and I've been trying not to eavesdrop, but we need to get this show on the road. I've got to get Holland to the airport and then get myself back to the work site to oversee my apprentice electrician and make sure he doesn't do anything stupid that'll set back the entire build.

Here we go. Movement.

I stand up straighter as Holland and Poppy embrace in what appears to be a tight hug. Now he's leaning away, taking her hands. I can tell she's giving them a squeeze. She's nodding. If I had to guess, this is the part where she's assuring him that she'll be okay while he's gone. He's going in for the kiss.

I look away.

Just like I'm not trying to see Holland's girl naked, I also don't need to see them making out.

I refuse to acknowledge the slight twinge in my chest. How would I define it? A prickle? Of what? Jealousy? Maybe. Only because it would be nice to have a partner...someone who was sad to see me go and anxious to welcome me home. I'm not sure that's in the cards for me. Not since Tricia.

I slide into the driver's seat and wait, drumming my thumb against the steering wheel. I don't put the key in the ignition because I don't want to rush the happy couple. I'm considerate like that.

Holland is only another minute. As far as goodbye kisses go, that one must have been pretty tame. I side-eye Holland and wonder if he realizes how good he's got it. Not that I approve of this whole situation. I mean, he asked a woman to move all the way across the country to his hometown just before he heads off on a grueling pro-golf tour circuit. There's no way this set-up is going to work, right? It has disaster written all over it.

And yet, this is Holland, and everything he touches turns to gold, so maybe I'll be eating my words when the two of them wind up married with a baby on the way in a year or two.

"All set." Holland reaches across his muscled upper body to buckle his seatbelt and then shoves his sunglasses down over his eyes.

I grunt and start the truck.

"Thanks again for giving me a ride. I wanted to leave my car so Poppy and her sister have a spare."

We've been over this, so I know his motives. I nod.

"What did you think of her? Pretty great, right? She told me about your unfortunate encounter this morning."

I shoot my brother a sidelong glance. Holland is grinning like it's the most hilarious thing he's ever heard. Some guys might get up in arms at the thought of another man seeing their girlfriend in nothing but a towel. Not Holland. He's too used to being the golden boy for something like this to faze him. His head is so high above everyone else's—mine included—that he doesn't realize that if I were the type of man to lust after my brother's girlfriend, I could totally be disrespecting her right now.

Good thing for him—and for her—I'm not that type of guy.

"She seems fine," I offer, which is true. I don't have much to go on, but I admit to being impressed by Poppy's poise. She was flustered at being caught outside in her bath towel, but she didn't make a fuss. She didn't apologize, except for waking me up. She just desperately wanted to get inside. I'm glad I could help her with that.

"She's more than fine. Poppy is literally the best. Like, the coolest woman I've ever met."

I grunt again, and Holland takes that as his cue to continue.

"I mean, can you believe my luck? There she was, like a fountain of water, and I, a man crossing an arid dessert—"

"Finishing a training session at your posh gym?"

Holland continues, not bothering to answer my clarifying question. "I think it was love at first sight, and everything fell into place from there." He sits back in his seat with a happy, carefree grin on his face.

I fight an eye roll. I love my little brother. I do. He's a hard worker, which is a good thing because if he got everything he has coming to him and didn't work for it, he would be wholly insufferable. As it stands, he's about fifty percent insufferable.

Sixty percent.

Seventy-five percent.

And a half.

"So you think it's going to work out between you two?" I'm trying to keep my voice light—as light as my bass-like timbre can sound, at least.

The thing is, I have my doubts. In fact, I'm fairly sure this relationship is doomed to fail. Nothing against Poppy.

Well, maybe I'm throwing a little shade her way for getting swallowed up in the glitz and glam that is Holland Bradley, enough to move herself and her sister to a different part of the country. But I'm sure she's perfectly fine as a person.

I know my brother, though. There's no way he's ready to settle into a serious relationship.

"We're going to try to make the best of it, that's for sure." Holland shifts in his seat so he's looking at me. I feel his gaze on the side of my face as I drive along the Cashmere County coast, heading toward the airport. "I'm going to need your help."

"My help?"

"With Poppy."

"With Poppy?"

"What are you, a parrot?"

I frown. "What do you need from me? I'm already putting her up in my place. My in-need-of-some-serious-TLC place."

What Holland doesn't realize is that with Poppy and her sister living next door, I'm going to be more pinched for time to fix up that half of the duplex. My spare time is minimal as it is, and now, instead of being able to pop over there and work on a project whenever my schedule allows, I'm going to have to clear it with them. It's going to make getting the apartment up to par that much more challenging.

"I've already told you not to worry about that. Poppy is used to making do with less-than-ideal living situations." Holland waves me off, and I'm suddenly wondering what other places Poppy has lived. Maybe getting locked outside in her towel by a sticky door is a blip for her. No biggie.

"She'll try to help you with some of the renovations," Holland continues. "That's how she is. She's such a helper. She makes everything better." He leans back in his seat with a sigh, and I can almost see the hearts floating out from his eyes.

"You really like her?"

"She's easy to like."

I make a humming sound. "What did you need from me?"

"I need you to be her friend."

I cough toward the dashboard. I never know what to expect where Holland is concerned, but that request catches me off guard. "I don't really do friends."

"Bull." Holland holds up his hands, ticking items off one finger at a time. "You're friends with Piper and Ed. You're friends with your electrician buddies. You're friends with all the little old ladies around town. You're friends with Collin."

"That's not the same thing at all."

"Come on, man. You're like a hermit. But you can be sociable when you want to be. I know you've got it in you to be an affable host. I don't know why you choose to be reclusive and grouchy the other half of the time."

Of course Holland doesn't understand. In his defense, not many people understand me.

"Piper is family. My coworkers are different. So are the little old ladies. And Collin and I go way back. I don't do new friendships, Holland. You know that."

Especially not with women.

My track record there...well, let's just say I don't have a record because I tripped coming out of the starting blocks, face-planted in front of the whole town, and never raced again.

"You'll like Poppy, and with her living next door, I told her she could count on you for whatever she needs, so you're kind of stuck with her. She's expecting you to drive her to family dinner on Sunday."

I sigh. "Great."

"Just be nice and look out for her, okay?"

"No promises."

Holland laughs, but I skim my gaze away from the road and toward his face at the sound, because there's some strain in it.

"What is it?"

"There's one more thing I need you to do for me. And for Poppy."

"And that is?"

"I promised her we would email."

I raise my brows. "And?"

"She set up this whole account for us. One email address for her. One for me. She said it would be like the equivalent of the old timers writing letters while they were separated. It's her way of keeping us connected. She knows my time will be taken up with trainings, practices, travel, and everything that comes with being on tour, so she thought this would be a good way for us to keep in touch and sort of get to know each other. We haven't been dating for that long, you know."

You don't say.

"Since it's over email," Holland continues, "it won't be time-sensitive information or anything like that, but we'll be able to read and respond to each other whenever our schedules allow."

I'm trying to follow my brother's explanation here, trying to figure out what any of it has to do with me. I've got to admit, Poppy's idea is cute—in a sickly sweet sort of way. It seems like just the thing Holland would be all over.

Very movie-esque.

"That sounds, um, nice."

"I'm glad you think so." Holland slaps me on the shoulder, which is awkward, because I'm driving and my back is up against my seat, so he ends up hitting my bicep. He shakes out his hand. "Jeez, man. You've been working out?"

"Pulling wire cables." I'm an electrician. My workout is built into my work.

Also, I've discovered this YouTube trainer whose workout videos are dance-based, and I secretly love them. Think choreographed dance routines to music from Taylor Swift, Beyoncé, and the *Hamilton* soundtrack. It's addicting, and there's no way I'm sharing that little tidbit with my brother.

"I need you to email Poppy on my behalf."

Here I am, minding my business, thinking about how my YouTube dance trainer said she was going to drop a new video set to Shawn Mendes music today, when Holland drops *that* bomb.

"What?"

"You. Need to email. Poppy. For me." Holland says it like he's ordering fast food at a drive-thru window, breaking apart the sentences into manageable chunks. As if that's going to help me process his request.

"What the heck, man? Why?"

"Because I'm going to be swamped. I'm going to be exhausted. I'm not going to have time to sit down and wax poetic to Poppy at the end of rounds upon rounds of golf. Any mental energy I do have left, I'm going to need to use for visualization exercises for my upcoming tournaments."

"I get it," I say slowly, trying to be agreeable, trying to make him see what a preposterous request he's making. "Why didn't you tell Poppy that? I'm sure if she's as great as you say she is, she'd understand."

Holland looks solemn, almost contrite. "She hasn't asked me for anything. I'd feel terrible denying her this. She's so excited about it. Of course I had to go along with it and be excited too. But there's no way I can keep up my end of the deal. That's where you come in."

Maybe I should be offended at my brother's assumption that I have all the time in the world. He doesn't realize that I'm working over sixty hours a week as an electrician, and on top of that, I'm the town's resident fix-it man. I've got more irons in the fire than I can juggle. Most of the time, that's a good thing. It's one of the ways I cope with the rumors that swirl around me every time I'm out. If I'm busy, then I'm too preoccupied to dwell on what everyone has to say about me.

But! None of that matters right now. What matters is that Holland is looking at me with puppy-dog eyes. He's begging me with his pupils to agree to this. It's pathetic.

"Come on, Mack. It won't be forever, and it's no big deal. You know everything there is to know about me. Our childhoods are the same, so fill Poppy in on the basics of my history. You don't even have to initiate. Check the account regularly, and when she emails, respond. Do your best impression of me. Easy peasy."

We're getting close to the airport now, and I'm panicking because I don't know how I'm going to be able to talk myself out of this preposterous scheme Holland has cooked up. The man is not used to hearing no. So much so, that I'm pretty convinced a negative response doesn't register in his brain. I make a last-ditch effort.

"It doesn't seem like a good idea to build a relationship on a foundation of lies."

"That's deep, Mack. Really deep." Holland rolls his eyes. "But I hardly think I'm going to take relationship advice from you."

I can practically feel the blood in my veins turn to ice at that backhanded barb.

Holland doesn't notice the way I'm clenching the wheel now. He's messing around on his phone. "You're making this out to be a bigger deal than it is. I'm still going to be texting Poppy and calling her when I can. I'll be home for the wedding next month, and we'll regroup then. It's all going to be fine. I need your help with this one simple thing. If you don't think you can handle it, I'll figure something else out."

I pull into the drop-off lane at the airport and exhale, ready to tell my brother to bite me. But then, I don't know what happens...

Maybe it's loneliness.

Maybe it's exhaustion.

Maybe it's a deep-seeded desire to prove to Holland—and everyone else—that I'm not such a big screw-up that I can't handle being someone's fake pen-pal.

But I open my mouth and out spill the words, "Fine. Give me the account information."

3

Nicknames Are Bestowed

Poppy

"**Y**ou know why it's called Cashmere Cove?"

I spin around to find my supervisor waddling into the room—waddle is her word, not mine.

Heather Arnold—also known as the director of the Cashmere Cove Parks and Recreation Department and my new boss—is nine months pregnant. I've known her for all of two hours, and what I've determined is that she's basically Superwoman.

So far this morning, she's recruited three extra umpires for the youth baseball program so they won't be short for games tonight. She's resolved a snafu with a concession stand order. The vendor sent the town of Cashmere Cove one thousand extra choco tacos, and Heather got right on the phone and told them they needed to come back and pick them up and issue the town a complete refund. "We don't have the freezer space for that size order," she told me. She proceeded to send me to where the boxes got dropped off to snag us each one of the sweet treats before they were whisked away.

She's officially my hero.

"No. I guess I don't." I take one last look at the water before returning to the seat on the opposite side of Heather's desk.

She plunks down in her seat and blows the strand of hair that has fallen from her messy bun out of her face, wiping her brow with the back of her wrist. "The sandy bottom of our stretch of the bay. People say it feels as soft as cashmere on your toes when you walk out into the water." She shrugs. "Or something like that.

I'm not an expert. All I know is it is hot, and the water is a welcome relief most days in the summer. It's also a source for a ton of our activities, so I'm grateful for it."

I'm accustomed to the white-sand beaches of Florida, which are stunning in their own right, but Cashmere Cove is a different kind of gorgeous. The blue of the sky blurs with the greens and grays of the rocky, tree-dotted shoreline. The buildings lining Main Street are quaint and welcoming. Each one has different colored siding and trim, so when you walk down the road, it's like you're on the inside of a rainbow. The whole town feels cozy and accessible.

Cashmere Cove is one in a myriad of towns dotting Cashmere County, a premiere tourist destination in northeast Wisconsin. The county spans the entirety of the peninsula that juts out from the state into Lake Michigan. Cashmere Cove is situated on the bay side of the peninsula.

I nod. "Useful and beautiful."

"Glad you think so. You're going to get up close and personal with it."

I sit up straighter. I want to make a good impression on this woman. I'll be filling in for her when she goes out on maternity leave...any day now. My position is only temporary at the moment. If I can prove myself an asset to the department, then they may extend me a full-time offer after Heather returns.

I fully intend to earn that offer. "What do you need me to do?"

Heather tugs open the drawer of her desk and retrieves a sheet of paper. She hands it over to me, and I skim the contents.

"The fifteenth annual Cashmere Cove Party in the Park," I read.

"We throw a huge end-of-the-summer bash every August. Those are the plans we've made so far. You'll have to take over as point person for me, coordinate the event, and get it across the finish line for us."

Heather levels me with a steely look. I can't tell if she thinks I'm going to be intimidated by this task, or if that's her resting facial expression.

This is a huge responsibility. Maybe I should be worried, but all I can see it for is a huge *opportunity* to prove myself. It's what I wanted and what I'm good at. A zing of excitement flies down my spine.

Thank you, Holland Bradley. I could kiss you right now!

I make a mental note to write Holland my first email in our special account later today and tell him all about how excited this job makes me, how grateful I am.

For now, I turn my attention back to Heather.

She's fanning herself with a notebook, and I feel a shot of sympathy for her, coupled with another huge helping of awe. Heather is growing a human, which means if the temperature outside feels hot to me, I imagine it feels like the inside of an oven cranked up to four hundred twenty-five for her. I really like her. She's got a no-nonsense attitude I can get behind, but there's a softness there too. And she's organized, which is my love language.

I've done my research and know the types of programming the Cashmere Cove Parks and Rec department offers. It's good stuff for the community—and for the tourists who flock to Wisconsin's Cashmere County each year. I want to be a part of it. I want to be on Heather's team. I'm going to do everything I can to make this woman's life as easy as possible.

"This sounds awesome. I can handle it." I finish glancing over the details on the page. "I don't see anything geared toward teenagers on this list. Am I missing something?"

Heather shakes her head. "We've always had a hard time attracting the younger crowd. Actually, we're good with kids because we have a whole host of kids' games lined up."

I nod, noting the games listed along with a contact person, one Tricia Reynolds.

"And the older crowd...think sixties and above...they like the musical acts and bingo offerings early in evening. But I think we miss out on capturing the attention of the teenagers—and their parents, for that matter."

I tap my finger to my chin, my mind already swirling with ideas. "Do I have your permission to try to pull a couple things together to meet these needs?"

"By all means. This is your project now. Sink or swim, it's all you."

I square my shoulders. I can swim. "What else do I need to know?"

I get out my tablet to take notes as Heather starts ticking off contacts around town who'll be helping me pull this event together.

"You'll want to talk to Collin at the police department about security. Inez at the bakery is great. She'll help you coordinate the food trucks. Don't wait to book porta-potties."

I chuckle, but my laugh dies on my lips at Heather's serious look.

"I mean it. They're essential to the day's success. As for getting the park itself ready—"

A knock on the door stops Heather mid-sentence.

"Come in," she calls.

The door swings open, and I turn and find myself looking at my next-door neighbor—or, as I've recently discovered, my landlord.

And also Holland's older brother.

The man who saw me practically naked.

Peachy.

"Oh, good, Mack, you're here." Heather stands from behind her desk to greet him, but Mack waves her off.

"Sit down."

She huffs and begrudgingly does as she's told. "I'm pregnant, not incapacitated."

"Still, no need to be a hero." Mack strides into the room and takes a seat in the chair next to mine. I catch a whiff of his minty scent, same as it was this morning. So much for my hope that I wouldn't have to see this guy too often.

"Poppy, this is Mack. Mack, Poppy."

I shoot Mack a look. He's staring back at me, and this is the first time I can see his eyes. When Holland introduced us earlier this morning, Mack was still wearing his baseball cap. He shook my hand and then gave Holland and me some space. I appreciated that.

Now, he's without his hat, and his eyes laser into mine.

I don't know what I expected, but I guess I figured he'd resemble Holland, who's got these golden-brown eyes that remind me of maple syrup. But that's not what I see when my gaze latches onto Mack's.

His eyes are charcoal gray. Like they were once lit, but the fire has been snuffed out.

"We've met." I extend my hand to him and try to arrange my face into an expression to match the moment. How do you say, *Hey, you've seen me in my bath towel, and that was weird for both of us, but let's please forget it ever happened and move on,* with a look and a smile?

Mack shakes my hand and nods once before turning his attention back to Heather.

"Of course." She looks up to the ceiling like she's kicking herself for not putting it together. "The Holland connection."

Mack grunts, and I beam.

"That should make things easier, then. Mack knows everyone in town, Poppy. You can go to him with any issues or concerns. He's in charge of getting the park in order for the day of the event. You two are going to be working together closely to make sure the Party in the Park goes off without a hitch in my absence. I would suggest meeting regularly to ensure you're on the same page. Mack, I'm counting on you to make sure nothing slips through the cracks. Poppy's good. Her resume precedes her, but she's not local. You know how things go around here."

I might be imagining it, but Mack's cheeks look like they've turned a pale shade of pink. He dips his chin in response to Heather.

I'm pretending to make notes on my tablet so that I look like I know what I'm doing. I *do* know what I'm doing. It's just that Mack's presence makes me a little nervous. If I'm being honest, I'd like for Holland's family to like me.

I glance up and smile at Heather before cutting another look in Mack's direction, doing my best to look polished and unflustered by our brief and embarrassing history. "Perfect. I appreciate any help you can provide, Mack."

He grunts again. That seems to be his baseline. I swear the man has not spoken more than five combined words to me.

Heather's door swings open, and a man I don't recognize pops his head in. "Arnold, let's have our meeting in my office."

Heather nods. "Be right there, boss. First, let me introduce you to our newest employee. Poppy, this is Mayor Witmore." She motions to me, and I stand, extending a hand. Mayor Witmore has a round belly, and he's wearing a blue polo shirt that's tucked into creased khaki pants. His cheeks are slightly rosy, and he's got a receding hairline.

"Nice to meet you, sir."

"You as well." He offers me a genuine smile. "Holler if you need anything. Happy to have you on board."

I warm at the welcome.

Heather makes to stand, looking between Mack and me. "You two will be great. Obviously, I'm around until I'm not"—she points at her watermelon-shaped belly—"so don't be afraid to ask questions while I'm here, Poppy. I'm happy to be a resource. Then, Mack can take it from there."

She makes her way out the door, and it snaps shut behind her.

I'm left sitting next to Mack, and the silence in the room is deafening. I need to do something to quell the awkwardness that's threatening to suffocate me.

"Okay. Can I have a do-over?" I turn in my seat and hold out my hand for Mack. "I'm Poppy Kasper. It's nice to meet you."

Mack takes my proffered hand. "Kasper? Like the ghost?"

I crack a grin. "One and the same. Except with a K."

"Alright then, Boo." Mack stands and heads for the door.

"Wait." I scramble from my seat and trail him into the hallway. "Did you call me Boo?"

"Yup."

"Why?"

He pivots. "Kasper."

He says my last name as if that's the answer to everything.

I can feel my nose scrunching up. "You think I haven't heard that before?"

He pauses in his stride. We're almost to the front of the P&R building. He shrugs. "You probably have. It's a perfect nickname."

I put my hands on my hips. "What if I hate it?"

"Nicknames aren't chosen by the named. They're bestowed."

I flinch back, both because that's the longest single sentence he's ever said to me, and because of his monotone delivery. It's like he's speaking gospel truth on the subject of naming rights. "So you're going to call me Boo?"

"Plan on it, yep."

"Well then, I'll *bestow* a nickname on you."

Mack grunts. "I've heard them all."

"Mack Attack?" I study him. "No, that's not it. Hmm." I mull over my options. "Mack truck?" I let that one sit on my tongue for a bit. "Good, not great. Mack Daddy!" I frown. "No, that sounds somewhat risqué."

He's stopped in his quest to flee the building, and he's staring at me now. If I didn't know any better, I'd say his charcoal eyes are glistening with a hint of humor, like maybe I'm amusing him with this little exercise.

Good. I can work with that.

I hold up my finger and look all the way up to meet his gaze. A surge of triumph courses through my veins when the perfect play on words comes to me. "Big Mack! Except if you're going to call me Boo, then I'm going to call you Big."

"Big?"

"Yeah. It suits you."

We stare at each other for a beat, and I'm pleased to say I'm holding my ground. No cowering here. Maybe Gran was on to something with the cute-underwear trick. I did spend some extra time picking out a perfect pair this morning.

Mack blinks first. "Let me give you my number. Call if you need anything."

I'm slightly embarrassed to admit how relieved I am at his offer. I almost drop my tablet in my attempt to grab my phone from my pocket, but I manage to save it at the last minute. We exchange information, and he turns to leave.

"Where are you off to in such a hurry?" I fight off a cringe at how nosy my question sounds, but I can't help it. This is a brand-new town with brand-new people. Like Heather said, it's sink or swim time, and I'm sort of hoping Mack will help to keep me afloat.

"Work."

"What do you do?"

"I'm an electrician."

"Ah." I nod. "You're working on those multi-unit complexes the next town over."

Mack quirks his brow. "How'd you guess?"

"The logo on your hat from this morning. I remember seeing signs on our way into town that matched it. I'm guessing the M-E stands for Mack Electric?"

He eyes me again, and this time, I'm sure there's a glint of something in the dark depths of his irises. I'd like to think I've impressed him. That, or I've drawn his attention back to our first meeting, where he wouldn't have been able to learn anything about me from my attire.

Because I was clothes-less.

I fight the urge to cower.

"That's me," he says after a minute, and he's halfway out the door. "See you around, Boo."

"It's not too late, you know," I call after him. He pauses and glances over his shoulder, his eyes narrowed. "You could always change your branding to 'Big Mack Electric'. Has a nice ring to it, if I do say so myself."

One side of Mack's mouth hitches up a fraction of an inch before he turns and stalks off.

It's not much, but I'm going to count that as a massive win for today.

$$4$$

Possessive Pronouns

Mack

To: hbradleypro@gmail.com

From: poppykallday@gmail.com

Subject: Email 1

Dear Holland,

Here goes nothing! Thanks for agreeing to this email-writing scheme. I'm sure after a busy day it's the last thing you want to do, but like I said, your effort means a lot to me. I'm writing this while I'm waiting to head to your parents' house for Sunday dinner. I'm nervous! Overall, I've had a good first few days in Cashmere Cove. From what I've seen of it, I love your hometown.

I know I've told you some about my background, so I won't get into it all again, but suffice it to say, the only place I've ever felt like I could call my own was the tiny little bedroom in the upstairs corner of my gram's house. The paint was the color of the sky, and there were crisp white sheets on the three twin-sized beds that my sisters and I got to sleep in. Gram didn't have much, but she loved us fiercely. The years we got to stay with her were the safest, most at-home I've felt in my entire life. I miss her every day. But I already feel like I could feel at home here in Cashmere Cove. What is it about this place that ropes you in? Is it the way the sun reflects off the water? The colorful buildings on the downtown strip? The lush green trees that surround all the parks? I don't know. Something about this town makes me want to stay awhile.

I don't say that to freak you out or put the cart in front of the horse with our relationship or anything like that. Mostly I wanted to say thank you. Thank you for everything you did to set me up with a job here (which I love so far!) and a place for Rose and me to stay (yes, it needs work, but we're going to make the most of it!).

I've always tried to look for the good in my circumstances, and right now, sitting on the deck, listening to the creek running through the backyard of this little duplex, it's not hard to find. I hope your day has been good too. If not, take a minute to look up—whether it's morning or it's night. It's impossible to feel bummed out when you're looking up to the sky.

Sending a hometown hug your way tonight!

Xoxo,

Poppy

• • • ● • ● • ● • •

I'm standing on the porch outside Poppy's half of the duplex, stalling.

As I was getting ready to come and pick her up to drive her to my parents' house for family dinner, my phone dinged. I checked it to find an alert from the email account she set up for herself and Holland.

Before I thought better of it, I read her message.

Now I feel icky.

Uncomfortable.

Wondering how to be when I interact with her.

I don't want to have this insider's lens into her life and her thoughts. It's not my place, and it's going to make things weird between us.

Isn't it?

I grind my jaw. There's nothing for it. I need to rip the Band-Aid off. She's expecting me to take her to meet the family. She's living in Cashmere Cove. We're bound to run into each other. I have to get over myself and—

The door swings open, and Poppy's standing there, grinning at me.

"Where I come from, people knock to be let in. I might have a ghoulish last name, but that doesn't mean I have a sixth sense that tips me off to your arrival."

"Uh, right." I step back, letting her walk out onto the porch and motioning her to where my truck is parked on my half of the driveway.

She takes the steps off the porch but then stops and looks to me. She does a half spin this way and that. "Do I look okay?"

This feels like a trap. I don't particularly want to focus on how she looks. She's Holland's girlfriend. I have been determinedly *not* focusing on how she looks—which, I might add, has been a feat. Poppy is not the type of woman a guy can easily ignore. She's like sunshine. Unavoidable in her luster. I can hardly ignore her question, can I?

"I wasn't sure what the dress code is for Sunday family dinner. I've never been," she goes on. "To yours or anyone else's. This is already weird with Holland not being here, right? I want to make a good first impression."

She's smiling, but I can tell by the way she's shifting her weight between her feet that she's anxious.

I *do* feel for her. She's right. This is a bizarre situation. Here she is, in a brand-new town, about to be introduced to her boyfriend's family by me.

Her boyfriend's brother.

I blow out a breath and give her a once-over, not letting my gaze linger on any area in particular for too long. She's wearing one of those dresses that looks like it's made out of a man's button-up shirt. But it's sleeveless. Her arms are toned and tan against the light-blue wash of the dress. She's got her dark hair up in a ponytail. Loose strands fall on either side of her face, and she's donned simple earrings that keep glinting in the late-afternoon light. Basically, she looks put together but not like she's trying too hard.

She looks gorgeous, okay? Effortlessly elegant.

Dang it.

I don't want to be thinking about how attractive Holland's girlfriend is.

"You look fine," I say, angling my body toward the truck. "We should go."

"Right." She nods, hops into the passenger seat, and gives my truck a once-over. "Thanks for the ride. Your parents live closer to the water, right? This place is so gorgeous."

She chatters on as I make the quick drive through town. Cashmere Cove is split into an upper district and a lower district. The upper district is where many of the traditional neighborhoods are, like the one that houses my duplex as well as the day-to-day businesses like the Pick 'n' Save and a Walgreens. The lower district, all along the water, is comprised of the historic downtown strip, vacation rentals, area small businesses, and larger homes, including the house where I grew up.

"This whole town was snatched from the pages of a storybook." Poppy's head is almost hanging out the open window. "Look at these mansions! I can totally imagine who lives in that one!"

She points to a house with lavender siding and a black roof. "I bet it's a single woman's property. She's wealthy and dignified. She's made her millions in the perfume industry. And"—Poppy lifts a finger in the air as if a lightbulb went on in her brain—"there's a man who has been begging her to marry him for the last twenty years. But she's still in love with a young page she met in England when she was a teenager and worked as an underling at Jo Malone."

"Jo Ma-who? What are you talking about?"

Poppy looks at me and laughs. "Sorry. I got caught up in the game."

"Uh…" I'm at a bit of a loss. "Care to enlighten me?"

"An electrician joke. Nice." She holds up a hand for a high-five, and when I just stare back at her, she slaps her own hand. "It's a game I made up for Rose and Noli, my sisters, when they were in high school. Our living circumstances were…not ideal. So we'd drive to ritzy neighborhoods, get out of our car, walk around, and imagine who lived in the houses."

As I'm trying to wrap my brain around everything she's said—and let's face it, there has been a lot—she goes on. "So, am I close? Who lives there?"

"Ernest and Willow Dunlap. He comes from a long line of meat packers, and she's one of our local librarians."

Poppy bursts out laughing. "Not close, then."

"No."

I pull into my parents' driveway, and Poppy gasps. "This is your family's house?"

I glance up at the stately white siding and black shutters of the two-story house where I grew up. The green, striped lawn is meticulously kept, right down to the putting green my dad has been tending along the side yard ever since Holland showed true potential to be a legitimate golfer.

"Home sweet home." I cut the ignition.

Poppy steps out of the truck and brushes down her dress. "Any advice?"

I walk around the front of the truck, and she's staring at me with her big, baby-blue eyes.

"Nope." Her shoulders sag, and it's like I popped her birthday balloon. I don't like the feeling, so I add, "My parents will love you. You've got nothing to worry about."

She perks up and blows out a breath. "Okay. I can do this."

I walk around the side yard, knowing on a gorgeous day like today my parents will have the backyard set up picnic-style for our weekly dinner.

My mom spots Poppy and me first.

"There they are!" she squeals and hurries over. "You must be Poppy." She gives Poppy a brisk hug. "So lovely to meet you, dear."

Poppy eases out of the hug. "Thank you so much for having me."

My mom is looking her up and down with a delighted expression on her face. "Aren't you cute as a button? I hope my Holland has been treating you well?"

Poppy blushes, and I look away.

Because it's weird to think about my baby brother treating any woman in any way, but also because it's always like a knife to the side when my mom refers to Holland as *my Holland.*

I've never been *my Mack*—or at least, I haven't been for a long time—and that's okay. I've made my peace with it. But sometimes it gets under my skin. Like a sliver. Or a bee sting.

Or a bee sting on top of a sliver.

"Come with me. I want to show you around." My mom turns, linking her arm with Poppy's, only to pause and glance back to me. "Thanks for getting our Poppy here, Mack. The guys are inside."

She turns Poppy in the direction of my cousin Piper and her fiancé, Ed, anxious to make introductions. Poppy tosses me a small smile over her shoulder, and she looks so relieved I can't hold it against her that less than five minutes into knowing my mother she also has already earned a possessive pronoun.

I tell myself I don't care. It's my least favorite part of speech.

I wander inside to find two of my employees, whom my parents have adopted as surrogate children. Patrick Casterro and his wife, Mia, are standing around the island in my parents' kitchen along with Lou Boggs. I greet the guys and give Mia a quick peck on the cheek.

"Your mom and dad are so kind to keep having us over," Mia says as she grabs another carrot from the vegetable platter.

Since she and Patrick moved to town six months back, they have been Sunday dinner regulars. It's kind of my mom and dad's thing. They take in anyone new to Cashmere Cove and make sure they feel at home.

"They'd be offended if you didn't come," I assure her.

Mia smiles. "I'm going to head back out and mingle. You boys behave."

She leaves through the screen door, and I make my way to the fridge for a beer. "You guys good?"

Patrick and Lou raise their drinks.

"So what's the 411 on Cashmere Cove's newest—and prettiest—residents?" Lou asks.

"Holland's girlfriend and her sister," Patrick helpfully adds, in case, you know, I missed Lou's hooked thumb in the direction of where Poppy is standing, chatting with my mom and dad on the patio.

I pop the top on my beer. "What do you want to know?"

"Are they nice?" Patrick asks.

"Are they single?" Lou says at the same time.

Patrick slaps him on the back of the head. "Dude. Poppy is dating Holland."

"Which is weird, right?" Lou asks, unfazed. "Like, she moves to town as he's moving away? Doesn't seem like the smartest way to set up a lasting relationship."

"It's unconventional," I agree.

"But is she nice?" Patrick asks. "Do you think Mia would like her?"

Mia is a gem, but also very shy. I know Patrick worries about her making friends.

"I think so. She's..."—I search for the right word and land on—"bubbly."

"Bubbly?" Lou echoes. "Like champagne?"

I roll my eyes. "Not what I meant."

"You're going to have to spell it out, boss. Not all of us are poets."

I ignore the poet comment. "Bubbly like she's in good spirits...happy most of the time."

"So pretty much she's your opposite," Lou jokes.

"Pretty much."

Patrick and Lou laugh.

Patrick slings his arm over my shoulder. "For a grouch, you sure are lovable."

"Yeah, yeah." I shake him off.

"What about her sister? Is she single?" Lou asks.

"No clue. Haven't met her."

"But they're living next door to you, right?"

I nod.

"You can find out for me, then." Lou holds up his hand. "I call dibs."

Patrick rolls his eyes. "You can't claim a woman like that, Lou."

"I'm expressing my interest," Lou argues, turning to me and pointing his finger at my chest. "I don't want Mack to swoop in with his broodiness and sweep the other sister off her feet before I get the chance, ya know?"

"I'm not interested in Holland's girlfriend's sister." Talk about complicated.

"All the better." Lou nods, but then he rubs his hands together. "We do need to think about giving them both a nice, Cashmere Cove welcome, yeah?"

I start shaking my head.

"Come on, man. It's tradition."

"You are not pranking the Kasper sisters."

"Not by myself," Lou says, looking affronted. "We'll do it together."

"No way."

"Why not?" Lou puts his hands on his hips. He's a good six inches shorter than me, but he looks like he's ready to rumble. "It's how we welcome everyone into the fold—or at least how we vet people."

The Cashmere Cove faithful have a custom of pranking people who move to town. I don't know who started the tradition, but it's been going on for longer than I've been alive to witness it.

It's not malicious. Mostly, it's a couple of harmless miscues that the locals enact on new arrivals to establish that the newbies can take a joke—that, and to add to the town lore.

That's the thing about Cashmere Cove…we don't take ourselves too seriously, and we love a good reminiscence. If someone moves to this part of Cashmere County, folks here want to break them in, make sure they can hang with the fun crowd. This is a small, close-knit community. Last I checked, our population hovered right around two-thousand people.

We don't get a lot of turnover, so I guess I'm not surprised that Lou is practically vibrating with excitement at the thought of putting together a prank for Poppy and Rose.

"I'm still pretty proud that we passed muster." Patrick puffs up his chest.

We toilet-papered their house until the trees looked like weeping willows. Then it rained. They were dealing with soggy toilet paper for weeks. To their credit, Patrick and Mia were excellent sports.

"I don't know," I say. "I'm sure Holland warned them. What's the point if they're expecting it?"

Lou brushes me off with a *pfft*. "That's all the more reason to get creative."

I feel my lips itch with a smile. I'm not sure why I'm fighting this so hard. Maybe it's some misplaced desire to protect Poppy. But I check it.

After all, this'll be a good chance to see if she's as happy-go-lucky as she appears to be. If she can't handle a little Cashmere Cove pranking, then she sure as heck isn't going to be able to handle my brother.

Speaking of Holland, he asked me to show her around town, and this is how we do things in Cashmere Cove.

"Fine. But this prank will not take place on my property."

Lou grins. "So you're saying there's going to be a prank?"

"Oh yeah. I've got a great idea." I step forward, and Patrick and Lou lean in.

5

HIPS FOr IT

Poppy

"**S**o, Poppy, how're you settling in?"

Holland's mom, Darla, has plied me with a plateful of broccoli-and-cheese casserole, a kabob of fresh fruit, and three different kinds of pasta salad.

I swallow and set my plate down. We're seated on the patio under an oversized umbrella. Darla has been nothing but doting since I got here, which is nice. It's obvious that she's very proud of Holland and predisposed to like me. I'll take it.

"Really well, thank you. Mack's duplex is..." I hesitate, trying to find the right word.

Darla scoffs. "Completely unsuitable. I told Holland you and your sister should have stayed here, but he insisted that you would appreciate your own space."

I nod. Holland and I haven't dated for long, but I'll give the man extra props for understanding that, as a grown woman, I don't want to live with my new-ish boyfriend's mother.

"So then I tried to put a bug in Mack's ear. 'Get that property fixed up for those girls,' I told him." Darla's forehead creases. "But that boy wouldn't listen to his mother if his life depended on it."

Darla continues to prattle on about Mack, but I've zoned out, only murmuring here and there when the lulls in the conversation merit it. I'm focused on the man himself. Mack and his two friends, who I've learned are Patrick and Lou, are off to the side of the yard, adding kindling to the fire pit. Mia, Patrick's wife, is there too, along with Piper and Ed, Holland's cousin and her fiancé. I was thrilled to meet them all earlier. I'll be at Piper and Ed's wedding later this summer, and Mia is Rose's boss. Honestly, she's been a highlight of this whole dinner. She could not be sweeter, and I think she and Rose will hit it off. Since Rose pretty much uprooted her entire life to come with me, I'm thankful she's got a job here that she'll enjoy. I make a mental note to thank Holland for coordinating that aspect of our cross-country move, as well.

I had been waffling over what Rose would do in Cashmere Cove and feeling guilty about the move. My middle sister has had a myriad of different jobs, including but not limited to being a cable company saleswoman, a coffee shop barista, and an NFL cheerleader, so it wasn't that I didn't think she could find something, but I wanted her to find something that she'd enjoy. That would make all the tumult worth it. When I randomly mentioned to Holland that Rose loves books and reading, he made the connection that Mia could use some help at Mood Reader, the local bookshop in Cashmere Cove. The rest is history.

Patrick has his arm around Mia now, and she's gazing up at him with hearts in her eyes. Piper and Ed are in similar formation on the opposite side of the fire pit. Lou is running his mouth at Mack, who is crouched down, focused on the fire. I wonder if he was a boy scout. He's got the look of a man who could fend for himself in the wild.

What look is that, you ask? I don't know. Like he knows exactly what he's doing. He's building a log cabin with alternating pieces of smaller-sized wood.

When Mack turns his back to reach for another piece of kindling, Lou reaches down, grabs a handful of the crushed gravel that's surrounding the firepit, and stuffs it down Mack's shirt.

I can hear Mack growl and curse from where I'm sitting.

"MacArthur Bradley! Language!" Darla shouts in a tone I'm guessing she's used on her sons since forever.

Mack swivels to face us and catches my eye.

I mouth, "MacArthur," and raise my eyebrows.

He narrows his gaze at me and shakes his head.

I take a bite of pasta salad to hide my grin.

"Sorry, Ma." He stands and lowers his shoulder, hoisting Lou up in a fireman's carry.

"Hey! Put me down." Lou is kicking his feet, and it's kind of hilarious. "I was practicing for the pranks."

Mack cuts another glance in my direction, and I can't quite read his gaze. His dark-chocolate hair is longer on the top, and a tuft has fallen into his eyes. He's carrying Lou as if the man weighs nothing. Lou isn't a giant, to be sure, but it's still impressive that Mack can hold him up there like he's a feather. His expression doesn't change when he sees me staring at him, but he mumbles something to Lou.

Mack spins so Lou—still upside-down—is looking at me. He gives me a giant grin and swats Mack on the butt. Mack tosses him down and goes back to stoking the fire.

They launch into some other conversation that I can't hear, but Patrick is doing a lot of talking with his hands.

I have no idea what pranks Lou was referring to, but regardless, they seem like a group of people I'd like to get to know. Like they like to have fun. I could use some fun friends, and I want to invest myself in this community.

I'm about to make my excuses to Darla and go join the crowd that's my own age when she says, "Then there's the whole Tricia situation. An absolute mess."

"Tricia?" I've tuned Darla out to this point, and I'm afraid I might have missed some information pertinent to Holland or the family history. I rack my brain to try to remember when and where I've heard the name Tricia before.

"Tricia Rattler. Well, she's Tricia Reynolds now. I don't know if I can ever truly forgive him for that."

It comes to me then. She's the woman who's in charge of kids' games for Party at the Park. I press my lips together. I've missed something. "I'm sorry. Forgive who?"

"Mack. For ruining his life—not to mention his reputation, and spoiling the Bradley name—by breaking that girl's heart. He should have married her. I could be a grandma by now."

I blink. This is a lot of information to take in. Here's what I've gathered:

1. Mack dated a woman named Tricia, who is still around town.

2. There must've been a messy break up if it affected his reputation and the entire Bradley family.

3. Darla Bradley wants grandchildren.

She's eyeing my relatively flat mid-section as if it is a launchpad to all of her dreams.

"Do you want kids, dear? You look like you have the hips for it."

I nearly choke on a chunk of watermelon. "Uh ... I do. Someday. And ... thank you?" I'm going to assume Darla had good intentions and was issuing me a hip-focused compliment.

She beams at me. "Excellent. Excellent. Holland does too. He's going to be a wonderful father. He's so caring, and kind, and good looking."

"Very good looking," I echo, though I'm not sure that has any bearing on him being a good father. My dad was quite handsome, and look where that got us.

I blink to clear my mind. This conversation is getting out of hand. I can't say I expected meeting Holland's parents—without him—to be without incident, but I didn't prepare myself for a frank discussion about family planning, Holland's merits as a future father, and my childbearing hips.

6

SURLY AFTER ALL

Mack

I should be doing something productive, like sleeping. Instead, I've dinked around my house since dropping Poppy off after family dinner, and I haven't been able to focus. Dinner was fine. Fun, even, with Lou and Patrick. Poppy seemed to have a nice time too, which is good, I guess.

The problem lies with me. I always end up coming home after Sunday dinners feeling unsettled. It's like all the walls I've built around my heart to keep my insecurities from spilling out into the open fall away, and I'm left raw and exposed.

Family can do that to you, I guess.

So, here I sit. I'm outside on my deck, listening to the crickets chirp from the wooded area and the creek that runs through my backyard. I'm staring up at the sky because I haven't been able to stop thinking about that since I read Poppy's email earlier today. I'm realizing that she's right. The sky is so majestic—so expansive. The stars, when you stop to think about them, will blow your mind.

I spot the Little Dipper when the back door of the adjoining duplex groans open.

"So then she tells me that I've got great hips for childbearing."

It's Poppy. I wince, though her tone is more amused than offended. I wasn't privy to her conversation with my mother, but that sounds like something my mom would say. The woman means well—at least that's what I keep telling myself. But she has about as much of a filter as a colander under a full sink—by which I mean none.

There's a burst of laughter, and I can picture Poppy settling in on their side of the deck. I sigh. So much for my quiet moment of solitude.

"She seems nice, though. She wants you to come to Sunday dinner next week," Poppy says.

"Great. I can't wait to hear what she says about my figure."

This is a new voice, one that I assume belongs to Poppy's sister Rose. It's lower and more dry-sounding than Poppy's constant chipper tone.

"Stop. You're gorgeous," Poppy says, defensive. In spite of myself, I smile. The Kasper sisters seem to be close. It's nice.

"Maybe, but I have zero hips to speak of," Rose says. "I guess it's a good thing I'm not dating one of the Bradley brothers."

"There's always Mack."

Heat instantly floods my cheeks, and I feel all sorts of guilty for listening in on their private conversation.

"Not my type," Rose says without a second's thought.

Rude.

Poppy chuckles. "Strong, silent, surly men aren't your type, eh? Noted."

Poppy thinks I'm surly? I frown but then shrug. I guess I deserve that.

"Although, that's probably a good thing in Mack's case. Darla mentioned an ex-girlfriend. Tricia or something. Sounds like it was a messy break-up."

I stand up so fast the chair rattles against the deck.

I freeze, the only sound my own breathing.

"Big?" Poppy says my nickname like a question.

I grunt. I can hardly ignore the fact that I'm out here now. Leave it to Tricia to continue to put me in impossible situations...after all these years. "Uh, yeah," I say.

"What are you doing?" Poppy asks.

"Sitting outside."

She's silent, and I can imagine the conversation she and Rose are having with their eyes.

"Well, come over here. I want to introduce you to my sister."

I heave a sigh and stride around the dividing wall between our two decks.

Poppy is sitting with her back against the exterior siding of the duplex. Her face has been scrubbed clean of its makeup and she's changed into shorts and a white V-neck t-shirt. The woman next to her has raven-black hair chopped to chin length. She's wearing leggings and a tank top and eyeing me with blatant scrutiny.

"Big, this is Rose, my younger sister. Rosie, this is our landlord and Holland's brother, Mack Bradley."

Rose is twiddling with her necklace with one hand, but she holds up her opposite hand to wave. I nod my head.

Poppy is staring at me, and when I lift an eyebrow, she grins. "Or as I learned this evening, MacArthur Bradley."

"No."

She laughs. "Come on. It's such a distinguished name. Had I known about it, I could have come up with a whole lot more nicknames."

"No," I say again.

She rolls her eyes. "Fine. Big it is."

I give her a firm nod.

We lapse into silence. I'm trying to figure out how to address how much of their conversation I overheard, but Poppy beats me to it.

"Sorry I called you *surly* just now." She squishes up her nose in a way that's both self-deprecating and apologetic.

"It's fine. It's true." I dip my chin and clear my throat. "Your hips are fine."

The second the words are out of my mouth, I wish I could swallow them back in. I needed to address my mom's comments, but seriously...that's what I came up with?

"Fine hips. I'll add it to my resume." Poppy's eyes sparkle. "Big! You charmer, you."

I run my hand along the back of my neck. "I haven't noticed your hips. I haven't looked."

Poppy's eyebrows keep raising a half inch at a time.

"I'm sure they're great hips." *What is wrong with me right now?* I cough. "I mean, I'm sorry my mom sized up your potential to adequately give her grandchildren on your first meeting. Totally inappropriate."

Poppy and Rose exchange a look and then burst into giggles. Poppy waves me off. "No need to apologize. I'm mostly glad to have her stamp of approval."

"And your mom *is* right," Rose chimes in. "Poppy's hips don't lie."

Poppy shoves Rose's shoulder. Rose tips to the side and snickers. "What? You can do a killer Shakira impression. Mack, ask her to show you sometime. Then you can give your truthful opinion."

Poppy's eyes go wide. "Rosie!" She shakes her head before giving me another rueful look. "Anyway! It was a fun night. I like your friends and your parents. Thanks again for the lift."

I nod. "I'll leave you two alone."

"Night, Big." Poppy waves.

I stroll around to my side, and before the back door closes, I overhear Poppy say, "I take it back. I don't think he's so surly after all."

Her assessment of me makes my stomach do a weird wiggle. Because here's the thing. Contrary to the impression I give off, I'm not a grouch. I mean, I am. But it's a role I've taken on over time and due to the experiences of my youth. It's a coping mechanism, if you will. Keeping to myself, building up a hardened outer shell, stops me from getting hurt by all the subtle commentaries of the people in this town who are quick to judge me for my past misdeeds.

Some of that judgment is merited.

Some of it is most definitely not.

In any case, it's easier this way. I function quite nicely all by myself, coming out of my shell for air often enough not to choke.

But that doesn't mean that I don't feel things—or that I don't care.

The fact that Poppy saw through my front when very few other people have makes me feel some kind of way.

I'm not going to unpack that right now, but suffice it to say, I like Poppy. And her sister seems pretty cool too. It almost makes me feel bad about the pranks we've planned for them.

Almost.

7

EXPLODING TOILETS

Poppy

I'm at the office early on Monday morning, trying to get through some work, when I hear my phone vibrating like crazy in my desk drawer. By the time I pull it out, I've missed about ten messages from my sisters.

Noli: Sooooooo, how's life in the north?!?

Noli: Miss you guys bunches and bunches.

Rose: Aww, Noli! Miss you too. Life in the north is interesting...

Noli: ... Good interesting or bad interesting?

Rose: We've taken to calling our apartment "The Downer." This morning, literal plaster rained down on me while I was showering.

Rose: <gagging emoji>

Noli: OMG do you feel like Indiana Jones in the caves?!

Rose: Umm, no. I feel like I'm a third wheel who followed her sister to live in her boyfriend's hometown only to discover the living quarters are basically at *Little House on the Prairie* level.

Noli: I bet you'd look cute in a bonnet, though.

Noli: How's Poppy?

Rose: Fine, I think. She's already at work today...putting us to shame, as per usual.

I'm doing a rapid-fire scan of my sister's text message exchange. I try not to text while I'm on the job, but this is the first time we're hearing from Noli since we moved to Wisconsin. We left her back in Pensacola, Florida, and I'm feeling majorly guilty about it.

I've always been close to my sisters. In a lot of ways, our closeness has been out of necessity—we are all each other has.

But it was also easy to stay close since we all lived in the same house—at least until Noli moved in with her boyfriend.

I'm trying not to be overly critical of that decision. She's an adult, and it's important that she sees me as a sister now that we're grown up. Old habits die hard, though. I'm used to being the authority figure in her life. Mostly, I don't love the thought of her shacking up with a dude who is the definition of *not good enough for her*.

Gram is probably rolling over in her grave knowing that Noli and Nelson are living together. She always wanted us to be able to stand on our own two feet, and she'd have all sorts of things to say about Nelson having no need to buy the cow if the milk is free.

I've never liked that metaphor. I mean, don't call a woman a cow, right? But still, Gram's point stands—or at least the point I *think* Gram would be making.

I refuse to think about what Gram would say about me moving to another state for a man.

Anyway, I'm getting distracted. The takeaway here is that I love my baby sister. I want what's best for her. And I'm glad she reached out.

I cast a look out my office door. There's no one here except Patrick and Lou, who've been lingering in the hallway of the P&R building all morning. I'm not sure why. I type out a quick message in reply.

Poppy: I'm right here. Some of us have day jobs... <side-eye emoji> It's good to hear from you, Noli! I miss you.

Poppy: Are you eating? Are you sleeping? Are you wearing sunscreen?

Oops. My pseudo-mom card is showing. Noli will call me on it.

Noli: Down, girl.

See.

Poppy: Sorry! <angel-face emoji> But seriously, how are you?!

Noli: All is well here. Nelly is good. Work is good. Not much to report on my end.

Rose: Pfft, boring!

Noli: I know...such a bummer.

Poppy: No! Boring is good!

I much prefer boring, let me tell you. I dealt with both Rose and Noli through their teenage years, when hormones were raging, and tempers were flaring, and life was the opposite of boring. Noli threw all of Rose's clothes out our apartment window at one point. All because Rose kept leaving socks on the ground. It was brutal, and we barely made it through without murdering each other.

I'm only two years older than Rose, which makes me three-and-a-half years older than Noli, but you grow up quick when your mom dies in a freak car accident, your father abandons you, and the grandmother who took you in passes peacefully away in her sleep three years later.

Let's just say, I've had enough tumult in my life to last me a good, long while. At the risk of sounding like a killjoy, I'll take boring any day of the week.

At least when life is boring, nothing is hanging in the balance.

Noli: Yeah, yeah. That's why I need to live vicariously through you two. How's the dreamboat? How is driving his fancy car??

I roll my eyes.

Poppy: You make it sound like I'm using Holland for his car, which I'm not. He's very generously letting us borrow it. And he's good, thank you for asking!

Silly beads of sweat pop up along my hairline. I *think* Holland's good. We've texted, and he sounds good—excited about his golf game and his upcoming tournament play. I can't help but second-guess every one of our interactions, though. Am I being supportive enough? Am I giving him enough space? I don't know how to date a pro-athlete. I still can't believe I *am* dating a pro-athlete. Like, why would Holland want to date little ol' me?

It's all so surreal, and this relationship has been such a whirlwind it feels sort of fake.

Hopefully he has a chance to respond to my first email sometime soon. I told him there was no rush and he should check that account and reply when he's able, but it'll put my mind at ease when he writes to me.

Rose: In other news, Poppy met Holland's brother, Mack, while she was wearing nothing but a towel. <crying-laughing emoji>

Noli: OH! Juicy!

I feel the heat flood my cheeks.

Poppy: Hardly. I blame The Downer—which, ironically, Mack owns, so it was his fault. I blame him.

Noli: <sweating-face-laughing emoji> That is totally something that would happen to you, Pops. I can see it now.

Rose: Don't picture it! I'm still scarred from the experience.

Noli: Bahahahaha.

Poppy: Glad I can provide you two goons with some comic relief. <eye-roll emoji>

I glance out into the hallway because I can feel Lou and Patrick staring at me. When I meet their gaze, they look away, pretending to be very interested in the bulletin board Heather has arrayed with all the Parks and Rec programming information. Patrick points to one of the flyers, and Lou nods like he totally thinks they should take in that activity. I narrow my eyes.

I studied that bulletin board and have it memorized. (What can I say? I like to be prepared!) And I know for a fact that that particular flyer is for the mommy stroller warriors.

Poppy: As much as I'd love to continue to listen to your mocking, I've got to get back to work. Keep in touch, Noli.

My hand hovers over the keys, but then I think *screw it*, and type out what I'm thinking.

Poppy: And behave down there! Let me know if you need anything.

Noli: <eye-roll emoji> Yes, Mom!

Poppy: <sticking-out-tongue emoji> You love me!

Noli: I do! <hug emoji>

Rose: Love you both!

Noli: Byeeeeeee

I send a quick kissing-face emoji and then stow my phone in my desk. Patrick and Lou have moved away from the bulletin board that's right outside my office door. I hope they didn't think I was ignoring them. I'd like to chat, but I pull up my calendar and curse under my breath. My conversation with Noli and Rose ate up all the time I was going to use to prepare for the meeting I have with the volunteers who'll be chaperoning the zoo trip the P&R department has scheduled for next week. Heather has put me in charge, though she's still in the office. Her words: *I draw the line at chasing children around the zoo at nine months pregnant.* And honestly, good on her.

I'm excited to go, but I want to make a good impression on the volunteers, so I need to hurry.

I chug the rest of my coffee, tuck my tablet in my bag, and head out the door, pausing to lock my office. I have enough time to swing into the bathroom before I head to the meeting room. Patrick and Lou are talking to Abner, who is in charge of the Street Department in Cashmere Cove. They glance up at me as I approach.

"Hey, guys!"

"'Morning, Poppy!" Patrick sounds happy to see me.

Lou waves, and I'm relieved I didn't offend them.

I duck into the restroom that's off the hall, hook my purse on the back of the door, and peel off my tennis skirt, which feels like it's cemented to my legs thanks to the blasted Wisconsin humidity.

When I sit down on the toilet seat, I kid you not, it sounds like the entire bathroom explodes.

"SHI-OOT." I manage to curb my curse—a trick I learned trying to set a good example for Noli and Rose—as I bolt up and off the toilet, scooching my skirt up my legs as fast as I can and flinging open the door. "What *was* that?!"

Patrick and Lou are standing across the hall from the bathroom entrance. Lou has his cell phone out, and Patrick has his hand clamped over his mouth. His shoulders are shaking, like he's trying to hold back his cackle.

I'm panting, and I can feel my eyes flying in every direction.

Patrick lets loose a howl, and Lou pockets his phone to wipe the tears from his eyes. "Gotcha," he says.

"You...got me?"

"Pop-Its. The oldest trick in the book." Patrick turns to Lou, and they slap hands like they're freaking partners in potty crime.

"Your reaction was priceless," Lou says on a chuckle.

"You almost said"—Patrick leans forward, cupping his mouth with his hand—"*shit*, didn't you? That would have been perfect." He rocks back on his heels.

"I...my...how—" I cut off my own spluttering, forgoing words in favor of focusing instead on willing my blood pressure back to a normal range.

Abner comes out of his office—because of course he does. I do a quick feel of my skirt to ensure that it's not tucked into itself. What I don't need is to flash my new co-worker.

"So, it was a success, then?" Abner folds his arms across his chest, his eyes dancing. He's an older gentleman, probably pushing sixty-five. He's got a soft mid-section that lolls over the front of his belt. He's wearing a pale-yellow Cashmere Cove polo shirt tucked into black shorts.

"I'd say we hit pay dirt, all right." Lou is nodding as he gets out his phone. He taps it and shows it to Abner.

The video replay of my bathroom adventure plays back, and the three men chuckle.

"Are-are you guys hazing me?" My face is impossibly hot now. I don't know whether I'm on the cusp of laughter or tears. All I wanted to do was relieve my bladder, but I'm pretty sure I won't be able to pee again without some serious self-talk for the foreseeable future.

The guys snap their attention back in my direction.

Lou steps forward. "Didn't Holland warn you?"

"Warn me?" I feel a nervous prickle of sweat pop up on the back of my neck.

"Yeah. About the town tradition!" This from Patrick.

I shake my head. "'Fraid not. What *was* that?"

"That was your welcome to Cashmere Cove," Abner supplies.

"In the form of Pop-Its!" Lou looks all too pleased with himself.

"Taped up right onto the bottom of the toilet seat." Patrick sort of juts out his chest like he's proud of their efforts.

I glance between the three of them, floored. "You tape Pop-Its to the toilet whenever someone new comes to the Cove?"

They all look offended.

"Give us a little more credit than that! We change up the prank," Lou says.

"It's a rite of passage, Poppy." Abner pats me on the shoulder before turning to go back into his office. "Since you aren't swearing a blue streak or spitting mad, I'd say you passed with flying colors."

Lou and Patrick are nodding.

"Umm, thanks?" I don't know what to say.

"Wait until we show Mack this video," Lou chuckles.

"Mack?" I straighten. "He knew about this?"

"'Course. He planned out the whole thing. Too bad he couldn't be here to see your live reaction. But at least we got it on video."

I press my lips together. Maybe I should be offended. Maybe I should chew Lou and Patrick—and Abner—out for the PTSD I'm sure they just gave me. I swear, they scared the *piddle* straight out of me...because I no longer need to use the restroom. I could rant on them about how juvenile it is to pull a prank like that. How someone could have gotten hurt. I could have had a heart attack, for heaven's sake!

But they are staring back at me with looks of such pride on their faces that my shoulders relax, and a laugh bubbles up from deep in my chest.

Before I know it, we're all laughing together. I'm doubled over with tears streaming down my cheeks.

We watch the video four times, and each time, it gets funnier and funnier. My expression is priceless as I storm out of the bathroom, the door slamming the wall as I fling it wide.

Between gasps of air, Lou gives me a compliment that hits home, and I come close to hugging the man. "Welcome to Cashmere Cove, Poppy Kasper. You, my friend," he says, "are a keeper."

Toilet prank or not, that's all I've ever wanted anyone to feel about me.

* * * * * * * * * * *

To: poppykallday@gmail.com
From: hbradleypro@gmail.com
Subject: Re: Email 1
Dear Poppy,
I'm thrilled to hear you're settling in to Cashmere Cove. You don't have to thank me. You earned that job all on your own. I only made the initial connection. I have no doubt that you'll crush it in your role.

Speaking of rolls...here's an insider tip: be sure to stop in and see Inez at the Getaway Café. The cinnamon rolls are to die for (don't tell my coach! ☺).

To answer your question, I don't know what it is about Cashmere Cove—beyond Inez's pastries, of course—that makes it so special. I mean, no place is perfect, but there's a lot of good to be had in my hometown. I'm looking forward to getting back for the wedding next month. To see the Cove and to see you.

I took your advice and looked up at the sky. You're right. There's something grounding about that exercise. I think I'll make it a habit.

Before I sign off, I should give you a heads up that the Cashmere Cove faithful have a habit of breaking in new members of the community with some harmless pranks. Best to be on your guard!

Hugs,
Holland

∙ ∙ ∙ ● ● ∙ ● ∙ ● ∙ ∙ ∙

To: hbradleypro@gmail.com
From: poppykallday@gmail.com
Subject: Re: re: Email 1
Could have used that warning about eight hours sooner, Holland...

8

THE TRICIA INCIDENT

Mack

My eyes lock on hers, sweat cascading down my back.

"We're almost there," she says with a wolfish grin. "Don't bail on me now."

I'm too out of breath to respond with words. I force a wry grin in response. At least at this point, she's breathing heavily too. I'm not the only one working hard.

I gasp as we make the final push. I try (and fail) to match her rhythm. She's way out of my league. Different sport altogether, in fact.

"Come on," she coaxes, the tone of her voice giving me no choice but to keep going.

I squeeze my eyes closed, waiting to hear her glorious countdown.

Instead, I hear arguing coming from my front porch.

I bite back a curse and scramble for the remote to click pause on my YouTube dance fitness instructor. She freezes on my screen.

I needed this workout. I sent my first email to Poppy on behalf of Holland, and the nervous energy I'm feeling is out of this world.

Because I didn't know how to *be*. I didn't know what tone to use. I signed off with *hugs*, for crying out loud. Yuck. How lovey-dovey are they together? HOW SHOULD I KNOW?

The arguing is louder on my front porch.

"We are not going in there." I recognize Poppy's voice.

"Yes, we are!"

There's Rose.

What in the world are they doing on my side of the duplex?

I stride over to the door and tug it open.

Poppy must've been leaning against it, because she tumbles backward, arms pin-wheeling. She falls straight into me, her entire body now suctioned to my sweaty chest.

I reach out my hands, and they instinctively go to her hips, which we all know have been the topic of far too many conversations at this point in our short history.

"Sorry!" Poppy regains her footing and scrambles forward. She stares at my bare chest for a beat before she glances up and meets my gaze. "Why are you all wet?"

"Sweat," I say. "I'm kind of in the middle of something."

Both Poppy's and Rose's eyes go comically wide.

"I told you we shouldn't have interrupted him," Poppy hisses in Rose's direction. Her face is flaming red—like, Clifford-the-Big-Red-Dog red. "We...uh...we can come back. Rose thought...you know what? Never mind! Carry on! So sorry to interrupt. Enjoy yourself."

What?

Oh.

Oh!

Poppy starts to shove Rose down the porch steps.

"No." I raise my voice to catch her attention. "I'm not busy doing *that.*"

"You're...not?" Poppy turns. Her brow is knitted now. When she faces me fully, I can tell she's trying to peek over my shoulder.

"You thought something spicy was going on over here?"

Poppy smacks her palm to her forehead, covering her eyes, like she can't believe she's gotten herself into this predicament. It's sort of hilarious.

"That's exactly what she thought," Rose puts in, standing shoulder to shoulder with her sister.

"That's what it sounded like," Poppy admits.

"Get your head out of the gutter, Boo." I scoff as if I'm disappointed in her, but I'm fighting a laugh.

"Well, excuse me, *Big*! We heard lots of...suggestive talk going on."

"It's a workout video." I turn and walk back through to my living room, unpausing the TV in time to hear the trainer say, "Five, four, three, two, one, and REST!"

"See?"

Poppy primly folds her hands at her waist. "I guess that makes sense."

Rose takes a step into my side of the house. "So, this is how it's supposed to look, huh?"

"Rosie!" Poppy's voice holds a twinge of censure.

"What? I'm just saying!"

"No, she's right," I say. "Your side isn't done. I tried to tell Holland, but—"

"It's completely fine. Totally livable. We're grateful. Aren't we, Rose?"

"Eternally," Rose mutters.

Poppy looks heavenward before turning her focus back to me.

I grab for my t-shirt, which I tossed onto the back of my recliner mid-workout. I guess Poppy and I are even now. We've both seen enough of each other's skin to feel fully acquainted. "What did you need?"

"I was going to ask if you wanted to go do some door-to-door fundraising for Party in the Park with me." Poppy looks down, like she's almost embarrassed to ask. "Heather said she usually does it, and I thought I might get further with a local. Since you're the only local I know, I'm asking you."

Before I can formulate any type of response, Rose jumps in.

"And I want to talk to you about our side of the duplex." She bats her eyes with faux sweetness.

"Mostly, we'd like to go over the lease agreement. We thought we could grab an early dinner, and then you and I could hit up the town for some P&R funds—if you're not too busy," Poppy adds.

"I've got some time."

What compels me to agree to this plan, I don't know. But Poppy's full-faced smile makes me feel like I gave the right response.

They give me fifteen minutes to clean up after my workout, and then I'm driving us to Romeo's.

Poppy, who is sitting with her shoulder pressed against mine in the middle seat of my truck, ducks her head and peers out the windshield. Her whole body hums with excitement over this outing. I'm growing accustomed to her consummate cheerfulness, but it still leaves me a little off balance.

"This place is like nowhere else we've ever lived," she says with awe.

I scan either side of the road as I drive them along, trying to picture Cashmere Cove through a stranger's eyes. We drive past the granary, and of course, Poppy asks about it. I swear this woman has made me talk more in the past week than I have in the past year.

"Cashmere County was primarily built up around an agricultural economy back in the day. This grain elevator stored and protected food around the turn of the twentieth century."

"Fascinating," Poppy breathes.

"The granary fell into decay and was about to be demolished by developers, but the community banded together and got it listed on the National Registrar of Historic Places. It's been refurbished. There's a museum on the bottom floor, and the upper two levels serve as a top wedding venue in the area."

"Who knew small town Wisconsin could be so...exotic." Rose's tone is wry, but I see her taking in the sights with a keen eye.

"That's where Piper and Ed's reception will be held?" Poppy asks, ignoring her sister's sarcasm.

I nod.

"I love that. Gosh, I can't get over how darling this all is!" Poppy's head is on a swivel as she takes in the heart of downtown. Her face is shining in the late-afternoon sun. Even Rose, the more serious of the two, is eagerly peering out the front windshield.

Since I've lived here my entire life, the charming shops and picturesque views have become second nature, and I guess I take them for granted. Along the street, the sidewalks are wide and lined with planters overflowing with an assortment of seasonal blooms. Antique lampposts outfitted with modern electric functionality are strategically positioned on each corner. They're my favorite part of the downtown Cashmere Cove landscape.

The buildings are a mixture of brick and siding, and each has a wooden sign hanging perpendicular from its façade, announcing what business is housed inside.

"There's Mood Reader." Rose points to a long, narrow building with a wide front window.

Nearby there's also the hardware store, the flower shop, the ice cream parlor, several tourist-trap restaurants and souvenir shops, and of course, the Getaway Café—the best place to go for coffee in town.

"Oh! Holland mentioned the Getaway Café in his email. He said I should try the cinnamon rolls."

"You heard from Holland?" Rose shifts in her seat so she's facing her sister.

I cut a sidelong glance at Poppy. She's beaming.

"Yep!" she says. "Earlier this afternoon."

She looks so happy it makes my stomach hurt to know that it wasn't Holland who reached out, but me.

"Here we are." I park outside Romeo's, thankful to have an excuse to change the subject and not dwell on the email Poppy received (that, in a strange twist, I wrote!).

I lead the way to Romeo's, and Poppy falls into step next to me with Rose behind us.

We walk in silence for a couple beats, but then Poppy tugs on my arm. "Uh, Mack, not to be a paranoid Polly, but you aren't taking us somewhere to murder us, are you? This back alley feels a little sketchy, if I'm being honest."

Her gaze darts to the high walls of brick on either side of us.

"If you thought I was going to murder you, I don't think you'd be asking me about it."

"True. I'd clobber you over the head, Pops would grab your keys, and we'd make a break for it," Rose says without missing a beat.

Poppy nods solemnly, her big blue eyes wide.

I'm fighting a full-fledged laugh at the ridiculousness of this entire situation.

"Cashmere Cove has its local haunts and its tourist traps," I explain. "Unlike Mood Reader and the Getaway Café that have storefronts on Main Street, Romeo's can only be accessed through a back entrance. You've got to know it's here to find it. It's the best restaurant in town."

That means it'll also be full of at least half the town.

The good mood Poppy and Rose have me in disintegrates at the thought. Don't get me wrong, I prefer the locals to the tourists, but I also still run the risk of getting shunned by some members of the Cashmere Cove community every time I go out. That's what happens when you have a messy break-up with the town darling.

The daughter of the Cove's beloved police chief.

The one and only Tricia Rattler—or, Tricia Reynolds, now that she's married.

I hold the door for Poppy and Rose to walk in ahead of me, and once inside, I scan the dimly lit pizza joint. Mercifully, the place doesn't look too crowded. Pizza Master Kenny is in the kitchen. I can see him through the look-through window.

Yes, he goes by Pizza Master Kenny, or PMK for short.

We stop by the hostess's station, and a teenager leads us to a table tucked into a back corner.

"It smells amazing in here." Poppy beams and pulls in a deep breath.

"I'm starving," Rose says as she plops down into her seat, grabbing for a menu. "What's good, Mack?"

"Everything."

Rose hums. "I don't know, Pops. Should we trust him?"

I sit up straighter at that comment. What did I do to merit that?

She flicks her gaze to me. "I have it on good authority that you're partially to blame for the *disgusting* 'juice'"—she makes air quotes around the word—"I was subject to this afternoon."

Oh.

Mia works quickly.

I tug my lips into my mouth to keep my face straight.

"And I mean *disgusting*." Rose angles her head toward Poppy. "You know I try not to consume too much sugar, so I was only accepting the drink from Mia to be nice, to try to seem accommodating." Rose gags. "The joke was on me. It was macaroni-and-cheese powder dissolved in water. I mean *honestly*."

I snort but play it off like a cough.

"I'd take cheese juice over an exploding toilet," Poppy declares with a serious inflection to her usually upbeat tone.

I cough louder.

"Scared the you-know-what right out of me."

The two sisters pin me with identical glares. Looking at them like this, it's easy to see their similarities—the shape of their noses, the long eyelashes, and the crease of annoyance in their foreheads. But I can also point out their differences. Poppy's hair is lighter brown—more golden-bronze than Rose's dark, coppery-black hue. Poppy's hair is in its usual ponytail. I've yet to see her with it down...unless you count Friday morning when she was stranded outside post-shower. Rose's hair is cut to her chin. It's longer along her jawline than it is at the nape of her neck.

Their eyes are different too. Yes, they're both looking at me like they're ready to fight—playfully, I hope. But Poppy's eyes are a pale blue that reminds me of the color of the sky in the spring. Rose's eyes are like sapphires. Deep and moody.

"Do you have anything to say for yourself, Big?"

At Poppy's use of my nickname, I let loose a slight grin, but then I shrug. "I thought Holland would have warned you."

"He did. But not until it was too late."

"Cheese powder, Mack. I drank freaking cheese powder because of you." Rose throws up her hands. "Do you know how long that stuff will sit in my gut? It's got a shelf life of, like, five years." She pretends to wretch.

"I'll never pee in peace again." Poppy bows her head, as if she's taking a moment to mourn the death of her previous bathroom-going self.

I clear my throat. "You're being dramatic."

Poppy narrows her sky-blue eyes at me, tipping up her chin. "Have you ever sat on an exploding toilet?"

"Or drank cheese juice?" Rose adds.

I open my mouth, but I don't have a response to that.

Poppy crosses her arms. "Exactly."

"Watch your back, dude. We don't roll over very easily." Rose drags her thumb across her neck in the universal sign for decapitating.

I cock my head. "Are you threatening me, Junior Kasper?"

Rose crinkles her nose. "Junior Kasper?"

"I can call you Little Boo, if you'd prefer."

Rose snorts. "No."

I find myself relaxing in my seat. I like these women—the way they banter with each other. The feisty way they talk back to me.

"You've been warned. That's all we're saying." Poppy sets her menu down. "You'll never see our prank coming."

Rose nods, a closed-lipped smile making her look conspiring.

"That's not how it works. We prank new-to-town folks. It doesn't go both ways."

"There's no rule against it," Poppy says. When I narrow my gaze at her, she adds, "I've asked around. Now"—she claps her hands—"let's get down to business."

A waitress swings by, and we place our order—half sausage and mushroom for Poppy and me, and half veggie for Rose. We spend the rest of the dinner hour talking about the duplex and trying to figure out a schedule when I can work on the things that Rose has deemed "priority."

Poppy is playing mediator. "We're grateful for any work you do...whenever you do it. There is no rush at all."

Rose holds up her hand. "The bathroom is a must-fix, though. I can't go to work with plaster in my hair."

I grimace. I wish I could snap my fingers and make the place better for them. I truly do. But there are only twenty-four hours in a day, and I need about thirty to manage my current work load. Still, I find myself agreeing to come over this weekend to re-plaster the bathroom ceiling. "As long as there's no water damage, it shouldn't take me more than half a day."

Rose sits back and gives me a satisfied nod.

I turn to Poppy. "Boo, you got a top-priority request?"

"As long as I know the sounds coming from the AC unit aren't overly concerning, I can make do with things as they are."

I make a mental note to get an air conditioning technician out to check it.

After we finish our food, I head to the bar and pay, tipping my hat to Pizza Master Kenny. We drop Rose off at the duplex, and then Poppy and I embark on our Party in the Park donation-gathering spree.

Her enthusiasm is contagious, and she knocks boldly on each door, making conversation with everyone who answers, collecting pledges and cash on the spot. She doesn't need me at all, but I'd be lying if I said I wasn't having a good time. The sticky air is cooler now that the sun is lower in the sky. I can faintly hear the sound of the water crashing against the rocky cove in the distance.

"There's never been a dance at the Party in the Park, right?" Poppy asks me as we're walking between houses in the lower district.

"A dance?"

"Yeah, you know." She stops and jabs her finger in the air and then down to her hip.

"Not sure what that was." I gesture in her general direction, and she punches me in the arm. I smirk. "But no, there's not a dance—or there hasn't been one."

"We should do one this year." Poppy whips out her phone and makes a note. "Scavenger hunt for teens. Dance for adults. Perfect." She glances up at me. "I've been over at the park, and the courtyard right outside the lighthouse would be a perfect dance floor. Don't you think?"

"Maybe."

"Definitely," she says with a nod. "Who doesn't like a good town-wide dance? Besides, I bet you could make it a stunning scene with some extra lights. You're the best electrician in the county!"

Before I can respond to that, she marches up to the lavender-colored house we discussed on our drive to my parents' place on Sunday. When Willow Dunlap opens the door, Poppy beams at her. After making the requisite small talk, she asks, "Mrs. Dunlap, how do you feel about getting jiggy with it?"

"I've been known to bust a move," Willow says without missing a beat.

"Would you and Earnest like to help me coordinate the first annual Party in the Park Promenade?"

Willow pats her hair. "Well, now, I'd be delighted."

Poppy shoots me a triumphant grin as Willow goes to get her husband. We end up talking to the pair for a solid twenty minutes.

Willow has the idea that people can donate money to get songs played during the promenade—which is, admittedly, genius.

As we're saying our goodbyes, Willow turns to me. "Mack, dear, there's an issue with the self-checkout kiosk at the library. Do you think you could look at it for us?"

I mentally flip though my schedule for the next day. "Sure, Willow. I'll stop by first thing."

"What a good boy you are." She reaches up and pats my cheek.

We stroll back up the street to my truck, and I feel Poppy's happy energy next to me. "I'd say that was a success."

I nod. It almost feels normal to be out and about around town with Poppy. Everyone we've talked to has been generous and accommodating. No cold shoulder. It feels good. I feel good.

Too good to last.

I notice the silhouetted family walking at us before Poppy does, and I have a muscular-level response. What I mean by that is my whole body goes tense, from my scalp to the arches of my feet.

"What's wrong?" Poppy must sense a change in my bearing.

"Nothing."

"Big," she says, stretching out that one syllable like she's saying, *Don't lie to me.*

"It's fine." I steel myself as the family gets closer and closer.

"Well, well, well. Look what the cat dragged in."

The voice sounds like nails on a chalkboard. Is that too unoriginal? Well, then it sounds like the sickening break of a bone. All crack and snap. Everything out of place. Jagged. Painful.

Poppy glances at me. "Is she talking to us?"

Before I can answer, Tricia is standing in front of us, along with her husband, Terry, and their four-month-old son, Fennimore. Her eyes are flashing as she appraises me and then spins to size up Poppy. "What are you doing around here, Mack? This is my side of town."

My eyes are angled down at the sidewalk.

"Excuse me." Poppy's got her usual cheerful tone in place—the same one that earned her thousands of dollars in donations in the last hour and a half. I want to tell her to be quiet. There is no winning when Tricia is involved. But that would involve me speaking, and where this woman is concerned, I've basically forgotten how to do that.

I glance up to see Poppy giving a little wave. "I don't think we've met. I'm new to town. Poppy Kasper." She extends her hand in Tricia's direction.

Tricia's lips curl up, but her expression is tinged with disdain. "Holland's girlfriend, right?" She takes Poppy's outstretched hand and gives it a squeeze. "I guess I shouldn't be surprised to see you here with Mack. Someone should warn Holland."

Poppy flinches. "What's that supposed to mean?"

"Mack can't be trusted when it comes to women."

I'm grinding my teeth now.

"Excuse me?" Poppy shoots me a look that I can't read.

Before Tricia can say anything else, her husband, Terry, steps up alongside of her. "Now, sweetheart, is this worth it?"

He's talking to his wife, but his eyes are on me.

Tricia sticks her nose in the air. "No, it really isn't."

They make a move to go around us.

Poppy steps to the side. She's still smiling in their direction, but it's grown a little less authentic from what I can tell. "Looking forward to seeing you at the Party in the Park! The kids' game line-up looks spectacular!"

Tricia waves over her shoulder without looking around.

I turn and stride to my truck. Poppy has to jog to catch up to me.

"So," she says. When I don't respond, she adds, "That's Tricia."

"That's Tricia," I repeat.

"Want to tell me what happened between you two?"

"Nope."

"Figured as much."

And then, mercifully, she doesn't press me on it.

It's like she knows what I need—or rather, don't need—in the moment.

Instead, she starts prattling on about her ideas for the Party in the Park Promenade. "Don't you just love that name?" she asks. "Came up with it right on the spot. I think Willow was impressed with my vocabulary." Then, when the radio plays a Jonas Brothers song, she launches into a rendition of the choreographed routine she and her sisters made up to the tune of "Love Bug."

By the time we get back to the duplex and she hops out of the truck with a wave and a promise to see me soon, I can almost let myself forget about running into Tricia.

But then I walk into my dark house, and my fists clench at my sides.

It's not that I'm still in love with Tricia. Because I'm not. But she always wins. Everyone in town has taken her side—or at least that's how it feels. I should be used to it by now, but tonight it stings.

Why?

I toss my keys onto the counter and scrape my hands through my hair.

The answer comes to me in a flash.

Because I care about Poppy's opinion of me, and it's the first time in a long time I can say that I care about what someone else thinks. I don't know what it is about her, but I feel pulled in her direction. Like she's the moon to my tide.

I know, I know. I referred to her as the sun earlier, and now I'm comparing her to the moon. How am I supposed to categorize this woman? She's unlike anyone I've ever met. All I know is I want to be her friend, and I don't like the thought of her impression of me being skewed by the past.

9

Rumor Has It

Poppy

"So, how's Holland?" Rose settles into her chair across the table from me at Getaway Café, taking a long sip of her iced coffee and picking up a French fry.

"He's good." I loop my purse over the back of my seat and face her. "Tired, but energized, if that makes sense. It's cool to see him doing what he was made to do."

Holland and I were finally able to connect over a video call yesterday night after he finished his Sunday round. Not only did he make the cut and get to play the weekend, but he shot lower than anyone expected, made a nice chunk of change, and moved up the ranks.

Golf is a nebulous sport if you're not into it, but basically Holland earned a tour card, which allows him to play in PGO Tour tournaments. The Professional Golf Organization is the big leagues. He's got to keep playing well in order to keep his card, and each week's golf outing counts.

That's why he's so busy. He's focused on what's in front of him, and I can't fault him for that. I've been watching as much golf as I can so I can be as supportive as possible. Holland was happy to be able to talk through his game with me, and I was happy I could sort of understand what shots and holes he was referring to.

I'm not going to tell Rose that I feel absolutely zero romantic spark where Holland is concerned. It's unfair of me to think that at this point. Sure, he might have only talked about his golf game, but he seemed genuinely happy to see me, and he was nibbling on the snacks I sent him in my care package, so I know he appreciated that. While he didn't offer much by way of conversation outside of his game, he was very content to sit back and let me tell him all about Cashmere Cove and my first week in town.

All in all, we had a nice visit. I'm good with nice.

No, it's not a desperate, pining-after-each-other kind of romance, but it's steady, and it's still new. We started dating a month before I moved here. Our whole relationship has been on the fly, but he'll be back in town for his cousin's wedding, which'll be a great chance to reconnect.

"Don't you sound like the most doting girlfriend around?" Rose wiggles her eyebrows at me before continuing. "What did he have to say about"—she glances over her shoulder before dropping her voice—"Mack and Tricia?"

I look toward the counter area. We spotted Mack when we walked in. He was dressed in a Mack Electric t-shirt, was wearing his usual black M-E baseball hat, and had a tool belt around his waist. He was fiddling with a light switch behind the bar and looked up and nodded at us but returned his focus to whatever he was working on without so much as a word.

It's been a week since Mack took us to Romeo's for pizza, and he and I had what Rose has coined the Tricia Incident.

He's been like a ghost since then. He did come by the house to look at the drywall in the bathroom like he promised, but otherwise, we haven't seen heads or tails of him. He's been getting home late. I know this because, unlike Rose, who sleeps like the dead, I sleep like a zombie and am in a perpetual half-awake state. I always startle when his truck pulls in. That means I also hear when his truck rumbles away a little before six each morning.

"Holland brushed me off when I asked. He said Mack made his bed, and he's content to lie in it."

"What's that supposed to mean?"

"It's not really our business."

Rose looks affronted. "Don't be all high and mighty. I know you're curious about why Tricia said someone should warn Holland about you spending time with Mack."

"Excuse me."

Rose and I look up in unison to see a woman around my age waving at us from one table over. I recognize her from the volunteer meeting I held for the zoo trip chaperones. Ginny, I think. There's another gal in an apron—the same lady who was behind the café's counter, looking over Mack's shoulder when we entered, if I'm not mistaken—standing next to her.

"We couldn't help but overhear," the woman wearing the apron says. She tosses a look at the counter. "You're wondering about Mack Bradley, right?"

"We are," Rose says with no qualms about it.

"We don't mean to gossip," I hurry to add. "We had an interesting run-in with a woman by the name of Tricia last week."

The two ladies exchange a knowing look.

Rose's gaze flips to mine, and she raises her eyebrows before turning back to the other women.

"First of all, I'm Inez. I'm the owner here."

I shake the hand of the woman in the apron. She's got beautiful, deep-set, dark eyes and dark-brown hair piled high on top of her head.

"Holland told me I should try your cinnamon rolls."

Inez chuckles, all warm smiles and sparkling eyes. "He had me make up a tray of a dozen for him to take along before he left. The way to that man's heart is through his stomach."

"I'll remember that," I say, smiling back.

"I'm Ginny Douglas. Not sure if you remember me from the zoo volunteers meeting?" The other woman scoots her chair so she's seated at our table. Bold, but I'll allow it. I nod in response to her question.

She leans in. "I went to high school with Mack and Tricia, so I've got all the deets."

"What are the...deets?" Rose asks, shooting me another look.

I'm conflicted here because I'm both dying to know what's going on with Mack—there's something about him that's so intriguing—but I also want to respect the man's privacy. He must've had his reasons for not wanting to get into his history with Tricia with me.

"First of all, some background." Ginny settles into her chair, as if getting ready to tell us the next great American novel.

Buckle up, Boo.

I can almost hear Mack's deadpan voice in my head. Which is weird, right? I look over to where he is, and he's got his back to us. I exhale and focus on Ginny.

"Mack has always been a little rough around the edges. He got into some trouble as a kid."

"What sort of trouble are we talking about?" Rose asks, and I nod.

"The usual teenager stuff. Mostly harmless vandalism. Spray painting the old water tower. Egging a couple cars. That sort of thing. It was nothing to write home about—until he upped his game."

"How so?"

"He stole a necklace that was worth a couple thousand bucks from the local jeweler."

Rose's eyes bug.

"I know, right?" Ginny says. "It was a big deal. Rumor has it he was stealing it to give to Tricia, though Mack never confirmed that. They weren't officially dating at the time, but they got together shortly after. I personally have always wondered if she put him up to it to see how much he liked her."

"Sort of a *if-you-say-jump-I-say-how-far* situation, then?" Inez clarifies.

"Exactly."

Inez turns to Rose and me. "I moved to town after all this, so I'm not a primary source. I've only heard the story passed down."

"It's the juiciest of the Cashmere Cove history," Ginny says seriously.

"So, then what happened?" I ask, steering the conversation back to the point.

"No one knows who ratted Mack out, but the chief of police showed up at the Bradley house the day after the necklace was stolen, asked Mack to open the glove compartment of his truck, and *bam!* There the necklace was." Ginny shrugged. "Not the smartest idea to leave it there, if you ask me."

"Sounds like a set-up if you ask me," Rose muttered.

My sister reads a ton of mystery novels, so she would know. I can't help but agree with her.

"Mack admitted to taking the necklace, though," Ginny says. "The chief of police, who, I should mention, is also Tricia's dad, let him off easy. Lucky for Mack, he was only seventeen, so a minor. He was also different back then."

"Different how?" I ask.

"Charming. Happy-go-lucky. Not sure if you've noticed, but he's sort of…how should I put this…" Ginny pauses, as if searching for the right word.

"Surly," Rose suggests, flipping her gaze to me.

"Yeah, that's it." Ginny nods. "Anyway, he admitted his guilt and returned the necklace to the jeweler, who agreed not to take it any further as long as Mack completed one hundred hours of community service. Mack happily obliged, and that was that."

"Okay," I say. "None of that explains Mack's and Tricia's responses to each other last week. It was hostile, to put it mildly—at least on her end."

"Of course it was." Ginny nods knowingly. "There's nothing *mild* between Mack and Tricia, and this is where the story gets good. Those two started dating shortly after necklace-gate. They were together our senior year, and then well after high school. Mack stayed close to home here, working as an apprentice electrician, and Tricia went to school in Green Bay. Everyone thought they were going to get married and live happily ever after. Tricia talked about it all the time. She was counting down the days to the proposal. But then"—Ginny pauses and leans forward—"they broke up. Mack fled town, and word circulated that Tricia had found him in bed with another woman."

Rose and I both sit back in our chairs. This hits close to home. We have it on good authority that Nelson has cheated on Noli. Noli refuses to believe it, but Rose and I do.

"So his reputation was basically gutted after this all went down," Ginny continues.

"He's been blacklisted ever since, from what I've been able to tell," Inez supplies.

"Did he have anything to say for himself?" I ask Ginny.

"That's just it. You'd think he'd try to refute the claim or make an excuse. Defend himself. Something. But Mack turned inward. He got quiet and aloof."

"Surly," Rose and I say together.

"Most people think he's a prisoner to his own guilt. That's why he never fights Tricia on things around town. He takes a wide berth, like he's trying not to run into her, but when they inevitably collide, he ends up fleeing. Just like all those years ago. He hasn't dated anyone since. He's a certified bachelor."

Rose lets out a low whistle.

Holland's words about Mack making his bed and lying in it ring in my ears alongside Darla's. His own family has given up on Mack. That makes me sad.

"You're both Team Tricia, then?" I ask.

Ginny shrugs. "There isn't any other team to be on, is there?"

Inez avoids my gaze. Rose picks up on her shiftiness too and zeroes in on the café owner, channeling her best mystery novel amateur sleuth. "You look like you have other thoughts on the matter."

Inez gives a wry grin. "I've heard the legend of Mack Bradley's demise since I came to town, but I don't know. I hate judging someone for their past. I mean, I get it. Cheating on your long-time girlfriend is terrible. But is that what happened?" We all look at him, and Mack must sense our gaze, because he glances up.

I wave like an awkward elephant, and Mack furrows his brow.

We turn back to the table, and Inez lowers her voice. "Mack has been nothing but helpful as I launched this place. He brought all my electrical up to code in this building, and he gave me a steep discount. He's also always willing to swing by when I have an issue—like today." She nods at the counter. "All I'm saying is that he seems like a genuinely decent guy. I don't think I'm the only one who thinks so either."

I mull that over. "Interesting."

"Just my two cents. I've got to get back to work." Inez heads behind the counter, where Mack waves her over.

We're silent for a second, watching the pair, and then Ginny clasps her hands together. "Anyway. Make of that what you will."

"Thanks for filling us in on...everything," Rose says, and I nod, my gaze still on Mack.

"Sure." Ginny stands up. "I felt like it's your right to know...considering you're living next door to him and dating his brother and all." She flicks her gaze to me with the last words of her sentence. "If anyone gives you problems about that, know you've got a friend in me."

"Problems?" I bite my cheek, dreading her clarification.

"There are a lot of local ladies who would like to get their hands on Holland Bradley. Some of them aren't too happy an outsider swooped in and got to him first." Ginny must pick up on my unease, because she waves her hand in the air. "You know what? Forget I mentioned anything. I'm sure it'll be fine. You seem lovely." She glances around before adding, "Keep an eye out for people making mischief. There's this town tradition—"

"The pranks?" Rose rolls her eyes. "We know."

"Someone already got you?"

"Lou and Patrick," I say.

"And Patrick's wife, Mia," Rose puts in.

"With the help of Mack," I finish.

"Huh." Ginny looks thoughtful. "Well, that's good. You should be home free now. Unspoken rules state that once you're pranked, no one is supposed to pile on. The tradition would lose its fun that way, don't you think?"

"Guess so." I'm still not sure I'd consider the tradition *fun* to begin with, but I keep my opinion to myself for now. I'm willing to be a good sport about it if it means I'll be welcomed into the Cashmere Cove fold. From the way Ginny talks, it sounds like I'm going to need all the help I can get. My shoulders slump. I need the people of Cashmere Cove to like me in order to do my job well. What if they boycott the events I plan out of spite?

Anxiety tiptoes across my back, leaving me chilled. I can't stop myself from wondering if Holland would be better off with someone else. Someone polished. With a better background, or a shared history, or any number of appealing qualities. I mean, what's he doing with me in the first place? I've wondered that since he struck up that first conversation at the gym down in Florida. I was flattered that someone like him would want to be with someone like me. But I've got no business dating someone of his pedigree. And more to the point, are Holland and I compatible?

"I'm off. I'll see you for the zoo trip, if not before!" Ginny waves and saunters out of the café.

I blink at her retreating figure before facing Rose.

She's staring at me with her brows pinched. "Don't do it."

"Do what?" I twirl my straw in my drink.

"Second-guess yourself and your relationship with Holland."

I sigh. "Am I that obvious?"

Rose reaches across the table and wraps her fingers around my wrist, squeezing gently. "You get in your own head all the time, worrying about what other people think and what they need. But in this case, what matters is you and Holland."

"Long-distance relationships are hard," I say on a sigh. "How do I know if this is worth it or if it's right?"

Something I can't quite place flashes across Rose's face, but she masks it. "As long as the two of you are happy and committed to each other, the rest will all fall away. Put the blinders on, if you need to, but don't self-sabotage, Pops."

"That's the thing. I don't know if we are happy and committed to each other, because there's been no chance to find out."

Rose crosses her arms and studies me. I can't help but wonder if she's thinking I was crazy for moving us all the way up here when I've got my qualms about my relationship with Holland. Part of me thinks I *am* crazy.

"It's going to be fine, Poppy. If you and Holland are meant to be, that'll become clear to you with time. If not, then you'll figure that out too. But it's up to you ... not anyone else."

I sit back in my chair and stare at my sister. "When did you get so smart?"

"I learned from the best." She winks, and I smile.

"Thanks."

Rose leans forward and clasps her hands, all business. "Now, what do you make of the Mack situation? I have thoughts."

I swirl the straw in my drink. "I'm going to withhold judgment."

Rose stares back at me like she wants to say something.

"What?" I ask.

"Even if he's a cheater?"

I shift in my seat. I don't like the thought of that, but I also know how rumors can fly, and I'm willing to give him the benefit of the doubt—or at least let him speak for himself on the matter. "I'd like to hear his side of the story."

Rose frowns. "I guess there's always two sides in situations like this."

"Exactly. I can't put my finger on it, but Mack's body language wasn't that of someone who was guilty when he ran into Tricia. He was tense, sure, but it was like it was because he was holding something back, not because he was ashamed."

"You got all that from standing next to him on the sidewalk?"

"I don't know," I say, picking up my avocado-and-chicken sandwich. "I feel like I can read Mack. Maybe he'll tell me what really happened someday."

"Maybe," Rose says around a bite of her Mediterranean salad, not looking convinced.

I glance over her shoulder to where Mack is packing up his tools. Inez is arguing with him, and I'm guessing she's trying to pay him for his time, but he's shaking his head.

I can't put my finger on it, but there's something about Mack Bradley that screams *good guy.*

He catches me staring and holds my gaze for a heartbeat before turning and making his departure.

I feel a tug in my chest as the door swings shut behind him, and I recognize it for what it is. It's the same sort of feeling I get in my gut when my sisters need me—in those moments when I know I have to step up and go to bat for them.

Like when Rose was five minutes late for dance tryouts her junior year of high school because she was coming from her part-time job, and the coaches wouldn't let her audition because they said her lack of punctuality was indicative of her lack of dedication. You better believe I had a word with them about the meaning of dedication, and how Rose was doing a heck of a lot more than anyone else on that team when it came to her dedication to her family and keeping the lights on at our house.

Or when Noli was in tears because some mean girls kept making fun of her second-hand clothes. I called their parents up and told them they should be ashamed of their daughters' behavior. Yes, I was quaking in my boots to talk to adults who were a solid twenty years older than me, but I did it. Because I show up for my people.

I can't explain it, but I want to be there for Mack. I want to befriend him.

I only hope he lets me.

10

A MODERN-DAY BATWOMAN

Mack

To: hbradleypro@gmail.com

From: poppykallday@gmail.com

Subject: Email 2

Dear Holland,

I've been thinking a lot about forgiveness lately. And no, before you ask, you haven't done anything wrong! ☺ It's general ruminations on my part. When does someone deserve to be forgiven? And if we forgive, does it mean we're turning a blind eye to the wrongful behavior? I haven't told you much about my dad, but suffice it to say, he bailed on our family when we needed him the most. I've been trying to come to terms with that betrayal ever since.

I'm sorry if this seems heavy. I've been thinking a lot about how we form opinions of people and how we judge them. What's fair? What's not? How much of someone's past should we hold against them?

I'm going to stop there because I'm sure when you open this account, you aren't expecting to be accosted by deep issues of morality. I'll try to tone it down in the future. Thanks for letting me think out loud—er, on paper.

Sending a smooch,

Poppy

· · · · ● · ● · · · ·

My phone is screaming at me from the kitchen as I turn off the water in the shower. It's late—pushing ten o'clock. I got caught out at the job site, and then I ended up spending a half hour looking up at the sky. I swear, Poppy is on to something with that.

I hop on one foot and get into a pair of athletic shorts, looping my towel over my shoulders as I jog to my kitchen.

I manage to answer before the final ring. "Hey, Collin."

"I thought you were going to stand me up."

I chuckle at that, pitching my voice to sound like I'm baby-talking. "Aww, were your feewings about to get hurt?"

Collin is my best friend—has been for years. Maybe you're thinking it's weird that we talk on the phone at ten p.m. on a weeknight. Why not text like normal dudes? Who makes phone calls these days? I get it, but you know what? I say we need to normalize healthy male friendships. For Collin and me, phone calls work.

He's an officer on the Cashmere Cove Police Force. He works second shift, and when he goes out on patrol, he often calls me, and we catch up. He can't text because he needs to keep his head on a swivel, so most of the time, I'm on speaker phone while he's in his cruiser.

"I was close to tears, man. Don't ever leave me hanging like that again," Collin says this with mock sincerity.

I laugh. "How's the night shaping up?"

I can hear Collin stretching out in the front seat of his squad car. The leather creaks through the line as he launches into the happenings around Cashmere Cove. I jab at my phone and turn it on speaker while he tells me about how he pulled over Scott Wallace...again.

"I swear the man cannot drive under forty-five miles per hour. If he's not careful, we're going to revoke his license."

I murmur my assent as I bang around for a pot underneath my stove and put some water on to boil. I'm having mac and cheese for a late dinner. Don't judge. Although, I've been questioning my dinner choice after Rose's proclamation about how the cheese dust will basically never break down.

My entire stomach is coated with the stuff at this point, but there's nothing for it. I'm too busy to cook a meal, and by the time I get home, I'm too exhausted to wait up for take-out. So, fake cheese and noodles it is.

Someone next door, either Poppy or Rose, must be a good cook, because every night this week when I've come home from work, there's the scent of spices in the air. I've been giving the Kasper sisters their space since Poppy and I ran into Tricia. I don't know what Poppy thinks of me at this point.

"Mack?"

"What?"

"I asked how you are."

"Oh. Good. Fine."

"You sure? Tricia mentioned that she saw you out and about." Collin sounds hesitant.

I dump the raw noodles into my pot of boiling water and do my best impression of someone who is indifferent about life. "It's fine. Nothing to worry about."

Collin sighs. "I don't believe you. I'm sorry about Tricia. I...I don't... It's been a long time, you know. I wish she'd let it all go. For your sake."

Did I mention that Collin is Tricia's brother? Yeah. So there's that.

I sure know how to messy the waters, don't I?

"Tricia's going to do what Tricia's going to do, Collin. I can't control her."

I've been walking this line for years, trying not to bash his sister while also not heaping on any more dishonesty to the pile. I've had to choose my words carefully.

When everything went south between Tricia and me, and what felt like the entire town took her side, Collin remained a firmly neutral party. The man rivals Switzerland. I know it hasn't been easy for him. For a while there, we didn't speak about my relationship with his sister. We kept our conversations centered around other things. He didn't ask me what happened. I didn't offer to tell him.

Maybe I should have.

In the years since, the truth has been on the tip of my tongue more times than I can count, but I've always swallowed it back down. I was guilty in the eyes of this town before I had a chance to speak for myself back then. Who's going to give me the benefit of the doubt now?

Boo.

It's true. That's what I had been thinking about tonight, ever since I'd read Poppy's latest email to Holland. It got me wondering whether she might be the one to give me a chance.

A chance to explain. To come clean. To be me again.

That's what friends do, right?

And the fact that she'd consider forgiving her dad after whatever he did to her made me feel more hope than I've felt in years. Because maybe she'll keep an open mind around me, even if word about my past with Tricia makes it to her. I have no doubt that it will. It seems like it's the first thing people talk about in this town. But if Poppy is willing to withhold judgment—or at least willing to form her own opinion of me—then maybe, eventually, I could work my way up to telling her the truth.

She's also got me thinking about whether it might be time to forgive Tricia.

That was one powerful email. Holland has no idea what he's missing out on.

I give the noodles a stir, and there's silence on the line between Collin and me. I can tell he's grinding his teeth.

"Stop that," I say. "Your dentist isn't going to be pleased with you."

I hear him rub the stubble of his five o'clock—or, as it were, ten o'clock—shadow.

"My dentist is the least of your concerns. Does your doctor know your diet consists of one food group—preservatives?"

"That's beside the point."

"That is the entire point."

I drain the noodles, grateful to be back to a less weighty topic of conversation.

"How's Holland's girlfriend?"

"Fine."

"Fine? That's all you can give me?"

I shrug, though Collin can't see me. "Yeah, I mean she's normal. Nice."

"A change of pace for Holland."

I grunt. My brother has a history of dating loose cannons. "Poppy is different, from what I can tell. Holland asked me to show her around, but I'm still getting to know her."

Collin laughs at that.

"What?" I say, mixing in the cheese powder and trying not to think about it.

"Nothing. You aren't the first person I'd choose to be a part of the Cashmere Cove welcoming committee, that's all."

"Don't underestimate me."

"Wouldn't dream of it," Collin deadpans. "I'd like to meet her sometime. She has a sister, right?"

"Two of them, from what I gather. Only one's in town."

"Maybe you can set me up."

"Lou already called dibs, and I don't condone any of this. I draw the line at playing matchmaker—especially for you, Mr. Serial Dater."

Before Collin can answer, a scream pierces the silence of my apartment from through the wall. On its heels is another scream in a different register. The yelling continues. It's high-pitched and continuous.

"What was that? Mack?" Collin's cop senses are firing.

"I've got to go. Something's wrong at Poppy and Rose's."

"Mack! Do you need me?"

"I don't know. I'm going next door."

"Wait for me. You have no idea what's happening over there."

The screams are intensifying now. My mind is flying to worst-case scenarios. Did someone break in? Are the Kasper sisters in danger?

I toss my phone on my kitchen table and am out my front door in a flash. I can hear the screams louder once I'm outside. I scan the windows. The blinds are drawn, and the lights are out, but...is their front door open?

My heart rate kicks up as I creep forward. If there's an intruder, the element of surprise is my friend.

I sprint through the open door.

The sight that greets me is unexpected—mostly because I don't see anyone at all, at first. It's pitch black.

The screaming stops for a second, but then it picks up again.

I spot Rose crouched under the coffee table.

Poppy is holding a tennis racket in the air like she's Serena Williams. She's got herself wedged behind a floor lamp with a large shade.

"What is it? What's going on?" I have to raise my voice to be heard over their screams. "Are you okay?"

"Get down, Big!" Poppy takes a swing at something, and before I know it, a flying creature is headed straight for me.

I drop to the floor, hitting my wrists and knees hard. "What the hell?"

"We've got a bat!" Rose wails.

"Bats!" Poppy clarifies. "Multiple."

"You're screaming about a bat?"

"Not just one!" Poppy scowls at me. "Weren't you listening? There's a whole family of them. They dive-bombed us out of nowhere. What are you doing here?" she adds, as if only now realizing that I barged into their house unannounced. "And why aren't you wearing a shirt?"

I glance down. I sort of forgot I was just wearing my athletic shorts. "I'm here because you scared the crap out of me. I thought you were being ax murdered."

"Oh." Poppy's shoulders sink, even as her eyes don't leave the ceiling. "Sorry about that. And thank you," she says, "for coming to check on us. How're your reflexes?"

"My reflexes?"

"Bats do not play. We've got to get them out of here, and Rose is no help." She points the tennis racket at her sister.

Rose is reaching an arm out and grabbing couch cushions, one at a time, making a barricade around herself and the coffee table. "I want nothing to do with getting rabies. Haven't you read *Old Yeller*?"

"Now is not the time to flaunt your literary superiority, Rose," Poppy scolds. "I need to focus."

Two bats are flapping around overhead. I'm still on my hands and knees and offering no help whatsoever because now I'm paranoid about getting bitten by a bat and contracting a potentially fatal viral disease. I scooch to the side of the room where Poppy is. She's got the only weapon among us, so she's my best defense.

"How are you going to play this?" I ask, making it to her side.

Before Poppy can answer, Rose lets out a wail. "It gives me the heebie-jeebies. I'm never going to be able to sleep here again."

"Don't worry," Poppy says. "We'll get them out of here. Big will help me. Right?" She turns to me.

"Sure." I get to my feet, and I'm standing in her corner of the living room. "You ever taken on a bat before?"

Poppy's breathing is quickened, and I can tell she's got adrenaline pumping through her veins. "Not bats. Cockroaches, yes. An ant infestation, yes."

"Where have you guys been living?"

"You don't want to know," Poppy mutters, but then, in the dark, I see her square her shoulders. "We need to focus."

"Got another tennis racket?"

"No. I happened to bring this one home with me from work today. Lucky for me, right?" She swings at a bat I didn't see coming at us. The force of the air moving through her racket sends the bat on a different course, but she didn't connect.

"Are you trying to kill it or get it outside?" I glance at the door that's still open.

"I'm not picky." Poppy shifts, and now that my eyes have adjusted to their dark apartment, I can see the determination on her face. Her hair is in its usual ponytail, but it's half fallen out.

"Do you want me to try?"

She shakes her head. "Nah, I feel better with this is my hand. You can use the broom."

She nods her chin in the direction of the opposite corner. The bats circle around, and their tiny squeaks reach my ears. I don't particularly like the idea of leaving Poppy's side since she's turning out to be a modern-day Batwoman, but I figure two of us trying to get them out of here is better than one.

I tug the bath towel that's still around my neck up over my head. Can a bat bite through cotton? I don't know, but some protection is better than none.

I duck and weave across the room and grasp for the broom. As I'm turning to face Poppy again, I hear the sound of the tennis racket connecting.

Poppy shrieks, which makes Rose shriek.

"Got one," Poppy's voice wobbles.

"Is it dead?" Rose asks. Her voice is muffled. I'm pretty sure she's pulled a pillow over her entire head.

"Not sure," Poppy says, her attention returning to the task at hand. I've got to hand it to Holland's girlfriend—the woman has some hutzpah. If Holland were here, he would likely be hiding under the coffee table with Rose as opposed to taking on the bats with Poppy. I'll admit to being impressed with Poppy's ability to handle the situation at hand.

"We've got to get the other one," she says.

I nod. My eyes haven't left the other bat. I'm tracking it like my mom tracks the price of ground beef at the grocery store, waiting for a sale. I vaguely register the sound of emergency sirens in the distance, but I'm so focused on the second bat that I don't pay them much mind.

I chance a quick glance at Poppy. She, too, has all her attention on the bat. It's flown to the far side of the room now, so we're biding our time.

"Come on. Come on," I mumble.

"Wait for it," Poppy whispers from across the room.

She and Rose seem to be all screamed out, and my eardrums are singing hymns of thanks.

I creep forward a foot to get a better angle as the bat flutters back in my direction. I've got the broom held over my shoulder, and when the bat comes at me, I give a swing that Babe Ruth himself would have been proud of.

Then, several things happen at once.

I connect with something, but it's not a bat. It's a human, who lets loose a string of choice words.

Poppy swings her racket and nails the bat, sending it straight out the front door. She sprints forward and slams it shut, sinking against it, only to pop back upright and flip on the lights. "Who are you?"

"Collin?" I say at the same time.

My best friend is rubbing his nose, which I unceremoniously nailed with my broom.

"Who's Collin? Oh my gosh, did you call the police?" Poppy's eyes are wide as she takes in Collin's Cashmere Cove PD uniform. "Big! It was just a couple bats. I've seen worse. I had it handled."

"Then why were you yelling like that?"

"They startled us! It was a reflex." Her fists fly to her hips, and I can't help but notice how adorable she looks when she gets a little defensive. "By the way, can we make sure the flue is closed on the fireplace. Pretty sure that's how they got in."

I bite back a couple curse words of my own, kicking myself for not thinking to check that before the Kasper sisters moved in. Also, I give myself a mental talking-to for thinking that Holland's girlfriend is adorable. She's not for me.

"Sure," is all I say.

"Thanks." Poppy turns to Collin. "Officer, I'm sorry to have wasted your time. We have everything under control."

"No worries, ma'am." Collin takes his hand away from his nose. It's bleeding and already starting to swell. "Just doing my job." He levels me with a murderous look. "I could arrest you for assaulting an officer."

"Quit being dramatic."

"Don't tempt me."

"You two know each other?" Poppy looks between us.

"Best friends since forever. I'm Collin Rattler."

Poppy reaches out her hand but pulls back when she sees Collin's blood-covered fingers. "Come on in and wash up. I'll get you some ice." She moves to the kitchen. Collin scowls at me before following her. I can hear them chatting away. Poppy asks him a question about his work, and since I know Collin so well, I can tell when he relaxes into the conversation.

While they're occupied, I take a minute to study the living room.

This side of the duplex looks decidedly better than how I left it. There are bright-colored throw pillows on a slip-covered couch. Oversized tapestries hang from the walls, conveniently covering some of the cracks I know are in the plaster. Books are color-coordinated on the built-in shelves on either side of the fireplace, and the lamp Poppy hid behind is casting the room in a warm glow. It's welcoming. Happy. Nice. It feels like a home.

Something tells me Poppy made it this way. She seems to always be looking for ways to make things better.

Rose slowly emerges from under the coffee table. "Thank God we got that sorted. Took years off my life, but I can always count on Poppy."

I don't respond, but in my head, I can't help but think that anyone who has Poppy on their side is lucky, indeed.

11

Turtle Time

Poppy

To: poppykallday@gmail.com

From: hbradleypro@gmail.com

Subject: Re: Email 2

Dear Poppy,

You don't have to apologize for thinking deeply about things. I like hearing how your brain works. Mostly I'm glad that I didn't do anything to make you mad. ▢

As for forgiveness, I think it's one of the bravest things we can do—to acknowledge that we've been hurt but to also make the active effort to move forward by letting go. When we don't let what has been done to us rule over us, we can be free, and there's beauty in that.

In other news, Mack told me about the bat situation. I'm so sorry about that. What a mess! I did laugh when I heard about Collin taking a broom to the nose. I doubt his bruised nose will affect the man's swagger. Anyway, I told Mack to get his act together and fix some things up for you and Rose. Hopefully he does.

I'm looking forward to seeing you for the wedding. Soon!

H

• • • ● • ● • • • •

I am freaking thriving.

Holland's email put a pep in my step this morning. I don't know what it is, but I feel the elusive spark when he writes me. It gives me hope for us, which means that today—though I'm on a school bus with a whole bunch of six- and seven-year-olds and sweating my brains out—I feel good.

We're en route to the zoo, and this is the first official Parks and Rec event I'm on point for. Heather has been on maternity leave since earlier this week. No baby yet, but the prodromal labor has been intense, so we all sent her home. She wanted to ride it out. Mayor Witmore wouldn't hear of it. Mostly I think he didn't want the responsibility of being the one to catch a baby if it came to that.

Heather reluctantly obliged, so I'm on my own.

Today, I've got Ginny with me, along with another mom and dad who volunteered to chaperone. Collin Rattler is along with us too. Something to do with the police department's community outreach efforts.

And rounding out our crew of chaperones is Mack Bradley.

Somehow he got roped into being our sixth adult on this trip. He's sitting three rows ahead of me, and I've been watching him referee a couple of squirrely six-year-old boys for the entirety of our drive. It's hard to miss him.

Should I feel guilty that I can't get the image of him racing into our duplex during the bat debacle out of my head? It was nice to have someone come to the rescue for once. I mean, I was the one who ousted the bats, but it wasn't for lack of effort on Mack's part. I glance up at Collin, who's sitting two rows ahead of Mack and facing the back of the bus. His face looks like a children's finger painting—blues and purples all mixed together across his nose.

From Collin, my gaze settles back on Mack.

He is such an enigma to me. I've seen glimpses of his personality. Like when he bantered with Collin. And walking around town collecting money for the Party at the Park...at least before the Tricia Incident. I'm trying not to let my knowledge of his past color my perception of him. In fact, that aside, all I seem to notice about Mack Bradley—besides his impressive shoulders—is how helpful he is. The man is literally everywhere around town, doing all the things for all the people.

Inez at the café.

Willow at the library.

He met with the mayor about the Party in the Park earlier this week.

He's been working on our side of the duplex with renewed vigor since the bats descended upon us.

Now, here he is on a day trip to the zoo, and I'm pretty sure he runs his own business, so he's going to have to make up for being away somehow.

I don't think the man sleeps.

I check my watch. We've got another ten minutes before we're set to arrive, but I stand to make my way to the front of the bus. We hit a pothole as I'm passing Mack's seat, and I stumble into his lap.

"I'm so sorry." I scramble to my feet, bumping my hip into the seat in front of him, and careening back into him.

"Easy, Boo."

"Oh, gosh. I'm crushing you." I attempt to stand. Why is it that I'm a hapless, uncoordinated oaf when it comes to Holland's brother?

Mack scrunches his face up in a display of more emotion than I've ever seen out of him.

"What's wrong?" I ask, rearranging papers in my clipboard that had shifted in my fall and trying not to feel self-conscious. "Did I hurt you? I realize I'm not one of those dainty women who weigh less than a feather." I'm rambling. I always do this when I'm nervous. It's a terrible habit, but I can't seem to break it.

"You weren't crushing me."

"Oh." I laugh at Mack's monotone declaration. "Well, that's a relief. I'll be going now."

I turn to make my way up to the front of the bus, but I stop when I feel a hand wrapped around my wrist. I glance down to find Mack's hand against my skin, which suddenly feels sunburned. My gaze pops up to meet his.

There's a look in his eyes that I've never seen before—from him, or from any man...ever.

"You take up the exact right amount of space."

My mouth opens to respond before I register what he said. When I play it back, I snap my jaw closed. Mack hasn't taken his eyes from me. His gaze isn't uncomfortable, but it feels like he's imploring me to believe him. A swell of gratitude rises up in my chest. I shouldn't need any exterior validation that the space I take up—physically, emotionally, mentally—is valid. But it sure is nice to hear it every once in a while.

My shoulders relax, and I cock my head, a smile bursting onto my lips. I must catch Mack off guard, because he leans away and drops my wrist.

"Thank you for that. It was the perfect thing to say." I beam another grateful grin at him before I set off toward the bus driver.

I stop when I feel a tug on my shorts, and I turn to find a little boy doing the potty jiggle in his seat.

"Miss Poppy, I have to go to the bathroom!"

"Davis, can you make it five minutes? We're almost there."

He nods at me with wide eyes.

"Awesome." I make eye contact with Ginny, who is sitting right in front of him.

"I'll take him as soon as we arrive," she says, reading my mind.

"Thanks a million." I turn around and face the group, dialing up my best cheerful yet authoritative voice. "Alright, everyone! Listen up!"

The screaming and chatting doesn't stop. I hold my hands in the air and wave. "Hello! Can anyone hear me?"

A whistle slices through the rest of the noise in the bus, and I shoot Collin a smile. His whistle brought everyone else under control, so I take the window of opportunity to go over the groups we've split the kids into and to lay some ground rules.

"I expect you to listen to your chaperones. Stick with your group. Make sure you drink plenty of water, and most importantly, have fun! Now"—I tuck my clipboard under my arm—"does anyone have any questions for me?"

"I want to see the polar bears!"

"Can we go to the penguins first?"

"Do you think the badger will be out?"

The kids are launching inquiries rapid-fire. I hold up my hands. "Talk to you group leader, and listen to them. You'll get a chance to visit all the animals."

"I'm going to lick everything I can...like a lion." This from a kid sitting in the second row of seats. I think his name is Jameson.

I shake my head at him. "No licking."

"But you said to have fun! Licking is fun. And the lions do it."

"Leave it to them, then. Licking spreads germs. We need to stay safe, and we need to keep the animals and other zoo-goers safe. Keep your tongues in your mouths, please and thank you."

Chalk that up as a line I never thought I'd say in my life.

Mercifully, the bus pulls into its spot in the zoo parking lot.

Davis and Ginny bolt for the bathrooms, and I say a quick prayer that they make it. I did pack several changes of clothes, just in case, but if I can spare myself and Ginny having to deal with an accident within the first five minutes of arrival, all the better. Not to mention, I'm sure Davis would be supremely embarrassed.

I stand by the door of the bus as the kids file out, ticking them off my list and making sure they each go with their designated adult.

Ginny returns with a dry and relieved Davis and shoots me a thumbs-up. She takes the reins of her group, leading them into the zoo. Excitement courses through my chest. This is happening. I've coordinated this trip, and the kids are getting to go to the zoo. It might seem like a silly thing to be so giddy about, but it matters to me, and I'm thankful to be here.

I turn to my group of kids. I've got Jameson (the licker), Courtney, Autumn, Chuck, Wesley, and Barret and Bella, a set of twins. "Alright, my friends. Let's do this."

• • • • ● • ● • ● • • •

The day is going off without a hitch. The kids are having a blast, and I'm thoroughly impressed with the zoo myself. The company hasn't been bad either.

"Did you ever have any pets?" Mack leans against the railing, looking over the bison enclosure.

Our groups merged early on as we set out in the same direction. We've been meandering around the grounds for the better part of the day, and I'm shocked at how easy it is to talk to Mack. He doesn't say much, but when he does speak, it's to offer funny commentary or some insight that makes me think.

"No pets." I keep my eye on Jameson, who I can tell is dangerously close to trying to taste one of those binocular contraptions. He sees me eyeing him, and he drops his chin to his chest in defeat. "We didn't have one when I was little, and then after my mom died and my dad moved out, we lived with my grandma. She had a cat named Alvin, but he was terrified of my sisters and me. After that, we moved around so much the last thing I needed was to have to figure out whether or not the place I found us to live allowed pets. Too much extra work."

Mack nods.

"What about you?"

"Holland had a beta fish for a while. I accidentally killed it."

He grimaces, and I laugh. "Is there a story there?"

"Teddy the Betta fish died of overstimulation—we think." He looks bashful. "I rigged up his aquarium with these cool blinking lights, but while they looked sweet to us, they stressed the fish out. Holland sobbed for an entire day after we found Teddy floating at the top of the tank." Mack bows his head.

"Aww, Big." I pat his shoulder theatrically and try to keep the grin off my face. It's funny to picture these two brothers together as kids. "You guys are so different. Did you get along growing up?"

He side-eyes me. "What has he told you?"

I shrug. I'm embarrassed to admit I don't know Holland that well outside of his golf game and career aspirations. "Not a lot."

"When he gets around to sharing about the time he got stranded in the tree fort by the bay, know there are two sides to that story."

I laugh, and I'm about to ask him to tell me his side, but we're interrupted by a gasp from Jameson.

"That turtle is trying to stick out his tongue!"

"Turtles can't stick out their tongues," I say, ready to quell any attempts at licking. I read as much on the plaque nearby.

"Look! That one's climbing on top of that one. What are they doing?"

I find the object of study for our group of innocent children, and my stomach bottoms out.

Oh no.

No.

No. No.

No. No. No.

The turtles are mating—unabashedly, out in the open, for all the world to see. It's like the freaking Discovery Channel up in here, and this is way more than I bargained for.

"Um, my friends, let's move along. Nothing to see here." I'm trying to wedge myself in front of the kids. I glance over to Mack, who is staring with his jaw slightly unhinged. "Big. A little help."

The turtles behind me start making very loud, very specific noises. Noises that will haunt me for days, I'm sure of it. On the upside, this snaps Mack out of whatever trance the mating reptiles had put him under. He steps forward. "Hey, guys, the flamingos are over there. Come on!"

"But what are these guys doing?" Bella asks, her eyes so wide and innocent.

"They are...uh...playing. They're having fun."

Mack snorts, and I pin him with a *not now* look.

"Not fair. I want to climb on the back of a turtle!" Jameson is trying to peer around me as I shuffle the kids away from the turtle exhibit.

"I think that one is feeling sad." Bella has the puppy-dog eyes down strong. "He sounds like he's moaning."

"He's definitely not sad," Mack says under his breath as we corral the kids and walk away.

I let my head fall back.

12

FUN

Mack

The stars are out tonight. I lean back in my chair and stare up at the sky. It's become a slight addiction. After a long day, nothing clears my head like coming outside and gazing into the atmosphere. Today was long, but good.

After getting back from the zoo, I put in several hours at the build site. My crew made good progress, and I'm finally starting to relax, knowing we'll meet our deadline.

My mind flits to Poppy, and, as if I conjured her, the door on the other side of the wall divider squeaks open and then clicks shut. The deck boards creak, and then I catch a faint whiff of floral—it's gardenia, I think—which is Poppy's signature scent.

A tremor of guilt passes through me because I kind of think I might have developed a small crush on my brother's girlfriend. Spending the entire day with her solidified what I'd been learning about her from a distance. She's kind, and committed, and a little bit of a control freak but with the best intentions. She makes me laugh, and I'm going to have to be careful around her.

I'm not going to pursue Poppy. But I can't deny that I'm attracted to her. Big time. And I'm going to keep trying to be her friend. Holland asked me to, after all. And if friendship is my only option where Poppy is concerned, I'll take whatever I can get.

I stretch back in my chair, and my half of the deck groans beneath my shifting weight.

"Big? Is that you?" Poppy's voice is like a bubbling brook. It's always cheerful—always optimistic. She sounds almost excited at the prospect of talking to me. It's a nice change of pace compared to what I'm used to.

"Hey, Boo."

"Whatcha doing out here? It's late."

"I could ask you the same question."

Footsteps cross the deck board, and then Poppy peeks around the corner of the wall dividing our decks.

"Do you mind?" She motions to the second chair I keep on my side of the wall. Not that I have many visitors, but tonight, it comes in handy.

"Be my guest."

She drops into the seat. "That's what I told you the first day we met."

"I remember."

"It was memorable. I was a mess."

"You were fine."

She reaches back and tightens the knot of her ponytail. "A frazzled, blubbering mess."

What am I supposed to say to that? Because the truth is, I can still picture the curve of Poppy's neck as it sloped into the smooth skin of her shoulder. I can still recall the drip of sweat that fell from her temple and over her cheek. The sight of it made my mouth go dry. I don't think I've ever seen anything more beautiful than Poppy in her bath towel, with her hair looking like she'd been electrocuted, and her bright-pink cheeks looking like the kind of bubble gum I'd like to taste. Truth is, Poppy's impossible to forget.

"You seem to keep seeing me when I'm a mess." She says this like an observation.

I shoot her a look.

"That first morning. Then with the bat. Today."

"What about today? The zoo trip was great."

Poppy arches her eyebrows at me.

"The kids seemed to have a blast."

She cocks her head. "I think you're forgetting about the elephant in the room."

I wait a beat before answering. "You mean the turtle in the room?"

She buries her head in her hands. "That was mortifying. What if those kids tell their parents what they saw? They could sue the P&R department for scarring their children!"

"I don't think you'd be liable for the turtles'...um...*behavior*, so you're good."

Poppy lets loose a full-fledged giggle then. "Oh my gosh. The sounds they were making, right? I will never forget the sounds."

"Yeah. Could have done without all of that."

Poppy wipes a tear from the corner of her eye and tips her face up to the sky. "It's so peaceful out here. I love the sky, don't you?" Her face is almost wistful, with her chin tipped up, like she wishes she could reach up and touch a star. My fingers itch with desire to drag the strand of hair that's fallen over her cheek away so I can get a better look at her. Before I can answer, she continues. "There's something grounding about looking up and knowing that I'm a small part of it all. Mostly insignificant, but here for some reason, for some purpose, nonetheless."

I swallow, both grateful that she's sharing these musings with me and guilty that I already know how she feels about the sky because of her email to Holland.

She cuts me a glance. "I like it here."

I stay quiet, waiting for her to continue.

"In this town." She jabs her thumb in the direction of her half of the duplex. "This house. We appreciate all your improvements, by the way. Not sure when you're finding time to squeeze those in with your schedule the way it is, but thank you."

I shrug her off. It's the least I can do.

"Do you like it here?"

Her question catches me off guard. There's an innocent curiosity to Poppy's posture, and for whatever reason, I find myself wanting to open up to her.

"Yes and no."

She nods at me, encouraging me to go on with the openness of her expression.

I sigh. How do I explain this? "Cashmere Cove was a great place to grow up. Small town on the water. Basically every kid's dream. I still love how people here look out for each other. We have our traditions."

"The prank wars," Poppy cuts in with a rueful shake of her head.

"Among others. There's a real sense of community. I like being a part of it"—I pause—"even if people don't want me to be a part of it," I finish quietly.

Poppy is silent, nibbling on her lip in my periphery. I clasp my hands, feeling like I want to crawl out of my own skin for having said what I said. But there's something about Poppy. I consider her a friend—perhaps the first friend I've had, who isn't related to me and who isn't Collin, in the past ten years.

"Ginny told me about Tricia."

And *that* feels like a punch straight to the diaphragm.

I grind my jaw and chance a look at her. She's staring back at me, and I try to read her expression, but then she blinks and looks away. "We don't have to talk about it."

I exhale. I can't decide if I'm relieved or wishing I could spill the whole story for Poppy to hear. I hate that her opinion of me is already jaded. I'm dying to fill the silence of the moment, which is very unlike me, but thinking about Poppy thinking about what she thinks happened between Tricia and me is enough to make me want to puke.

Too much thinking is never a good thing—that's what I always say. Better to change the subject.

"What do you do for fun?" I ask.

Poppy cuts her gaze to me and then looks away. "I have fun with my sisters. Hanging out with them. It's been fun to decorate The Downer." She grimaces, shooting me an apologetic look. "We don't mean that name as a dig on you or your property. Truly, no offense."

"None taken. I sort of like the name. It's regal."

Poppy snaps her finger. "That's what I said. It's fun, right?" She settles back, crossing her bare arms across her t-shirt-clad chest, seemingly content.

"Naming the duplex you live in isn't what I had in mind when I asked you what you did for fun."

I spent most of today with Poppy, and that, coupled with the other times I've been able to observe her, has helped me create what I think is a pretty accurate picture of her life. I'm not quite ready to let her off the hook thinking that housekeeping and caring for her sisters constitutes *fun*.

"I get to have fun all day. It's in my job description. I come up with fun events for the kids and the community. Pretty much my entire life is fun."

She sounds so cheerful about it. I almost hate to burst her bubble.

Almost.

"You're curating fun. For other people."

"I—"

"When was the last time you let your hair down? Lived a little?"

She sucks in a breath, looking put out. "I do live."

"What you're doing isn't living. It's play-acting at life."

Poppy pushes her bottom lip forward in a pout. "That's a pretty big assumption from someone who doesn't know me all too well."

I know more about her than she thinks, thanks to the emails. But she doesn't know that.

The guilt is back.

All I do is shrug.

She holds me in place with a glare. It's not an angry look, so much as it is unflinching. Determined. It's a look that says I pushed her, but she's going to push right back.

"Speaking of living life to the fullest... Are you?"

I walked right into that one, I guess. I readjust my position in my chair but don't say anything.

She lets out a triumphant puff of air. "That's what I thought." After a beat, she adds, "My life is fun."

I can't help but wonder if she's trying harder to convince me or herself.

"I didn't mean to overstep. I've observed you the past couple of weeks, and I think you do a lot of living for others."

She opens her mouth as if to argue, but I hold up my hand.

"It's a good thing—don't get me wrong. But I was asking what you do for you. What fills up your tank and gives you the energy to be such a catalyst of joy for other people?"

Poppy blinks at me for a few long seconds before she dips her chin. "I guess I've always focused on what I can do for others because it's been essential to keeping my family afloat. Thinking about myself seems selfish and unnecessary. Noli and Rose have always come first, and that's translated to my work and other relationships too."

My mind flashes to Holland. How he's on the receiving end of her efforts. Does he appreciate her? Does he recognize how much she's going out of her way to care for him?

"There's a difference between selfishness and taking care of yourself."

Poppy twists her lips to the side, as if she doesn't know if she buys it.

"You can't keep burning for others if you don't add oil to the lamp."

Poppy snorts. "Was that an electrician analogy?"

I make a face. "A dated one, maybe."

Poppy grins at me. I can only see the shadows of her face in the dim light, but I'm glad to know I didn't offend her completely.

"I liked it," she says. "I better turn in. Another busy day tomorrow."

"Sure. Hey, if you and Rose are free, some of us are meeting around seven to swim at Wool Beach."

"Wool Beach?"

"A local treasure."

"Sounds...warm. And sheep-y."

"No sheep."

"Goats?"

"Not that I know of."

"Camels? Rabbits?" She pauses dramatically and widens her eyes. "Mammoths?"

"Are you trying to impress me with your knowledge of wooly creatures?"

"Is it working?" Poppy grins back, and my stomach swoops to my knees, leaving my midsection tingling. Poppy switches gears. "Just so long as there aren't any turtles." She shudders.

"I make no promises." My lips twitch, and I try to ignore that sensation in my gut. "I'll text you directions. You should come. You know, live a little."

If I'd been standing next to her, I would have nudged her shoulder. But thankfully, I'm not. Because that would have come across as flirty and playful. I can't be flirty and playful with my brother's girlfriend, even if she is making me feel...*feelings*. Long dormant feelings. It's inappropriate.

"Yeah, yeah." She sticks her nose in the air playfully. "I'll see if I can squeeze it into my schedule, around all the other fun I'll be having. Night, Big."

"Night, Boo."

She pads back down around the divider, and the door to her side of the duplex opens and shuts. The air temperature shifts and drops. Maybe it's because Poppy is no longer next to me. She radiates warmth, that one. But if she's not careful, she's going to run herself into the ground.

I stare up at the sky and play back our conversation. I'm glad I said what I said, but I hadn't counted on her throwing my own point back in my face. Can what I'm doing be called living? I thought I was content. I'd made my peace with my lot in life when I decided to take the high road. But my own warning to Poppy rings in my ears. Am I hiding behind my care for others? Am I so worried about Tricia—and her family—that I'm selling myself short? I've always been the deadbeat. The nobody. Holland is what most people consider the face of Cashmere Cove. I'm the backbone. I do a lot behind the scenes, but no one notices me. And I'm basically the butt of all the jokes. Which is fine. It's what I'm used to.

But then there's Poppy.

Around her, I see everything in a different kind of light, and I'm starting to wonder if I don't want more.

13

CHICKEN AND SILVERSIDES

Poppy

"Would you quit it?" Rose eyes me from the passenger seat.

"What?" I glance down at where my fingers are drumming a steady beat against the steering wheel of Holland's car. "Oh. Sorry." I flex my fingers.

"Why are you so nervous? This is supposed to be fun."

I stare straight ahead, focusing on the road instead of responding.

Fun.

Mack's questions last night have plagued me all day. I've gone from feeling defensive—*I'm fun! I have fun.* To depressed—*Who would ever want to hang out with me? I literally have nothing to show for my life but two sisters and a job.*

It's been a great little teeter-totter of emotion all day, and I sort of want to wring Mack's neck for putting me on it.

Then again, when I remember the kindness in his eyes when he was talking to me on the deck—the way he complimented me in his own, toned-down way—I can't be mad. Especially since I think he's on to something. Which is why I've been spending all my free time today thinking about what I like. What *is* fun to me? I don't even know. How pathetic is that?

I park the car in the lot Mack directed us to.

Rose wrenches open the car door and takes a deep breath of bay water air. "This is gorgeous." She practically skips across the grassy area that leads to the sand.

I pull in a deep breath of my own and follow her, taking in the water of the cove ahead.

Wool Beach *is* beautiful, tucked into a low spot of the bay, surrounded on the sides by jagged rockface. I know, based on the position of the P&R building, that on the other side of the rock is the populated, tourist-y beach area. But this little inlet is secluded. It took us a minute to find it, and I can see why the locals want to keep it to themselves.

I start sweating at the thought of Mack inviting us. Are we 'local' enough to merit an invitation?

"Hey! Poppy!" I turn to see Collin jogging down to where I'm standing. "I'm glad you and Rose came," he says. "It was good of Mack to invite you. First time he's done anything neighborly in years. Color me surprised."

"I think you've got enough color going on for now." I point at his bruised face, which resembles Van Gogh's *Starry Night*, grateful for his warm welcome.

Collin laughs a deep belly laugh. "Good one. Come on."

We wander down to the beach together.

Off to one side, a campfire blazes. There are sticks for s'mores neatly stacked nearby, along with a couple grocery bags, which I assume are filled with all the fixings. Rose has dropped the blanket we packed near a handful of multi-colored towels and shimmied out of her jean shorts and tank top. She's jogging toward the blue water of the cove, which looks incredibly enticing in the late-day heat. A group of people is submerged up to their necks. They wave Rose over as she splashes in up to her ankles.

I admire her lack of inhibition. She has no qualms about meeting new people, taking new adventures. She doesn't stop to think about what could go wrong. It's a good thing, really, and it's the gift I've tried to give my sisters. I worry about things so they don't have to. They can be carefree and innocent because I've dealt with the stress and seen the tainted nature of humanity on their behalf.

"Have you met Piper and Ed, Holland and Mack's cousin and her husband-to-be?" Collin asks, following my gaze and drawing me from my thoughts.

I nod my head. "At Sunday dinner."

Collin taps his temple. "Of course. Infamous Sunday dinner. How could I forget? Looks like Inez is here too."

I recognize the Getaway Café owner bobbing up and down in the water. I hear her laugh as Rose goes under and comes up for air next to her and Mia. Patrick is out there too. I can't mistake his tall figure. And the shorter guy next to him must be Lou. Across from the two of them, I recognize the figure of Mack.

He looks up at the same time, and our gazes connect. He holds up a hand and slowly begins walking in the direction of the beach.

Collin drops his gear near the beach towels and charges into the water in a full sprint. He tackles Mack, and I laugh.

Turning my back to the water, I set down my bag, and I peel off my cover-up. When I get it over my head and look back at the bay, I come face-to-face with Mack. He's dripping wet in a pair of teal board shorts that are slicked to his muscular legs. Droplets of water cling to the edges of his hair, turning its usual dark-brown color to midnight black. He looks like Holland but also, strangely, not at all like Holland. He's staring at me in that intense way that is unique to Mack.

Ironically, it's in this moment that I realize I've seen more of Mack's bare chest than I have of Holland's. I should feel like I'm getting the raw end of the deal, but I don't. Mack has a very nice bare chest. That's an objective fact. He's not as muscular as Holland, but where Holland's strength is earned through hours upon hours in the gym, I'd wager Mack earns his stripes—or his sinewy muscles—in his day job.

Or something. I don't know. Not my business.

"Hi, Big."

"Boo. You made it."

I adjust the straps on my bathing suit—a black bikini with high-wasted bottoms and a halter top. We moved from Florida, where we lived in swimwear, so this is like a second skin for me. In fact, I'd go so far as to say that being in a suit makes me feel like I'm taking Gram's nice-panties advice. I'm comfortable and confident.

"You know me. I follow the fun."

Mack's gaze follows my hand as I flatten the straps around my neck into place before he meets my eye. "Right."

"Speaking of fun, I've been thinking about what you said last night."

He tips his head enough that I know he's listening. I'm trying to decide how to explain to him what I've been turning over all day today when Rose yells to me from the water.

"Poppy! Mack! Come on!"

"Be right there," I call back before turning to Mack. "Are you staying out or going back in?"

"I could swim."

"Good. Last one in is a giant turtle." I toss him a grin over my shoulder and take off. He snorts behind me, which makes me smile bigger, but then I'm splashing into the cool, refreshing water of the cove.

Mack makes it to my side, and we wade out together toward Rose and the rest of the group. I chat about the wedding with Piper, and she asks how Rose and I are settling into town before she gets a mischievous twinkle in her eye.

"Alright, I challenge y'all to a game of chicken."

"Chicken?" I look at Rose, and she shoots me a small grin.

"Yeah, didn't they teach you to play down in Florida? I'll go up on Ed's shoulders, and you go up on Mack's. Rose and Collin can be a team. Mia and Patrick. Inez hates playing, so she can referee."

I glance at Inez who holds up her hands and nods.

"I'm going to go stoke the fire," Lou says.

"Good. So here's how it works." Piper puts her hands on Ed's shoulders, and he ducks under the water. Piper scoots her legs around his neck. When he stands, she's on his shoulders. "We'll see who can knock each other off first."

"Fun! I'm in." Rose nods at Collin, who ducks under her. Rose squeaks as he stands back up with her on his shoulders.

"You game, Boo?"

"Why not." I step around to Mack's back and boost myself up. He stands, and I feel steady as a rock up here.

"Alright. You guys ready?" Inez asks from below. "The two legit couples will go head-to-head"—she nods at Ed and Piper and Mia and Patrick—"and the two random couples will face off." She points at Mack and me and Rose and Collin. "Winner of each chicken fight will spar in the final round."

"Let's do this." Rose's voice is tinged with the fire of competition.

Piper rubs her hands together, and Mia looks entirely intimidated.

"Take no prisoners, Boo." Mack gives my legs a squeeze, and I grin.

"Let's go," I say.

"On the count of three. One, two, three." Inez claps her hands, and then Mack is charging. I squeal as he runs directly at Collin. My arms lock onto Rose's wrists, and I pull her forward as Mack backtracks. Collin is trying to keep up, but we get him in a vulnerable position, and he gets a face full of water. Rose falls forward off his shoulders.

"One down," I cry, and Mack swivels around to where Piper and Ed are lying in wait, having easily dunked Mia and Patrick.

"Piper will go for your boobs," Mack mutters as he and Ed circle each other.

"She and I don't know each other that well," I deadpan.

Mack splutters a laugh, Piper shoots me a wicked grin, and Ed uses that moment to make his move.

Piper is on me in no time, and like Mack said, she reaches for the tie of my bikini top. I'm expecting it, and Mack twists away from Ed but not before Piper draws first blood. She gets my suit untied, so I have to hold it in place with one hand, and I'm limited to only my other free hand to battle. "Low blow, Piper. Low blow."

Piper shimmies her shoulders. "If Holland were here, I'm guessing he'd be thanking me."

Mack back-pedals to give us some time to regroup, and I frantically try to tie my suit back on while I roll my eyes at Piper. The truth is, I haven't thought a lot about Holland lately. I've been busy, and so has he. Is it bad that I don't miss him all that much? Does that make me a terrible girlfriend? I need to send him another email—try to get back on the same page. I'll do it tonight when we get home.

Mack grunts from below me, and all thoughts of Holland flee. I'll worry about him later. For now, I want to win Chicken.

"Hang on, Boo." Mack jukes to his right, and I wrap my free hand around his forehead to stay in place. When he jukes back to the left and Ed turns to try to follow his movements, I let go of Mack's head, grab Piper around the shoulders, and tug her backward. She shrieks and tips off behind Ed.

I raise my hand and make a fist as Mack lets out a *whoop*.

"Victory is ours!" I call when Piper comes up for air.

Everyone else gives us golf claps from where they've started to retreat to the beach. Piper shakes her head, but she's smiling. I like her.

Mack ducks down and lets me ease off his back. My shoddy tie job means my suit balloons up in the water, and I have to shove it back into place before I flash anyone.

"No one wants to see that!" Rose yells from near the shore. "Put the girlies back where they belong, Pops."

My cheeks burn as I wrench my arms behind my back, trying to get a decent grip on the strings. I stick my tongue out at Rose, but she laughs and turns toward the beach.

"No licking, Boo," Mack scolds from next to me. "You're as bad as Jameson."

I laugh and turn my back to him. "Could you help me with this?"

He doesn't say anything, but the water shifts as he steps closer. I wait, and after a slight beat of hesitation, I feel his fingers, gentle against my skin. His warm breath tickles my neck, and goosebumps pop up on my arms. It's dumb, really. I spent the last ten minutes skin-to-skin with Mack, but now he's barely grazing my back, and I swear he's leaving a trail of fire everywhere he touches. I inhale and wait as he tugs the strings into a knot.

"How's that?" His voice is quiet.

"Good. Great. Thank you." I step away and try to shake off the tingly feeling in my stomach and the echo of his touch along my back.

Inez is waving at us from the beach where the rest of our party is sprawled out on towels around the campfire that Lou is still tending. "I've got leftover pastries from the café."

"You go ahead, Big. I'm going to take a minute." Truthfully, I need to get my pulse back under control because what *was* that physical reaction I had to him?

I flop onto my back, closing my eyes and dipping under the surface. The humming rush of liquid pressure that surrounds me, making me feel weightless, is at once soothing and powerful. The water of Cashmere Cove has a different smell than the ocean water in Pensacola. It's earthier. Heavier. It caresses my skin, and I can feel every inch of its push and pull...like I can still feel every inch of the surface area Mack touched.

Get a grip, Poppy. It was nothing.

I slowly let my head rise up and break the surface. I keep my eyes closed for an extra beat before clearing the water from my face with my hands. When I blink, I make a surprised squeaking sound. Mack is standing not too far off, staring at me.

"What are you doing?" I drop down so only my head is above the water.

"Waiting for you."

"Seriously? Go ahead. I'm sure you like Inez's pastries." I cringe. "That came out sounding more like an innuendo than I expected."

Mack's lips quirk, but he stares me down with one of his serious looks. "I don't like the thought of anyone out here alone after dark."

I glance up and around. The stone shrouding the cove and the dusky sky above has made the night appear darker than I expected.

"I'm totally fine."

"I'm not leaving. Forget I'm here if you have to, but I'll wait until you're ready to be done."

Mack isn't someone who's easy to ignore, what with his over-six-foot stature and perpetual broody stares. I stare back at him. I don't know why I'm trying to convince him to leave. It's sweet that he's looking after me. I'm not used to that out of anyone, and it feels good. "You know what?"

"What?"

"You're like the big brother I've never had."

Three sharp creases appear on his forehead as he frowns. "Big brother?"

"Absolutely. You're a classic protector."

"Not sure about that."

I skim my hand along the top of the water. "You are. I've seen you around town. You look out for everyone."

This is all making complete sense, and I feel better about my weird reaction to him already. *Of course* I'd be thrown off to have someone like Mack looking out for me, helping me. I've been deprived of it for so long it only makes sense. And it's the way Mack is. He helps people. It's in his nature.

Mack looks beyond me, out into the vastness of the bay.

"You don't have to be embarrassed. It's very endearing. You don't know you're doing it. It's like a personality trait."

"I don't think so."

"It is. And I'll allow it."

"You'll allow it?"

"Sure. I'm an independent, self-made woman, so you need permission to protect me. And I'm granting it."

"You sound like some sort of royal when you talk like that."

I nod, trying to look solemn. "Maybe I am."

All of a sudden, I feel something slimy around my toe, nibbling at my skin. I yelp and lunge forward, right at Mack.

"What *was* that?" I squeal.

Whatever it was has followed me to where Mack is standing. I feel it brush against my skin under the water, and I grab onto Mack's torso and start climbing up him, trying to get my full body out of the water. I'm clinging to him like a leech. "Get it away from me! What is it? Look out, Big!"

Mack stumbles in the water, his arms coming up to wrap around my calves as I tug myself up onto his back.

I peer over his shoulders, scanning the surface of the water, trying to determine what sea creature is lurking, but I can't see anything but waves and shadows. "Something was trying to eat me!"

Mack's body starts to shake underneath me. "It's only silver-sides."

"What?"

"Little fish that come up to feed at the surface at night. They're harmless, Boo."

I crane my head around so I can see his face. His eyes are laughing at me, and I can tell he's fighting to keep the rest of his expression neutral.

"Nothing about this is funny." I'm doing my best to sound stern when Mack scoots me up higher onto his back. I yelp, clinging tighter to his skin. "Don't you dare put me back in the water. I don't want to be fish food."

"You need me to protect you from the fish, princess?"

I scowl but don't respond because...yeah.

"Come on, then." He starts the slow walk to the beach.

Maybe I should let go and redeem myself as a strong, independent woman, but that feeling of fish slipping across my feet is giving me the creepy-crawlies, and being carried in Mack's strong arms isn't a bad way to get around. I'm going to let Mack have this one. "You know I'm doing you a favor here."

"Is that right?" Mack grunts, shifting me again.

"Like I said, you like taking care of people. This is a perfect opportunity, huh?"

"Yeah, just perfect."

"You're welcome." I pat him on the cheek.

The chuckle that rumbles in his chest vibrates against my arm. "You having fun yet?"

I pause. Being in the water, talking with Mack...it's been a lot of fun. More fun than I can remember having in a long time. "Yeah, but that reminds me of what I was going to tell you before."

I slide down his back when we make it to the shore, and he turns to me, waiting.

"Gardening. That's what I do for fun. I mean, it's what I used to do—what I would do if I had a place to do it."

"Gardening?" He stares at me, and the moonlight reflects off the water that's still shiny on his cheeks. He doesn't look anything like Holland right now. In fact, I don't know if Holland has ever studied me the way Mack is—like he's trying to read a barcode that's etched across my bones.

"Gardening," he says again, nodding.

• • • • ● • ● • • • •

To: hbradleypro@gmail.com
From: poppykallday@gmail.com
Subject: Email 3
Hey Holland,

I feel bad that I haven't emailed lately. Life here has been crazy. Good crazy, but crazy nonetheless. I know you've been busy too. I can't wait to see you next weekend for the wedding. I hung out with Ed and Piper tonight, and they're great. You've got a wonderful family. Mack has been helping Rose and me get acclimated to town, and he's been stopping by to fix up our side of the duplex as his time allows.

He asked me what I liked to do for fun, and it got me thinking about it. I used to love to plant flowers. Have I ever told you that? I love flowers. This is not some ploy to get you to send me them. I'm merely telling you something new about me...I promise! When we lived with my Gram, she had a beautiful vegetable garden and these lush flower beds all around her house. I would tend them with her. There was something about it that was so relaxing—the dirt under my nails and watching everything grow and change. I talked to all the plants too...like a goon. Anyway, that was almost a decade ago, but when I really, truly think about it, that's the last time I can remember doing something that was for fun. For me.

Is golf something fun for you? Or is it work and what you're good at?

Mack reminded me that there's a difference between what I do for a living and for others and what I do for me. I hope you take time to do one thing for yourself today...outside of golf. I'm trying to make a habit of it. Because I can't give off light from my lamp if I don't fill it up with oil every once in a while, right?

Xoxo,

Poppy

14

LOUSY LOVE

Mack

"**I** know it! I know it!" Poppy's in the passenger seat of my truck with her feet up on the dash. Her toenails are painted a deep red. Her hair is pulled back into her trademark ponytail. She's wearing aviator sunglasses, and right now, her lips are pressed together, humming along to the song on the radio.

"Hey, kids, shake-a loose-a feather," she sings.

"Those are not the words," I say at the same time as she screams, "'Bennie and the Jets' by Elton John!"

She pumps her fist in the air.

"You butchered the lyrics."

"Who cares? I got the title and artist. That's two points for me." She makes a pair of tick marks with her finger against an imaginary board and looks all too pleased with herself. "This is a great song." She juts her chin forward and back, enjoying it.

I'm convinced that Poppy has absolutely no idea how striking she is—not just physically, either, though she is that. I should know. Seeing her in a bathing suit last week. Having her in my arms—on a number of occasions—and the way her soft skin felt against my hands.

But more than her outward beauty, she's a cool person. She's delightful, the way she tells me things in such a whole-hearted way. How chatty she is. Her perpetual cheerfulness. I can't help but feel like if I can be near her, some of that warmth will rub off on me and leave me better than I was before.

Holland's got himself a real gem. I would feel guiltier about having these thoughts and feelings for Poppy if there was any chance that I was somehow luring her away from Holland.

She did me a favor when she likened me to an older brother. It had the effect of a cold shower. But—silver lining—it also took away any remorse I was feeling for spending time with her. She sees me as a friend and only a friend. There's no reason for me to check myself around her. I can have fun, and be goofy, and do whatever I can to make her laugh and make her blush. The only collateral damage is to me and my heart. I can live with that. So we're good.

"Oh! I know this one too. Michael Jackson!" Poppy plays the drum beat against the armrest as another song starts.

"Who would dance, if the girl's on the run?" she belts out.

"That is not even—"

"'Billy Jean!'" she yells.

"—close," I finish.

"This is the moonwalk song."

For a person who cannot string together accurate lyrics, she's been dead on when it comes to title and artist. And she knows a surprising amount of music history. We've been playing this game for the past thirty minutes, en route to Green Bay, and Poppy is smoking.

I should say she's smoking me.

I mean, she is smoking hot too. But we've been over this.

She's in a great mood, likely because we're on our way to pick up Holland from the airport. She hasn't seen him in almost a month. Of course she's happy.

Her phone chimes, and she stops drumming to pull it out from where she had it wedged under her leg.

Out of the corner of my eye, I see her frown down at the screen.

She types something and clicks the screen to black, but she's gripping it between her hands, not setting the phone back down.

"Everything okay?"

Her shoulders roll inward. "I think so. That was a message from Rose. She's visiting Noli in Florida this weekend since I'll be tied up with the wedding."

I nod.

"Neither of us are huge fans of Noli's live-in boyfriend. Rose got to their place and overheard them having a huge fight. She waited outside, and Nelson stormed off. He didn't see her, but Noli was pretty upset when Rose went in."

Poppy has completed deflated, and I hate it. "Anything we can do?"

Look at me, using the royal *we* when it comes to the Kasper sisters. I guess I've grown fond of them all. Mostly, I want to bring the light back to Poppy's eyes.

"That's sweet of you to ask, but I trust Rose to take care of it. She suggested to Noli that they check into a hotel for a spa weekend. They'll be fine."

She says this last line with authority—as if she can will it to be so.

I find myself wondering how many times in Poppy's life she's had to will things to go her way. I wouldn't bet against her.

She clicks around on her phone again. "Looks like Holland's flight is landing."

I glance over, expecting to see her expression, if not back to being as cheerful as it was, at least excited. Instead, she's chewing on her cheek.

"I'm sure you're looking forward to your reunion."

I know, I know. I'm asking a leading question. Don't give me that look. This isn't a court room. There's no judge here to overrule me.

Poppy sighs. "I guess. Can I tell you the truth, though?"

I wait, and she takes my silence as her cue to go on.

"I'm nervous. It's all been such a whirlwind. I don't feel like Holland and I have connected at all since he left, except through the emails."

I hate that I have to pretend like I don't know what she's talking about. I don't like being dishonest. I clear my throat, but when I speak, my voice still sounds pitchy. "Emails?"

"We've been writing back and forth. It was this idea I had. Holland probably thinks it's stupid and a waste of time, but I thought it would be a good way to keep our relationship moving in the right direction."

I clench my teeth together. I could punch Holland for not putting in the time to cultivate his connection with Poppy.

"Anyway, it's working...to an extent," she says.

"What do you mean?"

"Getting Holland's email responses has been a definite highlight, but he's like a different person over email than he is over the phone. It's weird."

I tug on the collar of my shirt, suddenly feeling like my truck's AC has given out. I hold my hand in front of the vent. It's still blowing cool air, so I guess it's just me. I'm burning in the hell Holland's created for me—or I've created for myself. "Huh. That is weird."

"I don't know what to make of it." Poppy kneads her hands together. "I'm rambling. Sorry. This is totally inappropriate and way more information than you need. But yeah, I'm nervous to see him."

I flex my hands against the steering wheel and exit to the airport. "I can always remind my brother that he needs to get his head out of his—"

"No, no." Poppy chuckles. "Please don't say anything to him. It's something I've got to figure out. Or he and I do, I guess." She pauses. "I hope I didn't put you in an awkward position."

"You didn't."

Holland did.

If this was Twister, I'd be spread-eagle with my feet in opposite corners and my arms crisscrossed in between...all thanks to my baby brother.

"You're just, like, my only friend right now."

Friend-zoned, for the win.

"I don't want to bug Noli and Rose with my complicated feelings," Poppy continues. "They think Holland and I are relationship goals."

"I've never understood that phrase."

"What, relationship goals?"

"Yeah. Isn't every relationship different? Wouldn't my goal in dating someone be different than yours or Rose's or Holland's?"

Poppy looks thoughtful. "I guess you're right. I think most of us hold up an ideal, and when we see two people who are happy and look like they're meeting that ideal, then we say that's the goal."

"But no one knows the real story from the outside looking in, right?"

What am I doing? She's looking at me like she wants to ask a very specific question. I can imagine it would go something like, *What's the real story with you, Big?*

But we're nearing the exit for the airport, and this is not the time to open up that can of worms, so I slam the lid on those little buggers and save them for a rainy day. "Enough of my philosophizing."

Poppy snorts, but then her eyes go wide. "I love this song!"

Just like that, her attention is tuned back in with the radio, and she's jamming to the Celine Dion classic "It's All Coming Back to Me Now."

"All the team stood to dance and I just knew my time had died and gone forever," she croons.

I'm pretty sure the actual lyric has something to do with tears turning to ash, but I'm going to let her have this one because she's feeling herself at the moment.

She starts banging out the rhythm on the dashboard with one hand and singing into a pretend microphone with the other as the verse builds to the chorus.

We end up serenading each other with the refrain. She reaches out and strokes my cheek dramatically—literally touching me like this.

I'm playing the part of a long-lost lover, and it's not that hard, to be honest. Especially when she looks at me with desperate eyes.

Pretend desperate eyes.

We're pretending.

When I don't think I can handle the feel of her hand on my skin any longer, she rips her fingers away and belts out the bridge.

I bust a gut when she sings, "It was more than all your lousy loooooove."

"Celine would not be singing so passionately if she was recalling a lousy lover," I remark during the brief instrumental interlude before the fade-out.

"Maybe he could have taken a lesson from the turtles."

We spitball back and forth, and by the time I pull into the terminal pick-up line, Poppy has tears streaming down her cheeks from laughing so hard, and my side aches because I've been right there with her. I haven't worked those muscles in years.

"Big. You're the best. I needed that." She leans over and kisses me on the cheek.

Like it's the most normal thing in the world.

Like she's a friend or a sister, and we're comfortable with each other like that.

Like she has no idea that her lips against my skin acted like a vacuum and sucked all the air from my lungs.

"There he is!" She unbuckles and opens the door. "Holland!" She waves.

In that instant, reality crashes into me with all the welcome of a lousy lover.

I glance away. I know I said I was okay with my heart being collateral damage, but a man doesn't need to see his brother get a welcome-home kiss from the girl he's majorly crushing on.

I give myself a mental shake and open my door. By the time I walk around my truck, Holland and Poppy are stepping out of an embrace.

"Hey, H."

Holland pulls me into a bro hug. He looks good. Tanner than when he left. Poppy is smiling at him like he can do no wrong, and I can't help but wonder if the sight of my little brother is enough to make her overlook all the reservations she shared with me. Holland has that sort of magnetism about him. He makes women forget themselves.

I load Holland's bag into the bed of the truck. Poppy climbs into the back of the cab, and Holland slides into the passenger seat next to me. I love my brother, but I'd say the level of company up front has decreased in its appeal by a solid sixty-five percent.

"Shoot. I've got to return my coach's call. Do you guys mind?"

Seventy-five percent, easy.

"Go ahead. Do whatever you have to do," Poppy says from the back, her voice all soothing and conciliatory.

"Mallory. I literally landed ten minutes ago. What could you possibly need from me?" Holland's tone is all stuck-up and whiny.

I chance a glance in the rearview mirror to see Poppy's reaction. She's looking back at me with wide eyes and shrugs.

We listen to Holland's end of a heated conversation about tee times for his practice rounds next week and his diet, and then he hangs up with a huff.

Poppy reaches forward and squeezes his shoulder. "Everything okay?"

Holland pats her hand. "It'll be fine."

We spend the next thirty seconds in awkward silence. I navigate out of the airport and am on a straight road heading to the interstate when Poppy pokes her head through the space between Holland and me.

"Your windshield is gross, Big. Can you see to drive?"

She's right. There are numerous bug splatters coating the glass. I press the button to dispense the windshield-wiper fluid and let out a curse.

Instead of the clear cleaning solution, I now have a rainbow of paint smeared across the front window of my truck.

From my side, Poppy lets out a cackle that could rival the hyenas in *The Lion King*. I am so stunned I don't have the wherewithal to flick off the wipers, so across they go again, smudging the paint into a cacophony of colors.

"Gotcha, Big."

I face her only to find her phone poised in what I assume is the *record* position. "Seriously?"

"We told you to watch your back." Poppy drops her phone and taps away at a text. "Rose is going to love this. Your face was priceless. Meme-worthy. You looked like a constipated cat."

"Really helping the ol' self-esteem there, Boo."

Poppy laughs.

"Um, what's going on?" Holland is staring between us.

I open my mouth, but Poppy beats me to an explanation. "Ever since Big played a hand in pranking Rose and me, we've been looking for a chance to get him back."

"I told you, that's not how Cashmere Cove pranks work."

Poppy waves me off. "Rules change."

"I should have warned you about the pranks." Holland palms his forehead.

Poppy looks at him funny. "You did, remember? In that email. You were too late, but at least you tried."

I clear my throat, and Holland catches my eye.

"Right." He clears the confusion from his face and instead looks apologetically at Poppy. "Sorry about that. Again." He nods at the windshield. "I hope it's washable."

Poppy looks affronted. "We're not cruel. It'll come right off."

I put my hazard lights on and steer us into the parking lot of the nearest gas station.

"I'm going to use the bathroom while you get this cleaned up." Poppy hops out of the car.

"Watch out for exploding toilets," I say to her back as she jogs to the door.

She tosses a grin over her shoulder, ponytail swaying with her momentum.

I reach for the squeegee and start cleaning, trying to wipe the mental image of Poppy's toned legs in cut-off denim shorts from my mind's eye. Holland steps out the passenger seat and slings his hands into his pockets. He's got his baseball hat on, and he looks like a movie star, even standing in a Podunk gas station parking lot.

"So," he says, "you and Poppy seem to have hit it off."

I shrug.

"What was all that?" he presses.

I glance over at him. He looks curious rather than upset. "We're friends."

"So I've gathered." Holland nods and then shoots me a grin. "She's pretty great, isn't she? Didn't I tell you so?"

I grunt to acknowledge that yes, he did tell me Poppy is great. I focus on the streams of multi-colored watery paint running down my windshield as I wipe back and forth and try not to think about the other adjectives I would use to describe her...because they're growing by the minute, and they go something like this:

Charming.

Adorable.

Brave.

Clever.

Sweet.

Kind.

Sexy as sin.

Holland paces in the parking lot next to my truck, scrolling through his phone, and I find myself in a mental war between honoring Poppy's request for discretion and also making sure my brother realizes how lucky he is to have a woman like her waiting for him at home.

"You really like her?" I ask.

"What?" Holland is staring at his phone.

"Poppy. You really like her?"

He frowns. "Of course I like her. I asked her to move to my hometown." He says that as if it explains everything.

I consider him for a minute as I stick the squeegee back in the hanging container of soapy water. "But that was for you. I'm asking if you like her, or if you like the idea of her."

Holland whips his head up. "Where is this coming from?"

I hold up my hands. "As her friend, and your brother, I don't want to see either of you get hurt."

Holland's phone vibrates three times in quick succession. He looks down at it, once again distracted. "I hardly think I need to take relationship advice from you, Mack. Leave Poppy to me."

I grit my teeth to keep my mouth shut, hating everything about the thought of Poppy in anyone's care but my own.

15

WeDDINGS Are For LoVers

Poppy

Ed and Piper's wedding ceremony was beautiful. They professed their vows in a quaint country church outside of Cashmere Cove, and the party moved into the restored granary that Mack pointed out to Rose and me our first week in town. It's airy and bright, with high ceilings crisscrossed with rustic wood beams and the scent of fresh flowers permeating the air.

The food—I had the salmon and mashed potatoes—has been divine. The bride and groom could not be more gracious or charming. Everyone's spirits are high.

Everyone's but mine.

I should be feeling giddy from all the love in the air, right? That's what weddings do. They get you high on the thought of happily ever after. They make you lean in closer to your partner and fall in love all over again. It's a whole thing.

My phone vibrates in my clutch purse, and I reach for it like a lifeline. I'm against being glued to my cell when I'm in a public place where there are plenty of other things to occupy my time and attention, but I'm desperate for a distraction from the fact that, though I'm at a wedding—the most romantic of all occasions—I'm not feeling any flashes of affection for my boyfriend.

The same man I moved across the country for.

That realization makes me feel sick to my stomach.

Rose: How's the wedding event of the Cove, Pops?

Noli: Send us a picture!

I scroll through the photos I covertly snapped during the ceremony and find one where Ed and Piper are smooching at the altar. I send it along.

Rose: They look stunning!

Noli: Agreed, but I meant a picture of you. Rose said you picked the sequined wrap dress. Let's see it.

I open my camera app, flipping the view around so I'm staring at myself. I might not feel good about my relationship at the moment, but at least I look good. I did a dramatic smoky shadow around my eyes, and that, coupled with the golden color of the dress, is making my eyes look more *storm at sea* than *everyday blue*, which is fitting my mood perfectly.

I give them my best Tyra Banks smize, keeping my lips closed and doing my winningest impression of a fierce-looking, cat-walk-strutting model. I send it to my sisters. Their responses are immediate, and just what I expected.

Noli: Dang! Smoke show!

Rose: <fire emoji> You've never looked better.

Poppy: I wish you both were here. Holland has left me to fend for myself.

I nibble my lip as my message sends. I don't want to worry my sisters, but I also need someone to talk to right now. I catch sight of Holland on the other side of the granary. He's surrounded by a circle of admirers, and he's regaling them with some story. They're hanging on his every word—and both his arms—and he's eating up the attention like a proud puppy. Would it be too much to ask for him to throw me a bone and introduce me around? I know literally less than ten people in attendance at this shindig: the bride and groom, who have more on their mind than little ol' me; Holland; Holland's parents; and—

A throat clears to my left.

I set my phone face down as relief washes over me. "Big! Hi!"

"Is this seat taken?"

I laugh a slightly manic laugh. "Um, no."

He sits down next to me, the starched fabric of his groomsman suit pulling tight against his thighs. Unlike the other groomsmen, who have been hitting the Miller Lite hard since they arrived at the granary, Mack's tie is still in place.

"You look like you need to loosen up." I reach over and tug on the knot at his collar.

He flips his gaze to me. "You have no idea."

He stares at me while I work the tie looser.

"There." I pat his peck. "Better?"

"Much. You having fun?"

My phone vibrates four times in quick succession. I'm about to ignore it, but then it goes off twice more. I can't leave Noli and Rose hanging, so I shoot Mack an apologetic look and reach for my cell. "Sorry. It's my sisters."

Rose: Do you need me to fly back and beat some sense into him?

Noli: What is his problem?!

Rose: Seriously, he may be semi-famous, but I'm famous for my right cross.

Noli: Are you sure you're okay, Pops? Sorry for stealing Rose away. I feel bad.

Rose: I love to know I'm in such high demand. I feel very needed at the moment.

Rose: Hey, where's Mack? You could hang with him.

I read through the sequence of messages, and my spirits rise. I love my sisters, and now that Mack is sitting next to me, things feel a little less bleak. It's amazing what a difference it makes to not be sitting by yourself in a corner. Patrick Swayze was on to something.

I scooch my chair closer to Mack's. I hold out my phone in front of us and rest my chin on his shoulder. "Smile."

I take the photo and glance down at it. Instead of looking at the camera, Mack has his eyes directly on my smiling face. It's a great shot of his chiseled jawline. "Look at your face!" I squeak. "Have you ever considered a side-gig as a model? People pay big bucks for your God-given bone structure."

Mack grunts. "What are you doing?"

"Assuring my overprotective sisters that I'm okay."

Poppy: Found a friend! Thanks for being here when I needed you. Love you both. <kissing-face emoji>

I stow my phone back in my bag and turn my full attention to Mack.

"Are you not okay?" he says.

I shrug.

He turns and follows my gaze.

A woman I don't recognize has her manicured hand on Holland's bulging bicep. She's leaning in and giggling, and he's eating up the attention. I wait for a pang of jealousy or anything to rise up in my chest, but I've got nothing.

Nothing except that sick feeling in my stomach that I upended my whole life for a guy who isn't for me.

I glance over at Mack, and I can see him grinding that perfectly notched jaw of his, offended on my behalf. The last thing I want to do is cause any beef between the two Bradley brothers. "It's fine. I'm fine. I can handle myself."

My phone vibrates from inside my purse, but I ignore it because, at that same moment, Mack turns his gaze on me, and his eyes are twinkling like he's Santa Claus on Christmas Eve.

"So you've said." He holds out his hand to me, palm up. "But do you grant me permission to protect you tonight?"

I laugh, recalling our conversation at the beach. I'm already reaching for his hand even as I push back a little. "Protect me? From what? I don't see any rogue waves or carnivorous fish."

He hauls me to my feet. "True. But see that guy over there."

I glance to where Mack tossed his chin, and my eyes land on a beefy gentleman with a full mop of curly brown hair.

"That's Cousin Albert. He tends to zone in on unsuspecting wedding guests—male, female, canine...it makes no difference to him. If you aren't matched up and happen to be looking lonely when he makes eye contact, he'll drag you out on the dance floor. He means well, but you won't get out of his sweaty grip for the rest of the night. I don't know what type of voodoo he uses, but I've seen him lure many a soul into his Macarena-dancing clutches at family weddings over the years."

I stare at Mack, registering that my mouth is hanging slightly open but not caring. "Are you pulling my leg?"

"I'm not. But Cousin Albert might try to if you're not careful."

I snort, and Albert looks my way. He gives a finger wave, and I suck in a breath.

"So, Princess Boo. Since my baby brother is falling down on the job, I'm asking if I have permission to protect you from our over-eager cousin Albert tonight?" He twirls me around and pulls me back into him.

My hand lands against his chest. It's warm and firm, and when I look up into his eyes, he offers me one of his rare smiles. It transforms his face from stony to soft. I like this version of Mack Bradley. I don't think he shows it to too many people, and knowing that I'm one of the lucky ones he's comfortable enough to let his guard down around makes my insides feel settled for the first time all night.

"Lead on, Big Mack."

16

GUILTY

Mack

I'm holding Poppy in my arms, and I don't know if I'll ever be able to come back from this. The damage is fully done.

She's prattling on and on about this true-crime podcast that she finished binging. I keep catching bits and pieces, but mostly I'm lost in my own thoughts. About her. About how I shouldn't want her.

But I do.

"...I don't believe he did it. I mean, I couldn't believe the way things were covered up. I also don't think I'll sleep ever again, but that comes with the territory." She flashes me a wry grin, and her eyes sparkle in the dim light of the granary.

And here's something funny. I thought I had a good grasp on the color blue before—you know, living a stone's throw away from the cove, with the Cashmere County sky overhead—but I feel like I never knew blue until I looked into her eyes. The color comes to life in Poppy's glittery gaze—all multi-dimensional and kaleidoscopic.

I'm doing my best to leave room for the Holy Spirit. I have my arms almost fully extended as we take up the age-old slow-dancing formation. My hands rest on her hips, and the fabric of her gold-sequin dress shifts as we sway. I'm actively *not* thinking about her gorgeous curves or the fact that her legs are mere inches from mine. One misstep and we'd be a collection of tangled limbs. I keep my focus on her face, on those eyes that have successfully ruined me for enjoying blue in any other capacity for the rest of my life.

"I'll shut up now." Her voice is tinged with self-deprecation. Before I have the chance to say something stupid like, *I could listen to you talk forever*, she says, "Let's just be quiet."

She closes her eyes and lets out the softest of sighs.

Tentatively, I readjust my hands. I'm fighting against an intuitive desire to hold her a little tighter. I can feel the warmth of her body heat through my white dress shirt, and I'm certain she can hear the pounding of my heart.

As I catalog every sensation of having her in my arms, it hits me that nothing about this situation feels awkward. It feels incredibly right. Her hands are clasped lightly behind my neck. It's a friendly position. Not overly intimate. She isn't doing any type of massaging, nor is she running her fingertips through my hair. And thank the good Lord for that because it might be my total undoing.

I catch a whiff of her floral perfume, and I tear my gaze away from where I've been staring at the way her eyelashes have fanned out across her cheeks. I pull in a fresh breath and try to clear my head as I look beyond her.

I scan the dance floor, and everyone is either too lost in the eyes of their partner or too drunk to notice Poppy and me.

Everyone except Holland.

My gaze snags on his. He's leaning against the bar, and from across the room, I can tell he's tense. He's staring right at Poppy and me, and I'm guessing he has been for a while. The posse that kept him busy and away from Poppy all night is nowhere to be found. A creeping sense of shame washes over me. I am majorly overstepping, aren't I?

Poppy must sense or feel a change in the rhythm of my heartbeats, because she eases away from me and opens her eyes. She arches her back and drops her hands from my neck.

I let go of her waist and run my palm over the skin that she was touching, savoring the fleeting warmth of having her so near.

"Have you seen Holland?" she asks.

I bob my chin over her shoulder. She spins around, and when she catches sight of him, she holds up her hand in a wave.

Holland weaves his way toward us. "Hey, you." He drops a light kiss on Poppy's cheek.

I clench my jaw and release it, working to keep my expression neutral. I nod at my brother and offer Poppy a tight smile. "Holland will protect you from Cousin Albert now."

She chuckles. "Thanks, Big."

Without another word, I make my way to the bar, both trying to erase the past few hours and sear them into my brain.

I plop down onto a barstool. "Shot of whiskey."

The bartender nods and gets out a shot glass. He fills it and pushes it at me. I down it without hesitation.

"What's going on?"

I set the shot glass down and turn to where Holland has angled himself next to me, leaning with one shoulder against the bar, his arms crossed over his chest.

"Nothing."

"That didn't look like nothing."

"I don't know what you're talking about."

"You were staring at my girlfriend like you—"

"Like I what?" I swivel on the barstool and pull my back straight, taking a smidgen of satisfaction in the fact that Holland has to look up at me. "Like I wanted to spend time with her? Guilty."

Holland opens his mouth, but I cut him off.

"Where is she anyway? Did you abandon her again?"

He narrows his gaze. "She's in the bathroom, and then we're going to head out. What is your problem?"

"My problem?" I scoff. "You've got an amazing girl on your hands, and you're taking her for granted."

"I am not."

I give him a disbelieving snort, but it's pointless to argue. He's Holland. He's not going to see that he's in the wrong, no matter what I say. "Look, you asked me to be her friend, and that's what I've done."

"That's all?"

I hate the way his voice is laced with disbelief. I tighten my fists and release them. "That's all."

We're in the middle of a stare-down when Poppy appears behind Holland.

"You ready?" she asks, glancing between us.

I clear my face of any expression that might give away the tornado of emotions that's swirling inside my chest.

Holland blinks and looks down at her. "Absolutely. Let's go."

He puts his arm around her shoulder and tucks her to his side.

I watch them go long enough to see her rest her head against his bicep, and the blast of jealousy in my chest rattles my sternum like a grenade. I turn to the bartender.

"Another shot."

17

A Trick of the Camera

Poppy

Holland insisted upon taking me from the wedding and showing me the view from the rocky edifice overlooking Wool Beach. I didn't have the heart to tell him I'd been there with Mack and his friends.

We're another half hour before we arrive back at The Downer.

He hops out of his side of the car and jogs around the front to open my door for me. It's a nice gesture. He means well. I know that. But I also know what I'm going to do next.

I step out onto the driveway and am blinded by headlights.

A car pulls into the spot adjacent to where Holland is dropping me off.

Mack gets out of the back. He must've Ubered home.

He slams the door, glances at us, looks away, and strolls up to his half of the duplex, disappearing inside before I can get any words out. I'm not sure what I want to say. I've already thanked him for a fun night.

Not only did he save me from Cousin Albert's clutches, but Mack kept me laughing and with a wine glass in hand. I had so much fun I almost forgot that I was at a wedding with a boyfriend who wasn't paying me any attention—the same boyfriend whom I need to break up with.

Whoa boy. If given the choice, I might let Cousin Albert have his way with me now, if only to prolong the inevitable.

But no. I can do this. I square my shoulders when Holland and I reach my front door and remind myself that I'm wearing fancy underwear.

"Look, Poppy. I'm sorry I was so distracted tonight. It's just my first time back in town. Lots of people want to hear what I've been up to…" Holland trails off when I put a hand on his chest.

"I don't think this thing is going to work between us."

Holland flinches, but I plow ahead.

"I think you're great. I mean, you're a star, Holland. You truly are. You're going to do amazing things, but this"—I gesture to him and then me—"isn't right."

"Is this because I left you alone at the wedding? Is Mack right?"

I feel my brow crease. "Mack?"

But Holland isn't listening. He rakes his hand through his hair. "Gosh, I think so highly of you, Poppy. Can't I have another chance?"

He looks genuinely distraught, and my hands tremble ever so slightly. I clasp them in front of me. The idea of dating him—of being in a relationship with a pro-golfer, of being wanted by someone like him—is so shiny and nice that my resolve wavers. But then I remind myself that just because the *idea* sounds good, it doesn't mean the reality is good.

"I don't think so, Holland." My voice comes out sounding gentle. "Our timing is off, and I don't think I'm the type of woman you need."

That's what I've been circling and finally realized tonight. Holland is willing to take and take from me without offering too much in return.

I'm a person who'll give and give until there's nothing left. I can already see that happening in the way I'm pouring into Holland, and he's not reciprocating, other than to say he's grateful. But words of gratitude aren't the same as actions of gratitude. Holland needs a woman who'll stand up to him. I need a man who'll be there for me. Someone I can trust.

Holland twists his jaw and glances over my shoulder at Mack's side of the duplex.

I awkwardly transfer my weight in my heels.

"If that's what you want," he says after a second. "What will you do?"

My stomach feels queasy again, because in the words of Sherlock Holmes, that *is* the question. I can hardly stay in Cashmere Cove. This is Holland's hometown. But the thought of upending our lives again after having only been here for a month is preposterous.

"I...I'm not sure."

Honest, if slightly terrifying.

He nods. "Take all the time you need to figure it out. I don't need my car for any reason, so you're welcome to keep using it, and I'm sure Mack doesn't mind the neighbors."

My stomach does a weird wiggle at the thought of moving out. Of someone else taking up residence in The Downer. I glance behind me. Mack's side of the duplex is dark. I turn back to Holland. "Thank you for that. For everything." I know he's always meant well, and that's what's making this break-up both harder and easier. "I truly am grateful for our time together. I'll always root for H. Bradley Pro!" I quip.

Holland furrows a quizzical brow. "H. Bradley Pro?"

"Yeah, you know. Your email handle?" I'd been pretty impressed with myself for coming up with that one.

He gives me a blank look, but then blinks. "Right. Of course." He leans in and kisses me on the cheek. "Take care of yourself, Poppy."

"You too."

He waits while I unlock the door. I give him one small smile before I walk inside, throwing the deadbolt behind me. I walk straight to my bedroom and flop onto my bed.

I can't believe I broke up with Holland Bradley.

I feel exhausted down to my core. I'm not sure if that's from the break-up, or the dancing, or the uncertainty of what comes next for me. I kick off my heels and crawl toward my pillow, pulling the covers up to my chin. The sequins on my dress scrape at my skin, but I'm too tired to care.

I paw for my purse and find my phone. Texts from Noli and Rose stare back at me.

Noli: Umm, you two failed to mention that Holland's brother is HOT.

Rose: There was no need. But that was before he started looking at Poppy like he wanted to memorize her.

I roll my eyes, which sends flecks of mascara into them. Don't come at me about the damage I'm doing to my pores by not washing my face. I know, alright. But Neutrogena can't save me now. My eyes are watering. Or maybe I'm crying. I don't know. I swipe at my face, trying to see clearly. I click over to the photo I took of Mack and me.

I have to squint one eye closed to stop the burning of my cornea from the errant eye makeup, but what I see gives me pause.

I've got a toothy grin on my face, and Mack's profile is all that's visible. His nose is poised a fraction of an inch away from my forehead, almost as if he's going to sniff my hair. He's staring down at me as if I'm the most precious thing he's ever laid eyes on. Like I'm the last sentence of his favorite storybook. His gaze is tinged with both longing and contentment.

Of course it's a trick of the camera. Mack isn't *actually* looking at me like that. I happened to catch him off guard. That's it.

I don't respond to my sisters. Not tonight. Not with burning eyes, and a muddled heart, and a future that looks about as clear as a dense fog advisory.

I drift off to sleep with my phone open to the photo of Mack and me clutched against my chest.

18

"DID HE HURT YOU?"

Mack

I'm wedged in a ninety-degree angle, with my feet on the ground and my upper body splayed the full length of a bookcase, when I hear the bell above the door to Mood Reader jingle.

"Rose?"

I slam my head on the shelf above me at the sound of Poppy's voice.

Biting back a curse, I pull myself out of the precarious position I'm in and stand up straight as a board.

I haven't seen Poppy since the wedding last weekend.

To be specific, I haven't seen her since she and Holland arrived home at the duplex. I bolted inside because the thought of watching them kiss goodnight was enough to make me upchuck, and I really, really didn't want to see her invite him inside. I've been trying not to think about it.

"I'm upstairs," Rose's voice echoes throughout the room of books.

Mood Reader is located in the Cashmere Cove historic district, the part of town nearest to the water. As such, the building is longer than it is wide, with weathered wood floors and quaint fixtures. There's a spiral staircase in the back that leads up to an open loft and adjacent apartment, and from the sounds of it, that's where Rose is working at the moment.

"I'm coming up."

Footsteps grow louder as Poppy approaches the row where I'm standing. Right as she rounds the corner, I manage to kick over the books I painstakingly removed from the shelf and piled in order on the floor so I'd have room to work.

"Big?" Poppy cocks her head at me. She's dressed in what I've come to consider her work attire. A black, sporty skort and a polo shirt. Her hair is pulled up and off her face, and the heavy makeup from last weekend's wedding is gone. She looks good, if a little tired.

"Uh, hey."

"What are you doing?"

Ogling you.

Being an idiot.

"Mia asked me to install undershelf lighting for all the bookcases." I gesture at my electrical toolbox and then the shelf.

An expression covers Poppy's face that I can't quite read, and when she glances at me with a look of admiration in her eyes, my knees turn to jelly. I'm not sure what I did to deserve that, but I'll take it.

She points to books that are spread across the floor like a paperback rug. "Do you want some help?"

"Nah. I've got it."

Poppy twists her lips to the side.

"It's all organized."

She narrows her gaze.

"I've got a system." I take a step back and knock another pile of books over.

She smirks. "If you say so."

"Yep. All good here." I go to rest my forearm against the bookcase, but instead of looking cool, calm, and collected, I knock my drill to the floor.

It hits the hardwood, and the battery pops out of place. I bend to retrieve it. Poppy does too, and we slam our heads into each other.

She falls backward onto her butt, letting out an *umph.*

I grunt and rub my forehead.

"Everything okay down there?" Rose calls.

"Fine," Poppy says, getting to her feet. "Sorry."

"My fault."

"Well, I'm glad I ran into you."

"Literally," we say at the same time.

Poppy laughs, and I swear that sound does something to my soul. It's like a ribbon wraps itself around my heart and lifts it higher in my chest.

She hands me my drill battery. Our fingers brush, and something like a shock passes between us. I deal with wires and circuits and lightbulbs all day, every day. I know how these things work, and there is no such thing as literal sparks flying between two people. But I don't know how else to describe the connection I experience with Poppy every time we're skin-to-skin. All I know is I want to experience it again and again.

But she's off limits, and the electrical current I'm craving is only one-sided, so really, I need to stop obsessing over it.

Poppy bends back down and picks up a book. "Gosh, aren't we on the same page?" She wiggles the book. "Get it."

I level her with a look that says, *That's not funny*, even though I think she's the most adorable creature in the whole wide world.

"Oh come on! Book. Page. Get it?"

"Ba-dum-ching," I deadpan.

She laughs again. "I've gotta talk to Rose, but then, can I pick your brain about Party at the Park?"

Before I can answer, Rose appears. "Hey, Pops. What did you need?"

Poppy slings her arm over her sister's shoulder. "Let's talk over here."

"Don't let me keep you two from your plans." Rose flips her gaze between us with a curious look in her eye. A look I can't place. She stares at me, and I stare back at her, but she shakes her head, turning her focus to her sister.

"No, it's important," Poppy says. "Big, can you wait?"

"Sure."

The sister's disappear into the tiny office behind the register, and a sense of foreboding washes over me.

• • • • • • • • • •

"This is such a cool venue." Poppy leans against the chest-height fence that encircles Lighthouse Park and stares out over the water.

She's been all business since we left Mood Reader. No small talk. No teasing. Just work and questions about Party in the Park. We've sorted out the timing of the assembly of the stage and who she needs to communicate with about permitting. I've assured her that, on my end, nothing about this event will be a surprise. My team has coordinated the set-up for the past two years. I'm not worried about it.

"And you'll add extra lights for the Party in the Park Promenade, right? Make the place pop?"

I fight an eye roll. She's leaning into making the dance romantic and—for lack of a better word—sparkly.

"If that's what you want, sure."

She nods, and I hope I've set her mind at ease. But as she stares out at the bay, she looks almost wistful.

"You okay?" I rest my forearms on the fence, keeping six inches of distance between us.

She gives me a sidelong glance before facing forward again. "Have you talked to Holland?"

I frown. "No. Why?"

My brother sent me a text the morning after the wedding saying his coach told him he had to get back for some extra practices. He didn't say goodbye in person, which is classic Holland. Is Poppy upset that they didn't get to spend more time together?

She sighs. "We broke up."

"What?"

"Easy, Big. You look like you're taking the news harder than Holland did," Poppy quips.

I unball my fists and try to relax my face muscles. I cut my gaze to her, and she's staring back at me with a small smile tipping up the corner of her lips.

"Did he hurt you?" My question comes out in a growl. Poppy might be the most exquisite human being I've ever encountered, and so help me, if Holland did something to dim her light, I will personally see to it that he makes amends.

"No, no. Nothing like that. It was my choice. Your brother was a perfect gentleman." She shrugs. "It's my own fault. I let myself get caught up in the idea of dating Holland. I was blinded by how nice it was that he was interested in me. But I should have paid attention to the reality of the relationship and our lack of compatibility. I could have saved us both a lot of trouble."

My head is swimming as I try to follow her train of thought, but all I can think to say is, "You're no trouble, Boo."

Poppy chuckles, but then it turns into a wince. "Tell that to Rose. She's not very pleased with the thought of upending her life...again."

I frown, and Poppy must sense my confusion.

"I told her I think we should move back to Florida." She lifts her shoulders and lets them drop. "But it's daunting...the thought of moving again.

My mind is still trying to catch up. "You're leaving?"

Cashmere Cove without Poppy is the color gray.

"I'll stay through the end of the summer. Until Heather gets back from maternity leave. That's what I committed to in the first place." She pauses. "But this is Holland's hometown. There's nothing here for me anymore."

Well.

If that isn't a metaphorical sucker punch to the gut, I don't know what is. I shouldn't take it personally, but all I want to do is scream, *Hey! I'm here! What about me?*

But then I'd sound like a Looney Tune, and I've made it a point to avoid acting like a fool whenever I can help it.

The thing is, Poppy's friendship means more to me than I would have thought a friendship of only a month and a half could. The thought of her leaving town—of not seeing her at the café or hearing her sing through our shared duplex wall—makes me feel hollow, like a rotted-out tree stump.

"I'll miss you." My voice legitimately comes out in a hoarse whisper, and I am a grown man. I clear my throat.

"Aww, Big. Are you getting soft on me?" Poppy elbows me in the side, but then pulls back and rubs her funny bone. "Ow. Nope, not soft. Jeez. How do you get abs like that? Is it your sexy-time workouts?"

"*Excuse* me?"

"What?" Poppy's eyes are wide and innocent. "It sounds very provocative every time you play those exercise videos. The walls in The Downer are paper thin. I hear everything. *Everything*, Big." She wiggles her eyebrows.

I stare at her, and when I realize my mouth is hanging open, I clamp it shut, but I can't help the quirk of my lips. How does Poppy do that? Make me feel lighter—no matter the circumstances. There is something so entirely captivating about this woman and how she speaks her mind.

Good thing I have nothing to hide. I haven't been doing anything to be ashamed of in my half of the duplex.

"It goes both ways, Boo. Think about that the next time you and Rose get in a fighting match over whose turn it is to buy tampons."

Poppy's cheeks blush pink—the same color as the sky behind her. She opens her mouth, closes it, and crosses her arms over her chest. "Female reproductive health shouldn't be taboo."

"I never said it was."

"Then you won't mind if I scream about periods and curse my ovaries in the future?"

"I'd welcome it. Let it all out. That's what I always say."

"Be careful what you wish for," Poppy mutters. "My hormones make me crazy." She pauses, and then adds, "And it *was* Rose's turn."

"I'll be sure to mention that next time I see her."

Poppy barks out a laugh, but when I glance down at her, she's staring at me with a serious look in her eye. She reaches for my hand and squeezes it.

"For what it's worth, I'll miss you too, Big. I think you've been the best part of moving to Cashmere Cove."

19

HanDSY anD HanDY

Poppy

"It's like the seventh layer of hell in here."

I stop to wipe the sweat from my brow and glance over to where Rose is sprawled out on the couch in front of our one oscillating floor fan. We've both abandoned shirts in favor of our sports bras. She looks like one of those Victorian women in paintings from time's gone by.

Half-naked and morose.

The day I feared since we first moved into The Downer has finally come—our air conditioning unit went kaput.

In the middle of July.

At nine o'clock at night.

Basically, there is no chance to get a technician out here until morning—at the very earliest—and I'm pretty sure Rose and I are going to fry in the meantime.

We've got the windows open, but I think that's making it worse. The air from outside is so hot and sticky it's seeping into our house and leaving a layer of moisture on every surface...including every inch of my skin.

"Popsicles. Antarctica. Snowflakes. Ice Cream." Rose has been listing off things that are cold for the better part of the night.

"Alaska. Refrigerated watermelon. Mountain tops. Diet Coke from McDonalds. My ex-boyfriend."

She's getting creative, I'll give her that.

Headlights flash into our living room.

"Big's home."

Is it weird that Mack's presence instantly improves my mood? Whenever he's around, I feel settled, confident that things will work out—or at least if they don't, I'll have some fun in the meantime.

I wait until I hear him toss his keys onto his kitchen counter, and then I bang my fist on the wall we share.

"What are you doing?" Rose props herself up on her elbow.

"Getting his attention."

"Why?"

"I don't know." I don't have a plan, but I want to talk to Mack.

"Me thinks someone has developed a little crush on her ex-boyfriend's brother." Rose wags her eyebrows at me.

"What? No way! He's a friend."

"Then why are your cheeks turning bright red?"

I feel my face, which does seem to be burning off. "Because, like you said, it's hotter than Hades in here."

Rose scoffs. "Keep telling yourself that. You're into him, Pops."

"I am not!"

"Don't be ashamed of it. It's cute. Nice to see you with a guy who's on your level."

"What's that supposed to mean?"

"As opposed to getting into a relationship that's doomed from the start."

"Wh-how? Why do you say that?"

"Because you always pick guys who you aren't that into."

"I do not! I was into Holland!"

"Were you, though?" Rose stretches her hands over her head. "Your chemistry was nil. With Mack, on the other hand..." She holds out her closed fist and opens it, miming an explosion.

I furrow my brow. "The heat is totally going to your head."

There's a knock on the door, and I jump, my heart flying to my throat.

Rose laughs. I scowl at her.

"Come in," I call.

Mack steps into the living room, looks around, takes in the sight of Rose and me, and frowns. "You rang?"

I wiggle my eyebrows at him. "Are you quoting *The Parent Trap*?"

"Maybe." His gaze locks onto mine for a fraction of a second, and my pulse surges. He looks around again. "Why is it so hot in here?"

"You tell us, dear landlord of ours," Rose sings.

"The air conditioning unit stopped working," I add, in case it wasn't clear.

Mack drags a hand through his hair and mumbles a curse. "Sorry."

"Not your fault," I say at the same time as Rose says, "You should be."

I shoot her a *behave* look, but she ignores me.

"We've only been saying something's wrong with it since the day we moved in."

I shrug apologetically at Mack.

He shifts his jaw. "You can sleep on my side of the duplex."

"You have air? Thank God." Rose peels herself off the couch, her sticking skin making a farting noise as she stands.

I cover my mouth to hold in my laugh, because apparently the heat is making me slap-happy.

"Real mature, Pops." She scowls as she saunters past me.

"Rose, wait." I turn to Mack. "We wouldn't want to invade your space."

"Shut up, Poppy." Rose looks at me like I've got a screw loose. "We're not staying here. We'll die of heat stroke."

"Quit being a drama queen." I roll my eyes.

"I'm not being dramatic. It's like Dante's *Inferno* in here."

"Again with the obscure literary references."

"That is not obscure! Everyone knows Dante."

"I don't."

Mack holds up his hands, silencing our bickering. "It's no problem. Rose is right. I'm not leaving you over here to melt."

I stare at him, but he's not flinching. I don't need much convincing. Rose and I pack a quick bag and practically sprint outside and through Mack's front door.

"Oh, sweet relief," Rose lies down on the rug covering the hardwood floor in the living room.

I glance around. It's sparse, but neat. His living room and kitchen share a wall with ours. I look down the hallway where I expect to see a pair of bedrooms and a bathroom, like we have, but instead, there are only two doors.

"This side is a little smaller," Mack says, reading my thoughts. "You guys can have my bed, and I'll sleep on the couch."

I'm shaking my head before he finishes his sentence. "Absolutely not."

He crosses his arms, giving me a full view of his tanned forearms. "Why?"

"Because we're already putting you out, and you're way too tall to sleep comfortably on your couch."

He looks down at himself, as if trying to find a loophole in my argument. There isn't one. He's got a good nine inches on both Rose and me. But he shakes his head and says, "I insist. There are two of you. It makes sense for you to take the bed. I'll be fine out here. It's my fault you're in this situation to begin with. It totally slipped my mind to call a technician and have your unit checked. That's on me." Mack looks like he's about ready to cry. When he meets my gaze, his eyes are pleading. "Take the bedroom, Boo."

The desperate way he says my nickname causes something to flutter right underneath my ribcage. A warm sensation trickles out from my core, and it's like I can feel the blood flowing through my veins. I absentmindedly feel my chest and look down, but then I realize I'm only wearing a sports bra, and there's no need to draw attention to *that*, so I drop my hand.

Rose, who has been watching Mack and me like a hawk, has a wicked grin on her face. "I'll take the bed, even if Poppy won't."

"Second door," Mack says.

"Thanks. Night, you two." Rose disappears down the hall.

Mack walks over to his refrigerator and gets out a glass container. "You hungry?" he asks.

"No. The heat zapped my appetite." I pull out a stool by his bar-height countertop. "I can keep you company while you eat if you want, though."

"I won't say no." He pops his food in the microwave, and the scent of leftover macaroni and cheese fills the air.

He leans back against the counter opposite of me, and I study him for the first time tonight. He looks rough.

"Long day?"

"You could say that."

"Want to talk about it?"

"Nothing much to say. We've got a deadline to hit with an inspection coming up, so I'm burning the midnight oil."

"Is that another electrician joke?"

He chuckles. "I guess."

"You know," I say, "maybe if you weren't so gosh-darn willing to be everything to everyone around town, you could focus on your own work."

Mack furrows his brow.

"You don't know you're doing it."

"Doing what?" The microwave beeps, and he turns to fetch his food.

"Let's see." I hold up my hand and start ticking off fingers. "I've seen you at the bakery, helping Inez. The bookshop, helping Mia. You wired your dad's entire garage since I moved to town. Not to mention all the time you're spending with me, getting stuff ready for Party in the Park." I drop my arm to my side and shrug my shoulders. "I'd say you're spreading yourself a little thin."

Mack shovels a spoonful of crusty mac and cheese in his mouth, and I grimace. "I don't mind helping out. I like to be busy."

By the way Mack isn't meeting my eye, I'm guessing there's more to the story, but I can tell he doesn't want to go into it. So, I shift gears.

"Have you always wanted to own your own company?"

He nods. "That was the goal since I started as an apprentice—to be a master electrician by the time I turned thirty."

"And you did it?"

"I did."

"How old are you now?"

"Thirty-one."

"An old geezer."

He looks affronted, and I laugh at his scowl.

"I'm only twenty-seven," I say.

"I'll have to start calling you Baby Boo."

I crinkle up my nose as a ball of heat flies like a rocket straight up my spine. I swear it splits into two fireballs that settle themselves on both of my cheekbones, because my face is flaming hot.

Note to self: best not to think too much about Mack calling me *baby*.

I clear my throat. "Do you like your work?"

"I love it. I never wanted a nine-to-five desk job. I like being out in the field."

I nod. "I can see that. You're very handsy." I blink. Swallow. "*Handy*."

Friggin' Freudian slip. What are the chances?

I blame the *baby* endearment. And Rose putting unnecessary thoughts in my head. It's all messing with me.

Mack's charcoal eyes are at once brighter. Like there's a fire lit in them. How is that possible?

He shrugs. "Both. And"—he pauses and stares directly at me with that intense look of his—"I'm good with my hands."

What the *what*, now?

That sounded a lot like an innuendo.

Right? *Right?*

"Right," I say. "Hands." My voice sounds a little squeaky. "Very important to be good with your hands."

Mack hums and crosses the kitchen in two long strides so he's standing directly in front of me, with just the counter separating us. He leans down to rest his elbows against it, and my lungs spasm.

I don't break eye contact as he reaches over and brushes a strand of hair off my forehead, tucking it behind my ear. Goosebumps erupt on top of my burning-up skin. His calloused fingers are gentle, and the thought of the actual electrical work he does with his hands sends a shiver through my nervous system. There is something about a man who is fully capable and in control. I imagine Mack is that on the job site.

And...elsewhere.

His face gets closer to mine, and for a fraction of a second, our lips are only an inch or two apart. I can feel his breath against my cheeks before he leans away.

"Very important," he echoes, his voice no louder than a rumble. Like the quiet purr of an in-tune engine.

My mouth goes dry. Is he flirting with me?

No way in Dante's inferno.

This is Mack. Sworn bachelor. Holland's brother. My *friend*.

Friends don't do...this.

Do they?

"Hands are good for lots of things, aren't they?" I start babbling, taking a play from Rose's book and listing off items related to the subject in question. "High fives. Crossing the monkey bars. Writing out checks." No one under the age of sixty writes out checks anymore. *Shut up, Poppy.* But it's like my mouth has detached itself from my brain and is running away from me like a mischievous child. "Kneading dough. Tying shoes. Putting on makeup, though I guess that one doesn't apply to you."

"No." Mack stands up straight, and he's smirking. "But I can think of some other things," he says.

The flicker in his eyes makes me feel like panting, and I have to physically tell myself to keep my tongue in my mouth. It's almost as if I can feel the sensation of his hands tangled in my hair. Brushing lightly up and down my sides. Squeezing my hips. Drawing circles on my skin.

"I can imagine," I whisper and then clamp my hand over my mouth. I did not mean to say that out loud.

Mack's face breaks into a full-blown grin.

It's dangerous, and delicious, and one hundred percent sexy. Suddenly, Mack's side of the duplex feels hotter than ours did, and that has nothing to do with a non-functioning air conditioning unit.

I push back my stool. "I should probably go to bed."

He doesn't take his eyes off me. "Right. Make yourself comfortable."

"Thanks." I nod. "Night, Big."

"Sweet dreams, Boo."

I make the quick walk down the hallway, stop in the bathroom to brush my teeth and splash water on my face, which—surprising no one—is redder than a tomato in September, and then push open the door to the bedroom.

Mack's bedroom.

Thirty minutes ago, my reservations about sleeping in here had everything to do with inconveniencing my friend. Now, as I stare around the space, a charge of electricity still circling me from my conversation with Mack, I have a bouquet of new hang-ups to contend with.

Front and center is the fact that I'm about to sleep in Mack's bed. The place where he lays down his tall, broad, muscular body each night. A body that I, all of a sudden, am seeing in a completely different way.

Why haven't I admired Mack's forearms, or the stubble along his jawline, or the way his grin crinkles the skin around his eyes before now?

Rose lets out a small snore, and it snaps me out of my daydream. I square my shoulders. I'm being ridiculous. Mack is my friend. He offered up his room out of the goodness of his heart, like any upstanding man would do.

He wants nothing to do with me romantically.

And I want nothing to do with him romantically.

Or I didn't.

Until he looked at me like that.

No.

I still don't.

Oh gosh, I don't know.

Things got confusing out there.

I close my eyes. I'm overtired and overheated and overthinking. Everything will be clearer in the morning.

I blink and walk over to the bed, slipping into the sheets. The cool fabric feels like a hug against my exposed skin. I take a deep breath and am hit with a scent that is so purely Mack—mint and sunshine—I whimper.

I close my eyes and say a quick prayer for dreamless sleep to overtake me ASAP.

But it's hopeless. My thoughts are totally and completely caught up in all things Mack.

20

A T-SHIRT'S WORTH A THOUSAND WORDS

Mack

I slept like garbage, so I'm stress cooking.

I know what you're thinking, and no, I'm not making mac and cheese. I can whip up a mean batch of homemade pancakes.

So yeah, though the sun hasn't risen, I'm in my kitchen...making breakfast. I've got my AirPods in, and I'm blasting Taylor Swift music.

Don't you dare judge me. The woman is a genius, and the lyrics to "Nothing New (Taylor's Version) (From the Vault)" will forever wreck me.

I said what I said.

(If you want to go give it a listen, I'll wait.)

Anyway, I have my griddle out and the first batch of pancakes poured onto it when I spin around, doing a little two-step to the particularly bomb bridge of "Mr. Perfectly Fine (Taylor's Version) (From the Vault)," and drop my wooden spoon.

Poppy is standing in the doorway to the kitchen, squinting at me with a goofy grin on her face. Her hair is in its usual ponytail, but it's mussed from a night of sleep. Her hands are on her hips, and her head is cocked to the side as she observes me. And she's wearing my t-shirt.

I repeat. She is *wearing. My. T-shirt.*

I'm frozen at the sight of her. I haven't said a word. I can't form a coherent thought beyond... *Her.*

Wearing my t-shirt.

I don't think I've ever seen anything that took my breath away like this. I'm light-headed and have to coach my lungs. *In. Out. In. Out.*

There we go.

I take a deep pull of air. "Morning."

"Nice moves." Poppy motions to me and assumes her position on the same stool she was sitting in last night before bed—when I lost my mind for a couple minutes and flirted with her.

I couldn't help it. One second, we were talking about work, and the next second, she called me handsy and got all flustered.

Her cheeks kept turning a deeper shade of red, and all I wanted was to kiss the stunned look off her face when I tucked her hair behind her ear.

But I didn't.

Because I have self-control, and I know better.

She sees me as a brother.

She's Holland's ex.

She's leaving town.

If that all isn't enough, I would never drag her into the muddied mess of my reputation.

Even if there was a small possibility she saw me as something beyond a friend.

Which she doesn't.

That's why I slept like crap.

Now, to solidify the truth of the matter, she's staring at me with a bright smile, as if she's been able to toss a wool dryer ball into the pile of static electricity that crackled between us last night and remove it all.

"You're wearing my shirt."

Naturally, since that's all I've been able to think about since seeing her, those are the words that tumble out of my mouth.

She glances down. "Yeah. I got a little chilly." She chuckles. "Ironic, I know." She sobers. "Is it okay? I can run next door and grab something of mine."

I bend to pick up the wooden spoon and swish it through the air. "It's fine."

Only Poppy could add layers of clothing and somehow seem sexier to me than ever before.

I shove that thought out of my head.

"Is something burning?" She sniffs.

I pivot to my griddle to find my pancakes charred. Serves me right. I toss that batch into the trash and pour more batter, keeping all my focus on the food. "How'd you sleep?"

"Great!" Poppy sounds so cheerful. I cast a quick glance at her to find her smiling back at me. She's like the actual morning sun. All bright and glow-y.

"Rose still asleep?"

She frowns at that. "Yeah."

"Everything okay with you two?"

Poppy sighs. "We'll be fine. She's still acting snippy about moving back to Florida. I can't figure out why. I mean, I get it. She loves Mood Reader and the people we've met here, but Noli needs us, so I don't know why she's being all irritated. We both decided we have to go."

I keep my attention on the pancakes. "Those we're closest to can push us the furthest because they know we won't leave."

Poppy is quiet for a minute, and when I look up at her, she's staring back at me with an unreadable expression on her face. She blinks. "You know, I never got a good idea of your relationship with Holland. Are you two close?"

I roll my shoulders and let out a puff of air. "That's a loaded question."

She shrugs, waiting on me.

I think for a minute before trying to explain it. "Holland's the golden boy. I'm not. My parents"—I angle my head at her—"who I love, don't get me wrong..."

She nods for me to continue.

"They're proud of him. Rightly so. And me... I've done some things they aren't proud of. I know they love me too, but sometimes it's all Holland, all the time. It's a lot to live with."

"So you're not very close, then?"

I consider that for a minute, and a pang of sadness hits out of left field. "Growing up, we were thick as thieves."

I never stop to think about how much I miss my brother. How much I miss what we used to have. But that's the truth of it. It doesn't help that Holland took Tricia's side—or at least never cared to hear my side of things all those years ago. I don't know if I ever got over that loss of loyalty.

"My sisters and me too. Though, I've had to function in a mom role." Poppy speaks quietly.

I flip a pancake onto her plate and set it in front of her, nudging the syrup in her direction and waiting for her to go on. I know some of her past from the emails, but I want to know more.

"My mom passed when I was a sophomore in high school. A car accident."

"I'm so sorry, Poppy." My heart constricts. My mom may give me a hard time, but I love her something fierce, and I can't imagine having already lived half of my life without her.

Poppy nods. "Thanks. She was the best sort of woman. Kind and sweet. My dad was sort of a loafer. She brought out the good in him, kept him on the straight and narrow, but then after she died, it was like the good stuff about him disappeared, and then after a couple months, he left."

"What do you mean he left?"

"Like, he walked out of our life. I haven't seen him since I was fifteen."

A deep rage forms in my gut at the thought of a man abandoning three daughters.

"Fortunately, my gram took us in. We went to live with her and had nearly two mostly blissful—if a bit quirky—years in her house." Poppy smiles as if a memory is tickling at her toes, but then she turns serious again. "She died right before I graduated from high school."

"I'm so sorry."

I don't know what I'm apologizing for. But there isn't anything else to say. We need a new word in the English language that means: *I don't understand why bad things happen to good people, and none of it is fair, and I wish I could make it better, but since I can't, know I'm here and I feel torn up on your behalf.*

Get on that, Webster's Dictionary.

"Thanks." Poppy takes a giant bite of pancake. Her eyes widen. "These are reawwly good." She covers her mouth and chews.

"I'm glad."

I add "feeding Poppy" to my mental list of favorite things, which is quickly filling with Poppy-related items. *Swimming with Poppy. Singing with Poppy. Dancing with Poppy.*

I could go on, but you get it.

"Anyway, after Gram died, all of my focus had to be on Noli and Rose. I was almost eighteen, but I couldn't bear the thought of the two of them somehow ending up in the foster care system, so I sold Gram's house, paid her debts with most of the profit, and used the rest to live off of for a little while. I took night classes at the local community college and took care of my sisters."

I've been eating pancakes as she tells me all this, but I'm pretty sure my fork has been stuck halfway to my mouth through this last bit. I set it down on my plate, and it clatters obnoxiously.

"You're incredible."

"Not really. I did what I had to do."

"No. I'm serious, Boo. You absolutely are. I just...that is a lot. A lot that you had to deal with. Alone. As a kid."

"There were some lean days, but we made it through. My dad texts occasionally. I sort of wish he wouldn't. It's like a stab wound to my heart every time." She squints at me. "Why am I telling you all this?"

"We were talking about our siblings."

"Right." She nods. "It's hard for me to remember that my sisters are all grown up now when making sure they survived high school and we all had a roof over our heads was my singular focus for so long. Noli and Rose are quick to call me out when I'm being too much of a mom." She rolls her eyes, but there's affection there. "Even though I know she agrees with me, Rose thinks I'm mom-ing Noli by moving back to Pensacola."

"Are you?"

She shrugs. "I want to be close by in case she needs anything."

"So that's a yes."

She sticks out her tongue at me.

"No licking."

Poppy laughs, but then her face falls. "Rose also thinks I'm phoning it in by leaving my job here. It's the first job I've ever found in the field I'm passionate about. I've worked at gyms and gotten to coordinate some youth programs, but mostly it was a lot of checking patrons in and rolling towels."

I consider this. "You could stay."

She looks at me with wide eyes.

"For the job," I add, and she blinks. "I'm sure they'd offer you a full-time position. Everyone thinks highly of you."

She smiles at me, but then it dips. "Thanks, but Noli needs me, and it's too weird with Holland."

She stands, as if that's all she's going to say about that, and moves around the peninsula. "You cooked. I'll do the dishes." She tucks in at the sink, directly next to me, nudging me out of the way with her hip.

I pile a plate of pancakes up for Rose to eat, whenever she decides to grace us with her presence, and stick it in the microwave to stay warm.

I move to stand next to Poppy, who hasn't started washing the dishes yet but is doing some sort of intricate prep work. She's stacking plates on one corner of the counter, utensils next to them, and she's got my dirty mixing bowl, spatula, and wooden spoon farthest from the sink.

"You know nothing is going to get clean unless you put it into the soapy water."

"Aw, look who found his sense of humor this morning." Poppy smirks at me. "You're cute when you try to be sassy."

It's silly the jolt of serotonin I feel when she calls me cute.

"I have a system," Poppy says, spreading her arms out wide.

"Clearly," I say. "I can help. We'll get done faster, and I'm pretty *handsy*."

"Oh my gosh, shut up." Poppy swats me. She's laughing, and I'm glad it's not weird between us. We're perfectly fine. Firmly in the friend zone, which is for the best. If she's leaving at the end of the summer, it's dumb to pursue anything...even if she was interested in me like that—which she isn't.

"Alright. Tell me what to do so I don't mess up your flow."

"I'll wash. You dry," she says. "And it'll be fun with music. It always is."

I retrieve my AirPods and hand her one. We each slip the little listening devices into opposite ears, and I press play. Taylor Swift's "The Story of Us" (Taylor's Version) starts up.

"What a banger," Poppy says. "Good pick."

We settle in, and I'm trying not to focus on the spark that crackles between us every time she hands me a soaking wet dish. It's against the laws of physics, or science, or whatever that we'd be able to generate any electricity with water in play, and yet, here we are.

I can only hope no one gets burned.

Poppy is oblivious. She's humming happily along, making small talk about work and the weather.

"What's that out there?" she asks during a song break. She's gesturing with her elbow out the kitchen window to the back corner of my lawn.

I have a giant tarp tacked down over a project I've been working on. It's not done, and I'm not sure if I'll ever finish it at this point.

"Nothing. Storage."

Poppy takes me at my word and gets back to the dishes. The song switches to "Enchanted" (Taylor's Version), and by the time it gets to the bridge, we're both belting it out. Poppy is botching lyrics here and there, which is so endearing. She sang, "These are the doors I held cracked as I was leaving, you'll see," and that makes absolutely no sense, but I kind of love it.

"Hey, Big?"

I turn to her, and with more speed than I would have thought possible, she reaches forward, grabs the spray nozzle, and points it directly at my face.

I'm soaking wet and spluttering as Taylor croons, over and over, about not being in love with anyone else.

Poppy is cackling. "I saw that online, and I always wanted to try it."

I splutter and wrench the sprayer from her hand, turning it on her.

She squeals and tries to sprint away from me, but I can be quick too.

I wrap my arm around her waist, and she lifts her legs off the ground, but I hold firm—her back to my chest. I point the sprayer directly at her.

I'm getting drenched as I spray her, but it's worth it to feel Poppy belly laugh and kick out as she tries to wiggle away.

My front door opens, and Collin saunters in. He takes one look at us and tips his head to the side. "What's going on here?"

"Collin, tell Big waterboarding is against the law," Poppy says as I set her down.

"Don't start something you aren't prepared to finish, Boo."

She puts her hands in fists at her waist. "Joke's on you. This is your t-shirt."

As if I could forget.

"I can come back," Collin says.

Poppy waves him off. "No, no. The more the merrier." She explains the AC situation and offers him pancakes. He settles in at the peninsula, and Poppy grabs the towel off my shoulder. It's pretty damp, but she dries her face and starts chatting with Collin about his plans for the day.

I love that she's so at home in my house. I love that she gets along with my friends. My mind takes me to a place where she and I are hosting all sorts of events—birthday parties, summer cookouts—here, together.

And then I can see us messing around, cleaning up the kitchen side-by-side long into the night.

"I should go get changed. I'll wash your shirt, Big."

The fantasy in my head is still so real it's like I'm looking down on us instead of standing here next to her, soaking wet. "Keep it," I hear myself say.

She freezes, her lips pressed together, but then she wiggles her eyebrows. "Are you afraid I have cooties?"

I don't dare tell her that I would gladly take any and all of her cooties, because that sounds weird any way you phrase it.

Poppy, I'd swap spit with you in a heartbeat. I'd welcome your germs. Lay 'em on me.

I mean, honestly.

"I have a million of those shirts," I say, all nonchalant. "All the guys wear them at my job sites."

"Wow, I feel so special. I'm just like one of the guys."

I shake my head because...no.

"What? You don't think I can pull it off?" She pops a hip.

The shirt rises up an inch on her leg. I'm sure she's wearing the same shorts she had on yesterday; I just can't see them. But I still can't seem to tear my gaze away from the smooth skin of her toned thigh. "That's not it."

"Then what?"

The challenge in Poppy's voice makes me meet her eye. We stare at each other for a weighty moment, until I can't take it anymore.

"You are completely different than one of the guys."

My voice is gravely, and Poppy sucks in a deep enough breath that I can see her chest move. She doesn't break eye contact with me, like she's searching my face for some sort of hidden meaning.

The hidden meaning is that she looks one hundred percent better than anyone else who has ever donned a Mack Electric t-shirt.

"Well, then," she says quietly. "Thanks." She blinks, and the charge around us dissipates. She beams and tosses me the towel. "Be right back."

She skips out the front door, and I watch her through the window as she hustles toward her duplex. I'm an astronomer and she's a comet I've been tracking for years only to watch it cross right in front of me. I don't want to let it—her—get away.

Collin, whom I forgot about, clears his throat.

When I glance at him, he's got a pie-eating grin on his face. "Well, well, well."

I throw the towel at him.

21

PICK ME UP

Poppy

I slam the door to Holland's car and march up to The Downer. Rose is working the evening shift at Mood Reader, so I have the house to myself.

There's no sign of Mack's truck, so I'm guessing he's still working.

I can't decide if I'm relieved or bummed by that news.

That's the problem with developing feelings for your friend.

He's the person I want to talk to, but I'm trying to keep my distance so I don't make things confusing.

I kick off my shoes inside the front door and storm into my bedroom. I rip my work clothes off and tug on a pair of denim cutoffs and a t-shirt—Mack's t-shirt, as it turns out. It's the softest, most comfortable shirt I own. That's all.

I stomp into the kitchen, wrenching the freezer door open and snatching the pint of cookie dough ice cream I always keep for such an occasion.

Mack's truck rumbles up in front of the house, and like a moth to a flame, I wander to the front door. Through the sidelight window, I watch as he steps out. He's wearing his work attire. Jeans and a forest-green t-shirt today. I feel slightly let down that we're not matching, which is ridiculous. He's got on a Mack Electric baseball cap and steel-toed boots. He takes his hat off and runs his hand through his dark hair.

I think I moaned.

Does he know how good he looks when he does that? How that little dip along the inside of his bicep muscle taunts me in my dreams?

As he walks to his front door, I can't help but notice something else about his appearance. The man looks dead on his feet. Don't get me wrong, he still looks incredible, but I can tell he's exhausted.

He catches me watching him through the window, and I hold up my spoon in greeting.

He changes courses and heads my way. I pull the front door open.

"Big."

"Boo."

"I've had a terrible day."

He waits for me to continue.

"Horrible. No good. Very bad. Just call me Alexander."

"What are you talking about?"

I flail my hands around. "You know, like the children's book? Gosh, the *one* time I make a literary reference, and Rose isn't even here to appreciate it." I want to stomp my foot, but I don't. Because I'm a grown woman. Instead, I take a huge spoonful of ice cream and shove it into my mouth. "Sorry," I say around the bite. "Ow. Cold!" I press my free hand to my head. "Brain freeze."

Mack crosses his arms, looking amused.

I swallow, and he bobs his head toward his truck.

"Come on," he says. "Let's go."

"What? Where?"

"For a drive." He turns and walks away.

I stow my ice cream and lock up the house. Mack has the passenger side door open, and I hop up next to him. There's a large, iced coffee resting in his cup holder. The condensation on the outside of the plastic cup is running in rivulets. Mack nods at it. "It's yours."

I should protest. I should tell him he bought it for himself and he should drink it. He looks like he needs the extra energy. He's being too nice to me, and it's making my throat all tight. I open my mouth, but before I can say anything, he reaches out, picks up the cup, and shoves the straw to my lips.

"Take a drink," he orders.

I wrap my mouth around the straw obediently and take a deep sip. Mack's eyes never leave me as I savor the splash of vanilla flavor that permeates the bitter, refreshing drink.

"Better?" His voice is hoarse, and he clears his throat.

I nod. Everything is better with him. "Thanks for that. But this is yours."

He shrugs. "We can share it."

He takes his own sip, and my stomach somersaults. Which is absurd. A shared drink does not mean anything. But it's the way the give and take is so natural with Mack that sets my nerve-endings rattling. I wonder if he feels it too.

He puts the coffee back down, wipes his hand on his jeans, and reverses out of the driveway, heading the opposite direction of the lower district. I have no idea where he's taking me, but I feel completely safe. I roll down my window with the hand crank on the door and stick my arm out into the rushing air.

Mack's radio is turned off, and tonight, neither of us makes a move to turn it on. It's him and me and the open road. Maybe I should feel awkward or self-conscious around him. But I don't. It's Mack. And it's me. I've never put my best foot forward where he's concerned, and yet, somehow, he enjoys my company.

Once we're outside the town limits, he side-eyes me. "You want to talk about it?"

I reach forward and take another swig of coffee before leaning my head against the headrest. "I ruined Party in the Park."

He lets out a disbelieving huff.

"I'm not exaggerating," I insist. "Heather warned me about getting the porta-potties taken care of early in the summer, but it slipped down on my list, and I've called everyone, and no one has units available."

"Units?"

"Like those individual little stalls. Toilet units. I don't know? What the heck are they called?" I fling my gaze in his direction to find him biting back a smirk. "Glad you're enjoying this," I grumble. "I should have known toilets would be my downfall. Toilet explosions. Porta-potty disasters. Everything's gone to pot for me."

Mack laughs outright at this, and I want to laugh too, but I feel traitorous tears burning in the corners of my eyes. I suck in a shuddering breath because I do not want to cry in front of him over freaking porta-potties.

"Hey. Hey," he says. "Boo, are you crying?"

I bury my head in my hands. "No. Don't look at me. I'm ashamed of myself. I'm crying about toilets. But it's more than that, you know?" A sob escapes. "I wanted to do this job well. To prove to Heather, and to everyone, and to myself that I deserved it. That I didn't get the position because of Holland. Now it's all falling apart. I know I'm leaving anyway, but still. I'd like to go out on a high note."

Mack reaches out and takes one of my hands off my face.

"Don't! I'm all snotty," I wail.

He squeezes my fingers and holds my hand in the center seat, driving in silence and letting me cry.

After I'm not sure how long, he pulls over. I take my hand back and pull the visor down. My eyes are red and puffy, and I try to wipe the mascara streaks from my cheeks before turning to face Mack.

"Feel better?"

I offer him a wobbly smile. "Actually, yeah. Thanks."

"I didn't do anything."

I scoot over and lay my head on his shoulder. I'm not sure when Mack and I crossed over into having a touchy-feely friendship, but if he can hold my hand in his truck, then I can do this.

"You did," I say. I take my first real look out the windshield and gasp. "Where are we?"

"The middle of a wheat farm field."

Everywhere I look is golden. There's no water in sight, so Mack must have driven me to the center of the Cashmere County peninsula.

The wheat stalks are blowing in the breeze, swaying as one, giant dancer. The sun hasn't quite dipped below the horizon. It hangs like a glowing ball of orange right at eye-level.

"It's a nice spot to watch the sunset," Mack says, reading my mind.

"It's beautiful." I rest my head back on his shoulder, and we sit in silence. The windows are rolled down, and the cross breeze ruffles my hair. "Sorry again for falling apart. It's not just about the porta-potties." I blow out a breath. "My dad texted."

Mack shifts, so I have to sit upright and face him. "Are you okay?"

I shrug.

"Does he reach out often?"

"Hardly ever. He picks the worst possible moment to remind me that he exists. The first time he reached out after he left us alone was the day Gram died. He called her house phone. I told him she was gone and begged him to come home. To help us. To help me. He stuttered something about needing to go and hung up. I didn't hear from him again for another two years."

"Boo," Mack says my nickname with righteous indignation laced within his usual low tone. It feels good...to have someone like him on my side.

I muster up a wry grin. "It's fine. I'm okay."

"What did he want?" He starts rubbing my back ever so gently.

I relax at his touch. It's soothing, like the first sip of an iced latte on a hot summer day. "I'm not entirely sure. His text said he heard I moved."

"Did you respond?"

"I texted *yes*, and he didn't reply to that." I massage my temples. "I wish I knew his end game. Does he want to see me? To see my sisters?"

"What would you do if he asked?"

I bite the inside of my cheek. "I honestly don't know."

"That's okay."

I'm quiet for a moment, staring out the windshield. Mack's gaze bores into the side of my cheek. "This has been a question of my life for some time. I mean, who leaves their children without saying goodbye? With nothing but a note that says, *I can't do this?*" I hold out my hands, palms up.

"I still don't know what 'this' is, but I've always assumed he meant parenting. Basically, he said he couldn't handle my sisters and me. Or he wouldn't. Or he didn't want to. I don't know."

"That was an awful thing for him to do." Mack's voice is measured, but I can sense the undercurrent of anger on my behalf.

I shoot him a grateful look. "I've spent a lot of time being angry at him. Ticked off at the position he left me in, with Noli and Rose to look after. What if I would have thrown up my hands and said I couldn't handle it? I didn't have that option. I had other people relying on me. People who should have been able to rely on him. I should have been able to rely on him."

I pinch my eyes closed. "With time, some of my anger has faded and turned to sadness. Sadness padded with a lot of questions. Does he miss us? Does he regret his decision? I don't know if I'll ever understand why he left. I don't know if he deserves my forgiveness. But when he reaches out like this, it always starts me spiraling. What if he wants to come back into my life and asks for another chance? Should I offer it?"

I drag in a ragged breath.

Mack reaches up and wipes at the tears I didn't realize have started to fall from my eyes again.

I blink and savor his touch against my skin.

"It's okay, Boo."

And you know what? I believe him. This is the first time I've ever been able to confide in someone about my dad. Sure, Noli and Rose and I talk about him, but I'm careful not to burden them with these sorts of thoughts and feelings. I'm the oldest. I'm the keeper of the family. Whether I wanted to be or not, it's who I am.

But it sure is nice to have someone take care of me for a change.

I rest my head back down on Mack's shoulder, and he drapes his arm across my back.

After a couple minutes, he says, "I don't know what to say about your dad, but I can help with the porta-potty issue."

I raise my head and turn so I can look at his eyes. "You can?"

He nods. "Let me talk to the builders at my construction site. They contract with a company. I'm sure we can find some"—he clears his throat—"*units*."

I bury my head into the crook of his shoulder. "I should scold you for making fun of me, but I'm seriously so grateful. You think they'll be able to find some for us to use."

Mack grunts in the affirmative.

I sigh. "I should have known you'd come to the rescue."

"Why's that?"

"Because you're you. You help everyone."

Another grunt.

"You're a regular Mack of all trades."

I gasp and slap his arm. "Oh my gosh. I can't believe I didn't think of that one until now. What a missed opportunity!" He snorts as I lay my head back down. "Cashmere Cove is lucky to have you." Mack's arm muscle tenses under my cheek. I look up at him. "I'm serious."

He's quiet for a long pause. "Thank you for saying that."

"It's the truth."

"It doesn't feel like it all the time."

I sit up in my seat. If I'm baring my soul tonight, then maybe Mack will do the same. "Are you ever going to tell me—or any-one—what really happened between you and Tricia?"

22

A GOOD Man

Mack

"Y ou've heard the rumors."

"Yeah. And we ran into her together when I first moved here, remember?"

I do remember.

"You don't believe what you've heard?" I hate how my voice comes out sounding raspy. I hate how much I care about what Poppy thinks. I hate how much I want her to say she never believed I was capable of cheating.

"I believe there are two sides to every break-up, and I want to hear yours."

I stiffen. That wasn't the rousing show of support I was hoping for, but at least she hasn't jumped to conclusions.

I open my mouth, but Poppy starts talking again.

Shocking no one.

My lips quirk. Only she would be able to take some of the tension out of this moment.

"For the record, I got *good-guy* vibes from you from day one. I even told Rose. I think you're good down to your core, and I can't imagine you cheating. I've been wrong before, but I don't think I'm wrong right now. That's it. That's all I'll say about it."

I gently shift my weight so she sits up. "Come on."

"What are you doing?"

I open the truck door and step out into the field.

She follows my lead, slamming her door shut. "You brought me out here to murder me, didn't you?"

I stare at her as we walk around and meet behind my truck.

She shrugs. "It felt like the right joke to make in the moment. Not that there's anything funny about being murdered." She gives her head a small shake. "Anyway. I *obviously* don't think that's what you're doing."

"Yeah, no. I just wanted some fresh air. And we can see the stars better from out here." I hold out my hand to her. She takes it, and I pull her toward me. She dips her head, and I catch a whiff of her gardenia shampoo. I want to hold her close to me like this, chest to chest, fingers intertwined, for as long as she'll let me, but I owe her an explanation. I pull the tailgate down and hold out my hand to help her into the bed of my truck.

Poppy mimes wiping her brow. "Glad I didn't misjudge that one. I know I've only known you for two months, but it's a relief that I can read you properly." She winks and hoists herself up.

I climb up behind her, and we both lie back and stare at the sky. The wheat is rustling all around us, humming white noise, and it feels like Poppy and I are the only two people on the planet.

Eventually, I turn my head. She meets my gaze. We're shoulder to shoulder, so our noses are less than six inches apart. It's intimate. Safe.

"Feels like a lot longer to me—that we've known each other, I mean."

Her eyes are wide and glued to my face. She nods.

"I've never told anyone this, Boo. I swore to myself that I wouldn't. But you're right. I didn't cheat on Tricia." I swallow. "She cheated on me."

I turn my head and face the sky again.

Poppy finds my hand and holds it. She squeezes once, as if to say she's listening, but she doesn't speak. She's waiting on me to continue.

"We had been dating for several years at that point, and she was dropping hints left and right that she was expecting a proposal. I met with the local jeweler to see what my options were. He and

I went way back, and he was willing to give me a deal so I could get something real nice for her."

I feel Poppy's gaze on me.

I sigh and turn to her. "And yeah, if you've heard about me stealing that necklace, yes, it was the same jeweler. That's a long story in and of itself."

"I've got all night," Poppy says quietly.

I nod in acknowledgement, grateful she's willing to hear me out. But I've got to get the truth about Tricia out now before I lose my nerve. Why am I nervous? I didn't do anything wrong.

"Anyway. Tricia was home from school for winter break. Her parents were picking up Collin from school, and I showed up at her house to find her in bed with another guy."

Poppy squeezes my hand tighter.

"The thing is, Tricia and I were never together...like that. Her parents are super conservative, and we had decided to wait."

I feel more than see Poppy nod.

"So I was feeling all the things. Shock. Confusion. Betrayal. Anger. I left without a word, but Tricia ran out after me. She begged me to talk to her, begged me to promise her I wouldn't tell anyone. If her parents found out, she was sure they'd disown her. I shook her off. I couldn't talk to her then. I got in my car and drove away.

"I left town for the weekend. When I came back, I walked into Romeo's, and I knew instantly something was off. The stares. The dirty looks. The rumor was already swirling that I had been the one who was unfaithful to Tricia."

"Oh, Big."

"There was absolutely nothing I could do at that point. Everyone believed what they heard, and if I would have tried to dispute the rumor, I would have had to throw Tricia under the bus. I was upset and heartbroken, sure, but I had no intention of ruining her life over it. So..."

"So you stayed quiet," Poppy whispers, "for all these years."

I nod. *And ruined my own life instead.*

That's how it has always felt.

Until now.

Poppy makes me feel like all isn't lost after all.

"I haven't dated since," I explain. "Mostly because who would want to align themselves with a supposed cheater?"

She scooches forward. "Sit up, please."

I raise up onto my elbows. "Why?"

She yanks me fully upright. "Because I want to hug you."

She's freakishly strong when she puts her mind to something, and before I know it, she has her arms wrapped around my waist. She's squeezing me so tightly I feel my skin pulling underneath my shirt.

I don't think as I drag her into my lap. It feels so good to be hugged like this. To have someone care. To finally have the truth out in the open.

To be believed.

I've always wondered who would understand. Who would take the side of a dude with a slightly tumultuous past over the side of the town's golden child? Who would share the weight of the secret I've carried all these years?

It's Poppy.

I let the warmth of her embrace stitch up all the jagged edges of my heart.

When she finally eases back, she searches my eyes. It's only then that I realize my cheeks are wet, but I'm not embarrassed in front of Poppy.

She cups my cheeks with her small hands. "You, Big Mack Bradley, are a good man." She presses her lips to my forehead. "Thank you for telling me."

"Thank you for listening. Please promise not to tell anyone."

She stares at me. "Even Collin doesn't know, huh?"

"It would put him in an impossible position. I never wanted to drag him into it. He has his suspicions, but..." I trail off. "Mostly it's

Tricia's parents. Maybe it would be okay now that she's married and has a family, but I don't think she was wrong in thinking they would have been cruel to her had they found out when we were younger. Her dad sort of rules the family with an iron fist. Sometimes I worry about Collin, living in his dad's shadow at the police department."

"Like I said"—she presses her pointer finger into my chest—"you are a good man, and you have my word. I won't say anything."

She scoots off my lap, and I instantly feel the loss.

She lies back in the truck, and I follow suit. "Can we stay out here for a while?"

I stretch out next to her. I'd stay here with her forever.

23

Death by Drill

Poppy

I wake up and sniff. Something smells good. It's my pillow. Did I do laundry recently? It smells like soap and a hint of mint. It's soft and warm, and I press my nose further into it and burrow my head, rubbing my nose back and forth like I'm a little bunny rabbit.

When my pillow moves under me, my eyes fly open.

I blink. Blink again.

I'm in the back of Mack's truck. He's got his arms cinched around me, and I'm lying half on top of him. His shirt is my pillow.

I should have known something was off.

I am the worst at keeping up with my laundry.

I try to keep my body still, but my mind is the opposite of still. It's racing a mile a minute. How did this happen? We were talking and looking at the stars, and we must've fallen asleep.

I guess it's not surprising since we pretty much bared our souls to each other last night. We were both exhausted.

My brain switches gears and starts chronicling every inch of Mack. His breath is even and warm against my forehead. He's been hiding some serious abdominal muscles under his t-shirts, because I can feel the ab ridges from my position curled up here next to him. He's clinging to me with a grip that says he never wants to let go.

I don't want to move. I don't want him to let go.

My entire body bursts into flames at the realization.

I never, in the entire time I was dating Holland, felt the way for him that I feel for Mack—physically and emotionally.

Because that's the thing.

I'm viscerally attracted to Mack Bradley. It's long past time to admit that. But I'm more drawn to how he makes me feel. How I can be around him.

He cherishes me.

I pinch my eyes shut.

I can't let myself get attached to him.

It's a bad idea.

I'm leaving town.

My sisters need my full focus. They have to come first.

Besides, Mack doesn't date.

Except, now I know why.

I know the truth.

And I'd date Mack Bradley faster than you could say *dibs!*

But I can't. The memory of how my last long-distance relationship fizzled out faster than a Fourth-of-July sparkler is fresh. Oh, and let's not forget that that relationship was with Mack's brother, so there's that can of awkward that would be spilled all over the ground if this went any further.

Mack stirs beneath me. His hold on my waist tightens, and...did he nuzzle his nose into the top of my head?

Be still my heart.

I chance a glance up at his face.

He's staring down at me. "Morning, Boo."

"Hi." I scooch up to a sitting position, silently mourning the loss of Mack's warmth.

Game's over, Kasper. You've got to go back to your plain, old, boring pillow from now on.

Even with a washing, I'm certain it won't smell as good as Mack.

"Sorry. I guess we fell asleep."

"It's fine." Mack pushes himself upright. "It was...nice."

Oh no. He's looking at me with those eyes of his. I'm a weak, weak woman in the face of him.

I turn to where the sun is starting to rise over the cab of the truck, because if I don't put some distance between us, I'm going to jump right on top of him and kiss more than his forehead.

We sit there in silence, watching as the sun turns the wheat fields from sleepy amber to goldenrod yellow. I don't think I could have planned out a more perfect twelve hours if I'd tried.

But it's over now.

Back to reality.

"We should get back to town, huh?" I make a move to scoot toward the tailgate, but Mack grabs my wrist.

I turn, and he's staring at me like he wants to say something else. He looks sort of uncomfortable, and *oh my gosh*, he's worried that it's going to be weird between us since we cuddled.

Or...wait.

I meet his gaze, and I see something so much worse. Interest. Desire.

I can't go there with him, so I beat him to the punch.

"Don't worry, Big. We're good. I mean, what's a little snuggling between friends, right?"

His gaze bores into mine, and I'm certain my racing heart is turning my neck blotchy. I've got goosebumps making my arm hair stand at attention, and the skin on my wrist under his hand feels like it's permanently tattooed with his fingerprints.

Now that I think about it...a Mack tattoo might be the only sort of tattoo I would ever consider getting.

I'm afraid he's going to call my bluff, but then he blinks. "Alright. Good."

• • • ● ● • ● ● • •

Mack dropped me off at The Downer, and I got to work on time. He texted me at nine a.m. with the contact information for a porta-potty company. I called and reserved everything we needed for the Party at the Park.

Crisis averted.

It's almost noon, so I grab my purse and make the quick drive to Getaway Café.

I push open the door, and the rush of air conditioning feels good against my warm skin.

Inez is at the register. She waves. "Poppy, hey! What can I get for you?"

I study the chalkboard with the specials. "I'll take two iced vanilla lattes, a turkey-avocado bagel, and one of your loaded BLT sandwiches to go, please."

Yes, I fully intend to ply Mack with coffee and lunch on me as a giant thank-you for sorting out the toilet situation.

"You got it."

I step back to let Inez serve the people behind me in line, and I spot Willow Dunlap. She waves when we make eye contact.

"Poppy, dear. I am getting so excited about the Promenade, aren't you?"

"Beyond excited," I say with a smile.

"What's this?"

My spine stiffens as Tricia turns in her seat to face Willow and me.

"Poppy had this great idea to have a dance at the Party in the Park this year. I think it'll be so romantic. Who doesn't like to cuddle up with their love under the stars?"

My cheeks heat as my mind flashes to Mack and me in the bed of his truck last night.

Tricia sticks up her nose.

Willow doesn't seem to notice her skepticism, but I feel the need to defend our plan.

"We thought it would be a nice event for the adult crowd."

Tricia narrows her eyes at me, and I can't help myself.

"Mack is handling the lighting, and he's planning to make the pavilion by the lighthouse look like it's dripping with lights. It's going to be stunning."

Tricia scoffs. "Are you sure that's a good idea? That man can't be counted on. I'd hate to see your new event flop."

"Poppy! Here's your food," Inez calls from the counter, but I don't tear my gaze from Tricia.

"I'm not concerned. I trust Mack. Completely."

I stare at her for an extra heartbeat before I bid Willow goodbye and grab my food from Inez.

"See you later this week for girls' night?"

"Definitely!" I walk out of the café with an extra bounce in my step.

I may not be able to give Tricia a piece of my mind, but I can let her and anyone else who's wondering know that I have Mack's back.

That's what friends do, right?

And Mack and I are friends.

Friends who cuddle.

It's fine.

I drive in the direction of his job site.

When I pull up to the under-construction multi-unit building, there aren't a lot of trucks around. Dang it, I hadn't thought about the fact that Mack might not be here. If I'm taking my lunch now, it tracks that he might be too, and I didn't tell him I was coming.

I wanted to surprise him.

Mostly, I wanted to see him.

Again.

Does that make me a sucker for punishment? Maybe so.

The roughed-in eight-unit apartment complex that Mack's been working on for the past week appears to be deserted, but the sound of drilling is coming from somewhere inside, and through the open walls, I catch sight of a worker.

I cross the gravel walkway and step through some of the framing on the front half of the building, carefully picking my way over power tools and two-by-fours left strewn about the space. The drilling gets louder and louder as I approach. When I come around the corner to what I'm guessing is the unit at the back right corner of the complex, I stop dead in my tracks.

There's Mack.

He's drilling a sequence of holes through the studs of the walls. The drill he's using is like nothing I've ever seen before. It's oversized and requires both hands. I know what you're thinking, that sounds like a metaphor for something, but I swear it's what I see with my own two eyes. I cannot make this up. My gaze roves from his drill—the *actual* drill, people...I promise—over his arms, which are vibrating with the exertion of controlling the tool.

My word. This is a problem. My mouth is all of a sudden very dry.

I'm going to go ahead and blame that on the sawdust Mack is generating.

But what grabs my attention and refuses to let go is Mack's back.

Sweet honey and molasses.

He's in a familiar-looking Mack Electric t-shirt, but this one has been modified. The sleeves are cut off, and his shoulders are on display for all the world to see—or in this case, for me to see.

When he raises his arms and lifts that giant drill thing over his head to make a hole through the joist in the ceiling, my breath catches. Mack's lats are all strong hills and smooth valleys. I tell you what, I could pull up a chair and watch the man's muscles tense and release for the rest of the day. Is it weird that I sort of want to trace my finger across the grooves of his skin while he works—to feel the power under the surface? There is something supremely sexy about a man who can work with his hands like this—or, as it were, his arms. And his back.

I've been frozen in place and speechless since I came around the corner and Mack came into view, so when he turns and catches sight of me, his head snaps up in surprise.

And wouldn't you know it, his front is as good-looking as his back. The knob of his shoulders into his biceps is on full display, and his forearms are tense as he wields the drill. He sets it on the ground and removes earplugs from his ears.

"Boo, what are you doing here?"

I blink. What *am* I doing here...other than watching the best-kept secret in Cashmere Cove?

"I...uh..." I hold up the bag from the café, finally regaining my wits. "I brought you lunch."

Mack unloads a full-throttle grin and takes a step toward me. "Have you been here long?"

Have I? Who knows? What is time? I've forgotten how to read a clock. All I can seem to focus on is how powerful Mack's body looks as he draws nearer. There's sweat on his brow, making his hair stick to his forehead. He smells rugged and manly, and I kind of want to lick him.

No *licking*, I scold myself.

Mack chuckles. "What's that?"

Oh my gosh, I did not say that out loud, did I?

Apparently I haven't regained all of my wits.

"Um. Time was *ticking*," I say, trying to cover for my mouth, which is going off the rails, chugging away from the last of my brain cells that haven't dissolved in a puddle at the feet of Mack Bradley's drill. "You seemed very busy," I continue. "So I was, um, here. Watching you. I mean *waiting* for you. Ready with the make-out." I pull my lips into my mouth. My face is burning. The train is off the tracks, people. I repeat, the train is off the tracks. "Ready with the *take-out*. To eat the take-out. With you. If you need a break. My treat."

Is Mack somehow closer to me than he was before I started that absurd monologue that will haunt me for the rest of my days? I'm pretty sure he is. Because I can see the bead of sweat that is lazily making its way down his side. And in my head, a siren is wailing *obliques, obliques, obliques!*

"You okay there, Boo? You're looking a little flushed."

I tear my gaze away from the skin of his side when Mack reaches up and traces my cheekbone, tucking a flyaway behind my ear.

My mouth…the traitor…hangs open like I'm a panting poodle.

I snap my jaw shut. "I'm fine. Totally fine. It's blazing hot out here. I don't know how you work in these conditions." I shove the bag of food into his stomach, if only to put a little space between us. I don't want space between us, but I am in way over my head here. Not in my right mind. Clearly. So I need to buy myself some time.

Serves me right for being all flippant with this plan.

Oh, I'm Poppy, and I'll casually drop by to see my neighbor and friend on the job. What's that? He's a modern-day Superman with a drill? No biggie. I can handle it.

Not.

I cannot handle Mack like this.

"You get used to it," he says. "Come on. We can eat over here."

He takes my hand and leads me through some of the framing into a room with a couple folding chairs set up. We split up the food and eat in silence for a minute.

Mack is watching me over the top of his sandwich, and I feel the need to make conversation. I talk to fill the awkwardness. It's my toxic trait, I guess.

"Tell me about what you're doing here. What was that thing you were using?" I pop the final bit of my bagel into my mouth.

"You like my drill, eh?"

I nearly choke, swallowing hard. "Um. It seemed to, uh, do the job."

Mack quirks a brow. "Oh yes. It always gets the job done."

My face is burning again.

Fortunately, Mack has mercy on me. "It's called a Hole-Hawg drill."

Well, there's a new one.

Never—and I repeat, *never*—did I think the word *hog* would ever sound sexy coming out of anyone's mouth, but Mack went and proved me wrong.

"And what were you using the hog for?" I ask, trying to focus.

"Drilling the holes in the studs and joists for the home run wires we've got to run back to the panel." I swear he lights up as he talks about it. No pun intended.

"Home run wires?" I prompt.

"They're the big ticket wires in a house. One to each main room, and then individual wires from the panel to major things like your stove and microwave. Your washing machine, dryer, garbage disposal, dishwasher. It's the first thing we do after we have the layout marked." He crinkles up the paper from his sandwich. "I'll show you."

I stand and follow him back into the other room. He walks me around, showing me how he marked certain areas, drilled holes, and his team has the wires pulled to all the rooms. They've mounted boxes for outlets and switches, and eventually, they'll install all the light fixtures. For now, it's the guts of it, all plain to see.

"It's like a rainbow," I comment, noting the different color wires.

"Each wire has a certain job. Those white ones are 14-2s. They go to the bedroom and living room areas. The 12-2 yellow wires are mainly for the kitchen, where you need your midgrade appliances, like a dishwasher and garbage disposal. The orange 10-3 wire there is for the electric dryer."

"Why do they have those number combinations?"

"It's the wire. So a 12-2 wire is a twelve gauge with two conductors. A hot and a neutral, plus a ground. The 10-3 has three conductors. Two hot, one neutral, plus a ground. The lower the gauge, the thicker the copper, so it can carry more electricity."

I need to get with Darla and let her know that she has misjudged her eldest son's career choice. This is incredibly intricate and detailed work, and Mack is an expert. His mind on the job is as impressive as his body.

I can't help it. I start to fan myself. I think I could listen to him talk electrician to me all day. Who needs neutral and ground wires? It's all hot as far as I'm concerned.

"Hot."

The word is out of my mouth before I can stop it.

"What's that?" Mack's gaze is like a laser on me.

I shift my jaw. I could play this off. I *should* play it off like I'm echoing a type of electrical conductor or something. But a part of me wants Mack to know how impressive I think he is. His self-esteem has taken a hit since Tricia started those nasty rumors, and he should know that he's got a lot going for him—including, but not limited to, the way he wields a drill.

"It's hot. To hear you...or anyone," I add because *self-preservation*, "be a subject matter expert."

Mack's eyes roam over my face as he closes the distance between us. "Poppy Kasper, did you just call me hot?"

He stops an inch in front of me. The smart little part of my brain that knows this is a bad idea because I'm leaving town and he's Holland's brother is screaming at me to deflect. But its scream is being drowned out by the much larger part of my brain that's listening to my heart, which is currently saying, *You think he's gorgeous. You want to date him! Love him. Marry him!* Like Sandra Bullock at the end of *Miss Congeniality*.

A classic if ever there was one.

"I may have said that, yes." I tip my chin up. Because I am wearing fancy underpants today, and I will not cower.

Mack's gaze unlatches from mine for a fraction of a second to dip to my lips, and a firework lights up my spine. He puts one of his jean-clad legs between mine, and my hands find their way to his sides, and those glorious oblique muscles feel better than they look. His skin is warm and rough with dried sweat and sawdust, and I'm here for it.

I swallow, and my eyes fall closed as he erases the distance between us.

"Honey, we're home!"

My eyes spring open, and I jump back at the sound of Lou's voice. I whip my head around as he and Patrick and some other guys on Mack's crew come sauntering through the door.

And by door, I mean the open framing, which means they likely witnessed the kiss that wasn't between Mack and me.

Judging by the smirk Lou is shooting at Mack, I'd say the chances they witnessed us almost kiss went from *likely* to *most certainly.*

"Alright, gentlemen. Back to work." Mack's voice is gruff and all business.

I am a strong, independent woman wearing fancy underwear, but I may as well be a wilting reed at the sound of the command and control in Mack's voice. I shiver.

"Come on, Boo. I'll walk you out."

"Oh, you don't have to," I hurry to say. "I'll let you get back to work."

Mack doesn't respond, just puts his big, capable, manly hand on the small of my back and gently nudges me in the direction of my car.

Why is there something so irresistible about the hand-on-the-back trick? Is this something all men know? If not, they should. Want to make a woman feel like she's the most priceless thing in the world to you? Put your hand on her lower back. Even better, do it in a crowded room, when other people are around.

Every single man here—and woman too, because there are a couple, which is cool—is staring at Mack's hand pressed against the gauzy blouse I'm wearing. It's like, with that simple gesture, he's not only taking care of me but also staking his claim.

It's a win-win, as I see it, because I like both of those things equally as much. The heart-guided part of my brain currently winning out over the rational part is chanting, *Stake that claim, Mack Bradley. Be the astronaut to my moon.*

Okay, yeah, it sounded better in my head, but you know what I mean.

Mack guides me all the way back to my car.

"You didn't have to walk me out," I say, babbling again as soon as I manage to string two thoughts together.

"Just making sure you stayed safe. There are a lot of moving parts in there when everyone's working."

Hot and thoughtful. "Thanks, Big."

We stand there, alternatively staring at each other and the ground. I sort of want him to kiss me, but I also don't. Not now. The moment has passed, and the guys are watching through the unfinished build behind us. And the rational part of my brain is finally getting louder. I need to think long and hard about getting more attached to Mack.

I know darn well a kiss would take me to a place I couldn't return from. Would it be a blissful, wonderful, magical place? I have a good feeling about it. But it's not a good idea.

Lou and the guys did me a favor. Saved me a lot of angst.

I'm going to keep telling myself that, even though being so close to kissing Mack only to have the opportunity ripped away from me makes me want to whimper like a sad puppy.

I pull myself up straighter. I'm fine. Everything's fine. "I should go."

Mack nods. "Thanks for lunch."

"Thanks for showing me around. It was—"

"Hot," he says.

And then the man winks.

It takes everything in me not to jump him right there.

He takes two steps backward, staring at me with a lazy smile hanging from his lips.

I'm too stunned to say anything.

"See you later, Boo."

I watch him turn and stride back to work like he owns the place, which in my mind, he totally does.

I'm pretty sure my chances of finding any other man attractive after this run-in with Mack just died a slow, slow death.

I check my watch.

Time: One o'clock.

Cause of Death: Hot electrician. His drill. His back. His arms. His mind.

Rest in peace, me.

24

GHOST JOKES

Mack

"They look the same to me."

Poppy shoots me a sidelong glance and gives an exaggerated sigh.

We're standing, facing the long wall in the living room on her side of the duplex. The place feels so much different since she and Rose moved in. Sure, there's all the décor they brought along, all frilly and bright, but I'm talking about Poppy's presence. When she's around, the air hangs in a different way.

Like it's bursting with suspended bubbles, all sparkly and full of possibilities.

"Big. Work with me, will ya? Put your Chip Gaines goggles on." She makes circles with her hands and holds them in front of my eyes.

I squint at the wall where she's painted two giant squares of gray paint. She's finally worn me down, and I'm letting her help me with some remodeling projects.

First on her list titled *Ways to make The Downer less of a downer*: fresh paint.

"Can you tell me which one I should pick?" I ask.

"You don't see the difference? This one"—she steps forward and points to the paint splotch on the left—"is blue gray. And this one"—she hooks her thumb to the right—"is greige."

"Greige? That's a made-up color."

"It's a thing, I promise. Gray plus beige equals greige."

"Then why don't you call the other one gra-lue. Gray plus blue equals gra-lue."

"Doesn't quite have the same ring to it, does it?"

I fight back a smile, crossing my arms and turning to the wall. "I don't care."

She throws up her hands. "This is way harder than Joanna Gaines makes it seem."

"I guarantee Chip doesn't care what paint colors she picks for their projects."

"Maybe not, but he loves her enough to play along."

My chest compresses at that thought.

Love?

"Fine. I like the greige," I say, trying to mask the slight wobble in my tone with another eye roll over the made-up color.

She claps her hands. "Greige, it is. I think all your future tenants will appreciate your selection. You can tell them you picked out the wall color yourself."

"Or you could stay, and then I wouldn't need to hunt down a future tenant."

"You can't afford to keep me."

I snort. "Probably true."

We've fallen into a rhythm of this sort of banter all week.

I keep finding ways to tell her that she should stay.

Exhibit A: "*What will you do without Inez's coffee?*" I asked her yesterday when I showed up with her favorite iced latte in tow before she headed into the office.

"*Die a slow, miserable, uncaffeinated death,*" she quipped in return. "It's *my cross to bear.*"

Of course, Poppy thinks we're joking around. But I am very much not. I don't want her to go.

I've never experienced being around another person like Poppy. With her, it's like I'm who I'm supposed to be.

Corny, maybe. But it's true. She's seen me at my least glamorous. I don't have anything to hide from her. Not anymore.

Telling her about Tricia was so freeing. Waking up to her in my arms was enough to bring me to my knees. I want to wake up like that every day for the rest of my life.

Which can't happen if she doesn't stay.

We've spent quite a bit of time together since she showed up at my job site last week, but there hasn't been another opportunity to try to pick up where we left off with that near-kiss.

Poppy has been working like a madwoman to get the Party in the Park arrangements made, on top of all the rest of the P&R day-to-day work she's doing.

She still usually beats me home, and by the time I get showered, eat a quick dinner, and wander outside, she's out there, most often with Rose.

The three of us end up sitting for an hour or two, talking or not talking, about everything and nothing.

It's been comfortable. Nice.

Too nice.

I'm trying not to think too hard about how much I'm going to miss how nice it's been.

How much I'm going to miss the person who makes me feel most like me.

· · · · ● · ● ● · · ·

We make a quick run to the home improvement store for the two gallons of paint we need to coat the entire kitchen and living room of her half of the duplex. When we get back, the reinforcements have arrived.

Lou, Patrick, Mia, Rose, and Collin are all waiting with paint brushes in hand, and we set to work.

I'm using the roller in the living room, and Poppy is cutting the edges along the trim. We keep running into each other, and I know I should start working on an opposite wall—the duplex is small but not *that* small—but I like being close to her, so I'm milking this.

I roll paint above her head and step behind her, passing her position on the wall. I gently nudge her with my knee, and she tips forward, her hand landing in wet paint.

"Big, watch it!"

"What's that? Who's there? I can't see anything." I look around obnoxiously until I settle my gaze on her. "Could it be…a ghost?"

She stands up, walking to the kitchen. "Seriously? Can you quit it with the Kasper-related jokes?"

"Abso-*boo*-tly not."

She groans.

"Don't pretend you don't think I'm fa-*boo*-lously witty."

"I think I need some literal booze to handle you" she shouts from the sink.

"By all means, as long as the alcohol will make you shake your *boo*-ty."

"Pretty sure nobody wants to see that," she calls back.

"Doubtful. I'm guessing under your straight-laced skirts and collared shirts, you're the ghost-ess with the most-ess."

I hear her giggle, and then she reappears.

While she was washing her hands, I managed to drape the drop cloth over my head like a goon.

"What are you doing?" she says.

"Don't you mean, what are you *boo*-ing?"

"Oh my gosh. Can we be done?"

I pull the cloth over my head. "Boo-hoo." At her look, I hold up my hands. "Alright, fine. That was the last one, I promise."

"You guys are cute."

I spin around to see Rose in the entry to the hallway, smirking. Mia is nodding from behind her. They were painting the bedrooms. I have no idea how much of that little ghost show they saw.

Poppy claps her hand. "What's cute is this new paint color. Right?"

Her voice is an octave higher than usual, like she's slightly embarrassed that she was caught flirting with me.

Is what we were doing flirting? It wasn't laced with the romantic tension of her visit to me on the job, but I liked it just as much. I like being goofy with Poppy.

Like I said, she brings out the best in me.

We all turn to assess our paint progress.

"I think we're at a good stopping point for today," I say.

"Good. I'm hungry." Lou and Patrick appear from the kitchen and bathroom, respectively.

"Let's clean up and head into town. Romeo's. My treat."

Everyone nods and heads for their vehicles.

"Boo, wait."

Poppy pauses and looks at me expectantly.

"I want to show you something, if that's okay."

"Sure. What is it?"

I hold out my hand, and she takes it. I tug her in the direction of the backyard, the opposite way our friends went.

We step outside, and the evening humidity hits me like a wet blanket, but the weather is the last thing on my mind. I did something for Poppy that I hope she loves. But I'm nervous to show her. I was going to wait, but since she's leaving town, I want her to be able to get some use out of it.

"Close your eyes," I say.

She looks at me with a furrowed brow. "How do I know you aren't going to ax murder me?"

"Are you still on that?"

"Maybe you should stop being suspicious," she says, tossing her chin in the air.

"Would you just close your eyes?"

She squishes up her nose but does as I ask.

I lead her around the divider between our decks and into the back corner of my yard. "Wait right here," I direct her.

I hurry ahead and pull the tarp off of what I've been working on: two perfectly constructed raised garden beds. The cedar glistens in the late-afternoon sun, and the scent of the warm wood and the organic soil I filled the beds with late last night hits my nose.

Poppy sniffs, so I know she smells it too.

"Open your eyes."

Poppy blinks. Her gaze freezes on the garden beds, and she inhales, pressing her lips together. "What is this?"

"These are for you."

She brings her hands up and covers her mouth. "You remembered?" she whispers.

She says it as if I don't have every single one of our conversations tattooed onto the fissures of my brain.

I nod.

"How did you... When did you... I don't know what to say. This isn't *storage*, you big fat liar."

I step closer to her, and I can see her eyes glistening with unshed tears. A nervous wiggle worms its way through my gut. "Are you crying?"

Poppy swipes at her lashes. "I guess I am. Happy tears, I promise. I'm overwhelmed. I haven't gardened in years. Not since we sold Gram's house. And these raised beds. They look like the ones we had in her backyard. How did you..."

She swivels her head to face me, tears trickling down her cheeks.

I grab for her hand and give it a squeeze. I can't help myself around Poppy. "I guess you could almost say it's giving you deja-*boo*."

My joke lands how I hoped it would, and she croaks out a laugh through her tears. I wanted to do this for Poppy, but I don't want it to be so overwhelming to her that it makes her sad.

"I hope it's okay."

She wipes her eyes. "It's more than okay. It's perfect. It's more than I deserve."

I shake my head at that. She deserves everything. Doesn't she see that? Doesn't she know I'd give her everything if she'd stay?

Before I can respond, she stands up on her tip toes, cups my jaw, and plants a gentle kiss on my cheek.

"Thank you."

"Anything for you, Boo. Anything at all."

25

GOOD FOR HIM

Poppy

"I swear I'm fine. There's absolutely nothing to worry about," Noli says.

My facial expression is the definition of skeptical. I can see it in the tiny little thumbnail square at the bottom of my phone. I'm on a video call with Noli.

"I'm serious, Pops. Let's talk about something other than my personal life for a change."

I want to argue, but I think better of it. I don't want to drive Noli away. I roll my shoulders, trying to relax. "What would you like to talk about?"

"How about your personal life!" Noli sounds chipper all of a sudden.

I snort. "Not much to report."

"Where's Mack? He's always close by these days."

My gaze darts over the opening of the cove, across the bonfire, to where Mack is sitting. He gives me a salute, and I laugh.

I stand and walk around the fire pit, plopping down on the wood log he's sitting on. "Here he is, in the flesh!"

Noli wags her eyebrows. "Mack, what a surprise!"

She's being facetious. She and Rose have been insufferable since Mack and I spent the night together in the wheat field. When I didn't come home, Rose of course demanded all the details. When I gave her an abridged version, leaving out Mack's admission about Tricia, she filled Noli in, and the two of them haven't stopped talking about me and Mack ever since. Their efforts only intensified when he made me my flower beds.

I still can't believe he remembered what I told him at the beginning of the summer about gardening. And not only did he remember, he went and made a special place for me to do something I love. Since Gram died, no one has ever done something this thoughtful for me. I can't think fully about it because I already feel like my chest is under some sort of crushing force field.

But Noli and Rose have been thinking about it. Our group text has been filled with kissing memes and Marvin Gaye sound bites. My sisters are convinced that Mack is in love with me.

I, as per usual, have been trying to be the voice of reason.

Demurring. Deferring. Downplaying.

Even though a tiny part of me hopes they're right. I've never felt about anyone the way I feel about Mack. When I'm with him, it's like someone stripped away all the extra stuff I add to my personality to fit in—or the stuff I try to tone down to fit in—and what's left is me. The real version.

The thing is, I think Mack is a different version of himself around me too.

I mean, you don't see the man making ghost jokes on the regular around Cashmere Cove. The goofy side of him—the relaxed, playful side—only comes out on rare occasions. Or I guess since we've been spending so much time together, not quite so rare anymore.

Collin mentioned it when I was running through Party in the Park security with him earlier this week. *"You're good for him."*

I want to be good for Mack for a long time to come. But I'm going to have to do that from the position of a friend. I can't get romantically attached to someone I like because I have other things to worry about. Their names are Noli and Rose Kasper.

I stick out my tongue at Noli while also trying to use my eyes to tell her to cool it.

"Watch the licking, Boo." Mack pokes me in the side, and I yelp and nearly drop the phone. My entire traitorous body starts buzzing at his touch.

"Um, excuse me, Poppy, can you control yourself? I'm trying to talk to Mack here."

I right the phone and scowl at Noli. "Sorry." I swivel the screen in Mack's direction.

"Mack! Hi!" Noli beams. "Tell me, is Poppy obsessed with Rose's life, or does she save her special brand of overprotective big sister for me?"

I scoot closer so I'm in the frame with Mack. I'm invading his personal space, but that's been my favorite place to be lately, so I'm not mad about it.

"I resent that," I say to Noli.

"Yeah, yeah." She rolls her eyes.

Mack cuts a look in my direction, silently asking me what's going on. I lean back so I'm out of the frame again and mouth, "She loaned Nelson more money."

Mack keeps his face neutral like a champ, but on the phone screen, Noli starts swishing her finger between the two of us. "Hey, no. Not fair. Leave it to you two to already be able to talk without words. But none of this communicating behind my back in front of my face. If you've got something to say, say it."

I sigh and lean closer to Mack again, drawing patience and resolve from his strong presence. "We've been over this, Noli. I don't like to see you getting taken advantage of, that's all."

"I've told you, Poppy. I know what I'm doing. I trust Nelson. It's fine. Mack"—she shifts her gaze to him—"please talk some sense into my sister. Tell her she does not need to move back to Pensacola for me."

"I've already told her that," Mack says evenly.

He has. A number of times. We joke about it constantly. But he knows that I have to go.

I roll my eyes at him now.

"See, Poppy. Listen to your friend." Noli puts a heavy amount of emphasis on that word, *friend.*

Mack puffs up his chest, and I wonder if he noticed what Noli was implying.

"Yeah, Poppy. Listen to me," he says.

I nudge him in the shoulder. He sways away from me, but when he comes back to a resting position, he lands closer to my side. Our shoulders are pressed flush now, and I could think of worse ways to spend a Saturday night in early August.

"Seriously, Pops. You love it there. You've got a great job. You can't stop gushing about how gorgeous it is in town. And then there's Mack."

Mack cocks his head to the side.

Before he can ask Noli to please elaborate, I rip the phone back in my direction and stand up. "Okay! Well, I'm going to go."

I walk away from the fire pit and drop my voice. "Would you cut it out? I don't need things to be weird between Mack and me because of all these hints you're dropping."

"Don't be so sensitive! I didn't mean anything by it. I'm sure Mack knows that."

I glance over my shoulder, and Mack's watching me. I shrug my shoulders as if to say, *Sisters, am I right?* He smiles at me, and I feel it in my core.

"Whatever. Stay in touch, okay?"

Noli sighs. "Okay, *Mom.*"

I make an exasperated face.

"Quit worrying about me, and go have some fun. I know how hard you've been working."

I sigh and nod. She's not wrong about that. Party in the Park has been kicking my butt. I've been touching base with the kids' rides operators to coordinate their arrival, putting the finishing touches on my teen scavenger hunt idea, and trying to relay all the appropriate information to the food truck rally participants. Not to mention going over all the Promenade details with Willow, who, bless her heart, has requested three in-person meetings in the last week.

I do need a night to relax.

"Fine," I say, making the word more than one syllable.

"Good. I can't wait to hear about it!" She gives me a finger wave and blows kisses at the screen.

She hangs up before I can say anything else.

I stand, staring out at the water for a second.

Fun. I can do fun.

But fun makes me think of Mack. And his garden bed. And *him*.

My feet are leading me back to his side before I can think twice. Because it's right where I want to be.

26

we're Not Friends

Mack

Wool Beach is all ours tonight, and that's the way I like it. We're a smaller group than usual since Piper and Ed left on their belated honeymoon earlier in the week.

Patrick and Mia are swimming together in the dusky waters. Lou is napping on the beach. Rose strolled off with her journal about a half hour ago. I can see her up on one of the rocky hill crests. Collin walked back to his car to get his Bluetooth speaker so we can listen to music, but I'm guessing he got a work call or something, because he hasn't returned.

Poppy wandered away from me a second ago—I'm assuming to finish up her conversation with Noli in private. I'm trying not to focus on how much cooler the night got after she left my general vicinity.

But I am a pathetic man, who is cold-blooded unless Poppy is around. Then, my veins run with fire.

I replay the last thing Noli said before Poppy walked away: *And then there's Mack.*

And then there's Mack, what?

I would very much like to know how I'm factoring into whatever equation is in question. What has Poppy told her sisters about me?

I settle back onto my log, poking a large stick at the coals of the fire and trying not to read too much into the moment. Instead, I glance up at the full moon suspended over the water. It's glowing pure white and sending shadows dancing around the stone walls of the cove.

Poppy steps out from one of those shadows and sits down next to me again. A thrill scuttles through my body at the closeness, and my body temperature rises.

Like a freaking reptile.

"I don't know what I'm going to do with her." She sighs.

Poppy has confided in me about Noli and Nelson a lot over the past month, so the backstory is familiar to me, and it's not good. Nelson is a classic freeloader, and it sounds like he's manipulating and gaslighting Noli, who works a steady job as a 911 dispatcher, into funding his lifestyle.

I stir up some of the coals, sending fluttering sparks into the air, as I think about my response. "Sometimes people have to make their own mistakes."

"She could get seriously hurt or in major trouble, though."

"I know."

Poppy looks anguished.

I rest my hand on her knee. Her skin is soft under my calloused palm until goosebumps spring up. I stare at them for a beat...relishing the fact that I did that. Her body physically reacts to *me*. But then I mentally scold myself. She's worried about her sister. Now is not the time to be flirty. I give her leg a friendly squeeze and move my hand back to my own lap. She's leaving. I shouldn't make this any harder on myself by flirting.

Patrick and Mia walk out of the cove and head toward us. Patrick stops and stands over the top of Lou, shaking water droplets on him. Lou startles and swears, grabbing Patrick's ankle and dropping him onto the sand.

"Serves you right," Lou grumbles. He wipes his eyes. "What did I miss?"

Rose joins the circle, her journal tucked under her arm. "Nothing exciting."

"How would you know?" Poppy asks. "Big and I could have been having a very exciting time together."

"Oh yeah, Pops, and what would you have been doing with Mack that you'd consider exciting? Do tell me."

Poppy opens her mouth, but nothing comes out. She shoots daggers at her sister.

Rose smirks. "I could think of some things for you."

Poppy's cheeks are flaming, and I'm starting to wonder if maybe I haven't been the subject of one or more Kasper sibling conversations. If I'm not mistaken, both Noli and Rose have hinted at Poppy and me being something...more.

Right?

Or am I misreading the signals?

Lou gets a look on his face that I know from experience to be dangerous. It's his *I've-got-a-great-idea* look. His definition of *great idea* is always questionable at best.

"We have about an hour until fireworks, right?" Lou says.

Collin returns with his speaker and takes a seat on my other side. "Yep."

Even though we're creeping nearer to the end of summer, fireworks are pretty standard in Cashmere County until Labor Day. We always have a great view of them over the water.

Lou rubs his hands together. "Who's up for a friendly little game of truth or dare?"

I roll my eyes. "We're not twelve-year-olds, Lou."

He arches his brows. "You scared?"

I don't blink.

"I'm in," Rose says, sitting down next to Poppy.

Everyone else agrees, even Poppy, who says, "It sounds fun."

Lou levels me with a look, challenging me.

"Fine. Let's do it."

We set about playing the game, and for the most part, the dares are pretty tame. Patrick dares Lou to run naked into the cove, which he does without hesitation.

Mia dares Rose to read a page from her journal. She scowls at her boss-turned-friend, but then she does.

I had no idea Rose is an author, but she read us the first page of a chapter of a novel she's working on. It's good if you're into sports romances.

"Okay," Collin says, "my turn to ask. Mack, truth or dare?"

"Dare," I say without missing a beat.

"Kiss Poppy," he shoots back at me just as fast.

"What?"

"You heard me. Kiss Poppy."

Poppy is very still next to me.

"Collin, come on."

"He doesn't have to," Poppy says, her voice calm, as if she's doing me a favor, as if she thinks I don't want to.

"What? No. I was going to say I don't have to because"—I wave my hand at her—"I'm not going to force you to kiss me if you don't want to."

Poppy opens her mouth, but before she can say anything, Rose jumps in.

"I can make this easy. It's my turn next. Poppy, kiss Mack."

I whip my gaze to Rose who looks quite pleased with herself.

"See, no issue." She dusts her hands as if her work here is done.

"Unless you'd rather tell us a truth. I've got a question for that too." Collin stares me down. He would ask me about Tricia, and I don't want to go there. Not tonight.

"Oh!" Rose says, clapping her hands. "And I have a great question for Poppy, if she'd rather tell the truth."

Poppy presses her lips together and then meets my gaze. She gives me a smile and a shrug that says she's game if I am.

"You want to do this here, in front of them?" I motion to our crowd of anxious onlookers.

"Is there another option?"

"Back in the day, we used to play that if you were dared to kiss someone, you could have some privacy." Collin points off to the side. "So you can go around the rock over there, if you'd prefer."

"Uh, well, yeah, I guess I'd rather not kiss in front of all you guys."

"How will we know if they kiss?" Lou argues, staring between Poppy and me. He's apparently quite invested in this.

"Trust me. We'll know." Collin smirks.

I fight against the urge to flip him the bird. Because he's doing me a favor, and I think he knows it.

I stand and hold out my hand for Poppy.

She takes it, and I hoist her up. I don't let go as I lead her over to the rock wall.

Behind us, our friends are catcalling, and laughing, and being generally ridiculous.

"Take your time!" Rose calls, and Poppy mumbles something about how life would have been ten times easier if God would have given her brothers.

We stop when we're out of sight.

"How will Collin know if we don't kiss?" she asks.

"The man has known me forever, and then he went and got cop trained. He's pretty good at lie detecting."

Poppy chuckles. "I can't ever get anything past Rose, either, so I guess we're stuck going through with it."

"Guess so."

Poppy looks up at me through her eyelashes. "Why am I so nervous?" She bites her lip, and my knees buckle.

"You don't ever need to be nervous around me, Boo. It's us."

She closes her eyes and exhales. It's several moments before she meets my gaze again. I see a mixture of nerves and desire flickering in her pale-blue eyes. And that's it. I'm putty in her hands, and she has no idea.

"I want this. Is it bad to want this?" She breathes the last words so quietly I think for a second I misheard her, but she flicks her gaze to my lips and back up again, and there's no questioning it any longer.

I lean toward her as she rises up on her tiptoes, and together we close the gap between us. Our lips meet, and they sort of cling together. We both hold still, as if we're stunned. She moves first, or maybe I do. But someone nudges someone else, and suddenly we're exploring. Slowly. Carefully. Like we're savoring a delicious bite of chocolate cake, letting the flavor infuse every one of our senses before we swallow it away. I realize somewhere in the back of my mind that we could have settled on a quick peck. It would have fulfilled the dare. But I wanted more, and amazingly, so did Poppy.

Still, we're both tentative. A question and an answer with each pull and press. A wave of desire for this woman is rising up in me, filling my lungs until I'm sure I'll suffocate.

Poppy takes her hands, which have been resting primly on my chest, and laces them behind my neck. She tugs me closer, deepening the kiss, and the dam in my chest breaks. I move my hands to her hips and hoist her up. She wraps her legs around my waist, and I slowly walk her backward to the rock wall. The kiss goes from basic chocolate cake to molten lava cake in no time at all, and I cannot get enough of the feel of her body pressed against mine. The way her lips simultaneously give and take, both following me and guiding me.

My hands are tied up with holding her steady—a job I'm taking very seriously because I do not want to break this kiss for any-thing. She's using her freedom to explore my body to the fullest. Her hands dip down and rub over my shoulders. She stops to squeeze my biceps and then lets her fingers skim down along my sides. When they hit my belt line, she drags them back up, the hem of my shirt rising with the movement. For a second, her fingers are on my bare skin, and it might be my undoing. I growl, and she smiles against my mouth, innocently completing the path of her hands, bringing them back up to my neck where she starts to play with the hair at the nape. Every part of me that she's touched is singed, and her soft, gentle caress is driving me crazy in the best possible way.

This is Poppy. And it's like everything I knew and loved about this woman has been brought into acute focus. A dialed-in telescope on a breathtaking star.

The way she lives so fully is mirrored in the way she's kissing me for all she's worth. Poppy doesn't hold back her feelings. She's bold and vibrant and sparkling. All the time. For everyone. But right now, this is for me. Me. I've never been more grateful or more overwhelmed and in awe of a person—of a moment—before in my life. I don't want to hold anything back from her either.

A firework explodes, and it takes me a moment to realize it was launched off behind me and the crackle and pop didn't come from between Poppy and me.

Slowly, we pull back, the kissing cocoon we've woven around ourselves breaking open.

Poppy and I stare at each other for a long moment. I'm still holding her off the ground, and I can't help it. I kiss the column of her neck before I set her on her own two feet.

She reaches up to touch her swollen lips as I use the pad of my thumb to brush a strand of hair off her forehead.

She keeps looking at me with those wide, doe eyes. "Wow, Big. I mean, wow. What was that?"

I chuckle, running a hand through my hair. "That was..."

"It was good, right? Good for you?"

I look at her, and...wait, is she still nervous? Can she possibly think that that wasn't everything I have ever wanted in my life rolled up in one five-minute kiss?

I reach for her hand and squeeze it. "Boo. It was good."

She nods, as if coming out of a daze. "But a terrible idea." She blinks. "I'm leaving soon, and we're friends."

I can't help it. I shake my head. "We're not friends. Not *just* friends, Poppy."

I use her whole name to show her I'm serious, and it does the trick.

Her eyes go wide. "B-but you don't date anyone." She pauses. "Right?"

"True. I haven't dated anyone." I make sure I'm looking at her when I say what I want to say next. "But you're not anyone, and I'd date you. In a heartbeat."

"Big."

I hold up my finger and press it against her lips. She closes her eyes and trembles at my touch.

"Stay." The word comes out of my mouth like a prayer.

Her eyes pop open. "What?"

"Stay. Here. In Cashmere Cove."

"I can't."

"You can." I'm not sure where this is coming from—maybe it was her admission that she wanted to kiss me—but all of a sudden I can't help but try to convince Poppy to stick around. It's her own fault. She went and made me believe that I deserve to be happy. I'll be happy if I'm with her. "I know it's weird with Holland, and I know you might think your sisters need you," I admit, "but I need you too, and I'm asking you to stay. For you. And me. Because we're so much more than friends."

She's nibbling her lip, her eyes searching mine.

"You don't have to say anything tonight," I rush to say.

After a minute, she whispers, "I'll think about it, okay?"

I start. That's a better response than I could have imagined. I feel like I could fly. "Yeah?"

"Yeah."

Poppy steps closer to me, and I pull her into a hug. I've never been much of a hugger, but this woman—this amazing, incredible, kind, interesting woman—is changing parts of me that I thought were cemented in place. She's unlocking chambers of my heart and opening them up wide to new feelings, new beliefs, and an entirely new mindset about the future. I'm going to hug her every chance I get.

"We should get back, huh?" As she says it, she nuzzles into my chest.

She fits perfectly against me. I don't care if thinking that makes me the biggest cliché in the book. It's the honest-to-goodness truth.

"Probably." I ease her out of the hug but keep one of my arms around her shoulders. "Unless you want to make out again."

Her eyes widen, and I grin.

She swats my chest. "Don't tempt me, Mack Bradley."

I commit the sparkle in her eye and the pink on her cheeks to my memory as we stroll back to the fire pit, where everyone is sitting watching the fireworks.

As one, they all turn to us with pie-eating grins plastered on their faces.

Collin and Rose size us up and then give identical nods.

We've passed their inspection with the dare.

And the truth is, I've lost my heart to Poppy Kasper.

27

café kisses and Hard misses

Poppy

N**oli:** Poppy and Mack sitting in a tree, k-i-s-s-i-n-g <music-note emoji> <kissing-face emoji>

Poppy: Are we still on that? I told you Rose and Collin dared us.

Rose: Maybe the first time. But there's been lots of kissing since.

Rose: And YOU'RE WELCOME.

I glance up from my phone and shoot Rose a look. "You know, you could say it to my face."

The two of us are strolling through the Cashmere Cove historic district, nearing the Getaway Café. The colorful buildings that line this part of Main Street are glowing in the mid-day sun, and it looks like the backdrop of an artist's oil painting. I can hear the faint laughter and squeals of families echoing from down at the beach in the tourist part of Cashmere Cove, and a hint of bayside breeze hits my nose, though we don't have a view of the water where we're walking. It's another scorcher, and I can't wait for a tall glass of Inez's homemade lemonade.

"Where's the fun in that?" Rose shrugs.

A text from Noli comes in before I can retort.

Noli: So are you two official, then?

I sigh. I want to be. I want to be official so very badly. I haven't given him an answer about staying here in Cashmere Cove, but I'm leaning in that direction.

Rose: They're officially swapping saliva on the regular.

I shove Rose.

She laughs as she trips down the sidewalk.

Noli: So he really lights you up, eh, Pops? Get it, *lights*...because he's an electrician.

Rose: He definitely turns her on, that's for sure.

"Oh my gosh, can you not with that? Barf," I say, though it's making me think of teasing Mack when he happens to accidentally make electrician jokes, and I secretly love it.

Rose just laughs.

Noli: Sounds like he's the shock your system needed, Pops.

Rose: I've seriously been afraid the sparks between her and Mack are going to burn The Downer down.

My fingers hover over my keyboard. I'm so used to trying to shut down these sorts of playful conversations amongst my sisters, but in this case, yeah...Mack and I kissed. And yeah, it was beyond wonderful.

Rose: He also left her a bag of seeds on her windshield this morning along with a love note. <melting-face emoji>

Butterflies stir up in my stomach at the thought. It's been almost a week since we kissed for the first time, and every day, he's found little ways to show me he's thinking of me—to make me feel like I am a legitimate princess and all he wants to do is serve me.

I never thought I'd be into the whole fairy-tale thing...mostly because life had other plans for me. But honestly, it's been the best.

He's working overtime at his jobsite, and I've been putting in long hours at the P&R department, but he continues to show up for me.

The bag of wildflower seeds is just one example.

There's been iced coffees left on my porch first thing in the morning.

One of Inez's homemade pastries has magically appeared on my desk every afternoon when I need a pick-me-up.

After the Friday night Cashmere County weekly summer base-ball league game, he laid with me in the outfield, talking and looking up at the stars until we got kicked out.

He added crisscross string lights to our half of the deck behind The Downer.

And he left me a long, handwritten note detailing all the things he admires about me under my door.

Rose is right. It was a definite turn-on. And I'm not ashamed to admit it.

Poppy: Nothing's official between us, but I really like him.

Noli: Awwwwwwww <heart-eye emoji> <happy-tears emoji>

Noli: I hope this means you're staying in Cashmere Cove. Don't be an idiot about this, Poppy.

Rose: Co-sign.

Poppy: Watch your mouth, young lady.

Noli: <eye-roll emoji> Seriously, Pops. I'm happy for you. I can't wait to meet Mack!

The thought warms my heart. I want Mack to meet my baby sister too.

Poppy: Come visit soon!

Rose: As a consolation prize, I am also here, and you'll be able to see me.

"You're not a consolation prize," I say out loud to Rose.

"I know."

I side-eye my middle sister. I've been obsessing so much over Noli and how she's doing down in Pensacola that I've sort of taken my eye off Rose.

"You sure?"

"Of course. I'm awesome."

I stare at her for a beat, and she holds my gaze. She raises an eyebrow, and I nod. "As long as you know it."

Noli: Gotta run. Nelson's home. Love you both!

I shove down the pang of anxiety that hits my chest at the mention of Noli's boyfriend, choosing instead to focus on how much I love my sisters and how grateful I am that we can still be close even in different states. It's making me feel confident about the prospect of staying in Cashmere Cove.

Rose and I stow our phones and push open the door to the café. It's full of all sorts of people we've met since moving to Cashmere Cove a month ago. I love being plugged in to a small town like this. I scan the crowd and spot Mayor Witmore sitting at a table with Abner, the head of the streets department, and a group of townsfolk, who seem to be in a heated discussion about something or other. The new road project that's slated to begin next spring, perhaps?

I love that I know that.

Nearby, Heather is sitting with a baby stroller tucked in next to her table. Her little Kenny is two months old now. She's been texting me about Party in the Park details, and it's been great to be able to honestly say I have everything under control. I hope I'm doing enough to earn me a full-time gig.

Across the way is Jameson, the licker from the zoo trip, digging in to a platter of homemade mac and cheese. I catch his eye and wave, smiling at his dad who's sitting across from him. I feel a rightness about it all settle on my shoulders, made complete when I notice Mack tucked into a booth on the far wall.

He's wearing his Mack Electric baseball cap turned backward, so I can see his face. That means there's no question that his eyes are laser focused on me. When our gazes connect, his lips quirk up ever so slightly.

"Should I leave you to your ogling?" Rose says, breaking the trance Mack's attention has put me under.

"What? No."

"Then move forward. It's almost our turn to order." Rose points ahead, and I realize the line has advanced while I've been caught up in staring at Mack.

"Sorry."

"Don't be. It's sweet." Rose loops her arm through mine. "I'm happy for you, Poppy."

"Thanks. But enough about me. Tell me about the bookstore. What do you guys have going on?"

Rose's face brightens. "We're bringing Daisy Reid in for an author event and book signing early next week. I can't wait."

"*The* Daisy Reid? Your favorite author?"

Rose nods. "Turns out all my Instagram fangirling paid off. I was able to get in touch with her manager and get Cashmere Cove a last-minute slot on her book tour."

We make our way up to the counter and order our food, chatting about Mood Reader and other events Rose is looking forward to planning. "Now that you're thinking seriously about staying in Cashmere Cove, I want to stay too."

"I'm glad you're happy here."

Rose gets a look I can't place in her eyes, but she blinks it away before I can ask her about it. "I am."

We finish up paying and turn to find seats as the door to the café blows open.

Tricia saunters in with her baby on her hip and another woman, whom I haven't met yet, behind her.

I might be imagining it, but I swear the conversations in the café quiet a couple notches. Everyone swings their gazes from Mack to Tricia and back again.

Tricia zones in on Mack and squishes up her nose in a scowl. She turns to her friend and, loudly enough for most of the café to hear, says, "He's like a nightmare that I can't stop having."

My entire body tenses. I glance over at Mack, who has his head down. He's moving the remains of his food around with his fork. Darla is across from him, wringing her hands together as if she still can't believe that her son didn't end up with the woman who currently disses him every chance possible.

Something inside me snaps.

I stride to Mack's table, and he raises his head when he notices me in his periphery. His eyes widen when I plop down on his lap.

I grab his cheeks with my hands, enjoying the coarse feel of his beard under my fingers, and draw his lips to mine. I take my time with a slow, meaningful kiss. I can tell the moment Mack gets over being stunned. His hands tighten on my hips, and the muscles holding his jaw tense relax. He kisses me back, and my entire body sighs.

When I'm pretty sure I've given everyone enough of a show, I ease back and trail a line of kisses through the stubble of his five o'clock shadow and up toward his ear.

"I need a new t-shirt that says *Team Mack*," I whisper to him before standing up.

He doesn't say anything, just stares at me with flames of appreciation lighting his pupils. I want to tattoo this look of his onto the insides of my eyelids.

I turn to Darla and beam at her. "Hi, Mrs. Bradley."

She stares at me with her mouth hanging open.

"I'm going to go grab my food. Be right back." I wink at Mack, and his smile stretches the entire width of his face.

The whole café is watching my every move and buzzing about what just happened—which was sort of the point. That kiss was for show—for everyone to see. I went for the shock factor, and it worked.

But more than that, it was for Mack.

Heather mouths, '*Nice*,' as I pass her on my way to the counter.

Tricia is staring daggers at me, but I ignore her.

Honestly, I feel sorry for her...for a lot of reasons. First and foremost, it sucks that she felt so pressured by her parents and their expectations that she thought her only option was to lie about Mack to save her own skin. But that was a long time ago. I'm not going to continue letting her treat the man I'm falling in love with like dirt.

"You good?" Rose asks as I join her by the counter.

I nod, a little stunned.

I'm in love with Mack Bradley.

It hits me with the force of a wave crashing onto shore. It's terrifying and exciting, disconcerting and settling all at once.

Because I don't know what the future between Mack and me looks like, but I know I want to go to bat for him. I want to be close to him and support him.

Inez hands us our plates over the top of the high counter. "I think you just put the pieces of Mack Bradley together again. Would you look at his face?"

I grab my meal and look over my shoulder at the man who holds my heart. "He wasn't broken in the first place."

Inez cocks her head to the side. "You know what? You're right. Let me know if you need anything else. Enjoy!"

Rose and I wander back to the table where Darla is hissing at Mack.

"I don't believe this. You and Poppy? Did you think about informing me, your mother, about this development?"

Mack glances up and meets my eye. "There wasn't any development to report."

"It's true, Mrs. Bradley. I sort of sprung this on Mack." I take my seat next to him.

"Took complete advantage of me is more like it," he mutters.

I shush him and beam at Darla. "But I am very interested in dating your son. *This* son," I add with a wince because it bears clarification.

Rose snorts as she pulls out the chair next to Darla.

"He's incredible, don't you agree?" I ask.

Darla's mouth opens and shuts like a fish before she presses her lips together and gives me a firm nod. "Of course I do. He's my son. Now, if you'll excuse me, I've got some errands to run. We'll see you all for Sunday dinner, yes?"

"Wouldn't miss it." I grab Mack's hand and intertwine our fingers, bringing them up to my mouth and giving them a kiss.

Darla can't seem to tear her gaze off of our locked fingers. She has a dazed look on her face, but she smiles at me. It's hesitant—like she doesn't know if I'm in my right mind—but it's there. She nods and turns to leave.

I'm not meeting either Mack's or my sister's gaze because suddenly I'm bashful. Did I really do that? The underwear I put on this morning must be made of superhero fibers.

"You"—Mack tugs on my hand and forces me to face him—"are my favorite."

Just like that, I'm not self-conscious anymore. "Ditto."

"Hey! I'm right here!"

I chuckle. "Sorry, Rosie. You know I love you."

"Darn right. Now if you don't mind, I'm going to try to enjoy my lunch, and as much as I like this"—she points between the two of us—"I also can't eat with you guys being all mushy gushy."

"I actually have to go. I'm working this afternoon." Mack tosses his napkin on top of his plate and stands. He lingers behind my chair, setting his hands on my shoulders and massaging the muscles in my upper back.

I fight the urge to moan, because we don't need an *I'll-have-what-she's-having* moment in the Getaway Café. But it feels nice, and I could very much get used to this.

"See you later?" His warm breath tickles my ear.

I nod, and he places a quick kiss on my cheek.

"Bye, Rose."

"Later, Mack."

I watch him leave, and I can't help but notice that Tricia keeps her focus on her food and doesn't throw any shade his direction as he walks past her table.

Mission *freaking* accomplished.

Rose and I finish eating our delicious lunch and stroll out along Main Street. We window shop and pop into Mood Reader where Rose shows me a book on gardening that she makes me buy.

I can't remember a better day. Then again, I've been thinking that a lot lately.

"We should head back to The Downer." I tuck the book in my tote, giving it a tap. "I want to put some of this book knowledge to use."

"You're such a nerd."

"I'm going to take that as a compliment."

After a couple seconds of silence, Rose says, "So..."

"So, what?"

"Are you staying in Cashmere Cove?"

I square my shoulders. "Yes."

Rose whoops and hugs me around the waist. "Good choice, Pops. Good choice."

I sigh. It does feel right, and I'm grateful.

My phone rings, and I shrug Rose off so I can dig for it under my new book.

"It's Noli," I say, checking the display screen. "Hey, sister."

"Uh, Poppy. Right. No, it's Nelson."

I stop walking. An icy finger of anxiety flies up my spine.

"Nelson. What's up? Where's Noli?"

"Uh, she, uh—"

"Spit it out, Nelson."

At my tone, Rose grabs my hand. I click the speaker phone button so we're both listening.

"She had an accident."

"Is she okay?" I ask at the same time as Rose says, "What kind of accident?"

"Um, uh...she's on her way to the ER—in an ambulance," he not so helpfully adds.

I press hard against the bridge of my nose. "Nelson. Tell me what happened. How is she hurt?"

"Likely concussion. Possible skull fracture. She hit the edge of the railing."

My breathing is erratic. "Why aren't you with her?"

"I, uh, don't think she'd want me to be. But she was unconscious. I called 9-1-1. I didn't—"

Rose clicks the phone off. "I can't with him."

I nod. "I'm booking a flight." I pull up the airline's website as guilt rips me in two. I can't believe I'm not there. My baby sister needs me, and I'm an entire country away.

28

EMO EMAIL

Mack

I 'm blasting my Celine Dion Spotify station like it's a national anthem.

And maybe it is.

Heck, I'll be the one to love Poppy more if she'll let me, and judging by that very public display of affection, I think she's going to let me.

Could I *be* any more thrilled?

No. No, I could not be.

Also, I think if I hire Poppy to kiss me every day at lunch time, I will increase my afternoon's productivity by a solid fifty percent, because I am *cruising* through this work.

I'm finishing up installing the electrical outlet and switch boxes at a multi-unit complex. It's a menial task, sure, but it still feels good to get it done. I could have left it for my apprentices to take care of on Monday, but I want to stay on schedule, and I've made it a point not to have my employees do anything I'm not willing to do. The truth about running a small business is if you're not willing to get down and dirty, then you're not going to be successful.

This week, getting down and dirty means working on a Saturday afternoon, making sure all the electrical boxes are roughed in.

I stand up from where I drilled in an under-the-counter outlet box in what will become the kitchen of this apartment. My back aches. I wonder if Poppy would be up for a late-night trip to

Wool Beach for a relaxing swim. The water is still comfortable, considering the August temperatures will not quit.

Movement in my periphery catches my eye. Holland's car is tearing down the road. Looks like I'll be able to ask Poppy out on a proper one-on-one date sooner rather than later.

I start collecting my tools, tossing them into my toolbox and tidying up the workspace. When I hear the car door slam, I make my way through the framing to the front of the building.

I'm grinning like an idiot, but when Holland's figure appears through the glare of the late-day sun instead of Poppy's, my cheeseball smile falls away. He must've grabbed his vehicle from the duplex.

"Mack, hey."

"What are you doing here?"

Holland looks affronted. "What, I can't come see my big brother at work?"

"You know what I mean. You're on tour. Why aren't you golfing somewhere?"

Holland shrugs. "Didn't make the cut."

I stare at him, and his indifferent tone is undercut by his rigid posture. He's trying not to show that missing out on weekend play is eating away at him. I feel for him. Truly, I do. I can't imagine the pressure. The endless drive to try to be perfect. I should cut him more slack than I do.

"Oh. Well. Hi."

Holland nods. "Yeah."

We stand, staring at each other and the ground. We're both sort of shuffling our feet, and it's the definition of awkward.

At the sound of another vehicle, I exhale. I hold my hand up to shield the sun and see Poppy pull up in the car she and Rose share. Rose is in the passenger seat on the phone.

I wince. I haven't told Holland about Poppy and me. Like I said to my mom earlier, there wasn't anything to tell.

But now...

She shoves open the driver's side door, and I don't have time to worry about how this is all going to play out, because one look at Poppy's face and I know something is seriously wrong. Holland becomes a blur in my periphery.

I step forward and open my arms. She strides straight into a hug, burying her head into the center of my chest. She stands there—inhaling and exhaling—for I don't know how long before she leans back. In her eyes are unshed tears.

"What happened? Are you hurt?"

Poppy bites her lip. "It's Noli."

She gives me a brief rundown of what Nelson said when he called her.

"We don't know much more than that. Rose is on the phone with the hospital, pretending to be me right now."

"Why—"

"I'm Noli's medical power of attorney, so they won't talk to anyone but me."

I nod. That makes sense.

"I booked a flight. I'm headed to Florida in less than two hours."

These words come out in a rush, and I try to digest them. Of course she's going. She wouldn't be Poppy if she didn't. Her sister needs her.

I'm still crushed.

I just found her. We're starting something new and good and potentially life-altering, and it feels like someone has pulled the emergency brake and yanked us to a halt.

"What about Party in the Park?" I hear myself ask. It's a stupid question. The town end-of-the-summer party pales in comparison to what Poppy's dealing with right now, but I'm grasping at straws. Maybe she'll come back for it. She's worked so hard.

"I've already called Heather. I left her all my notes, and everything should pretty much run itself at this point. I know I can count on you for the set-up." A ghost of a smile haunts her lips.

"I wish I could be here to see what you come up with for the Promenade."

"I'll try to make you proud." Inside, my heart is shriveling up like a raisin. Party in the Park has never been my idea of a good time. This year, it was bearable because of Poppy, and knowing that she was going to be there made me semi-excited to attend for the first time since I found Tricia in bed with another man. But now, the forecast for the day looks as bleak as ever.

"Rose is riding with me to the airport, and then she'll bring the car back. She's staying here," Poppy says. "At least for now. She's got a big author event at Mood Reader next week, and I'm going to assess how things are with Noli, and then we'll figure out what our next steps should be as a family."

"Right. Of course."

Poppy searches my face, taking in the vulnerability I don't think I'm doing a very good job of hiding from my gaze.

"I was going to stay," she says in a whisper. "I want to be with you, Big. But I have to go."

I pull her into another hug. "I know. I understand."

"I wish it could be different. I wish it could be easy. I wish I didn't feel so responsible, but ever since Nelson called, I've had this rock in my stomach. It's sinking me. I feel like I'm drowning, and the only thing that's going to make it any better is to be there for Noli. To help her."

"She's your sister. Of course you feel like that. But it's not your fault."

"I know, but it still feels like I should have done something to prevent this. I mean, she fought with her boyfriend and ended up at the bottom of the stairs. It doesn't take a genius to read between the lines there. Right? I could vomit thinking about it."

I can feel my own blood boiling. I have never met Noli in person, but I love her because Poppy loves her, and if I ever cross paths with this Nelson character, well...I'd like to give him a piece of my mind.

"I'm so sorry." My apology feels measly.

"Not your fault either. Actually, you've reminded me that there *are* good men out there, and for that I'm more grateful than I can say." She checks her watch. "I don't have long. I have to get to the airport or I'll miss my flight, but I couldn't bear the thought of leaving without saying goodbye. I know in the movies the girl would dip out and the guy would be left in the lurch, wondering what happened or where he went wrong, but I had to see you before I left to tell you that you did nothing wrong. You did everything right. I don't know what the future is going to look like, but my feelings for you are real, and—"

I cut off her babbling with a kiss. Quick and firm and sure. She grips the front of my t-shirt as I spear my fingers through her hair, the loose ponytail she always wears coming further undone.

I know I have to let her go, but *gosh*, I don't want to let her go.

I ease us out of the kiss, and Poppy takes a deep, shuddering breath. It's then she registers Holland.

To be honest, I've forgotten about him too.

She shifts out of my embrace and holds up her hand in a small wave. "Holland, uh, hey."

Holland swings his head between the two of us. "Sorry to hear about Noli," he says, and then he gestures at me and then at Poppy. "I didn't know... I mean, you two..."

Poppy and I exchange semi-guilty looks, but I keep a tight hold on her hand.

"Yeah," Poppy says.

"We weren't anything when you two were together," I add.

"Of course not." Poppy sounds offended that anyone would think that, but I know my brother.

He's staring at us with nothing but a bewildered look on his face, so I don't know what he's thinking. I don't care much at this point, either. Poppy has bigger concerns. I'm about to usher her back to her car, but Holland's face cracks into a wide grin. "You know what? I think it's great. I'm going to take credit for it, as a matter of fact. Bet you're glad I put you up to those emails now, aren't you?"

He steps forward and slaps me on the back.

I close my eyes, suddenly nauseated.

"What emails?" Poppy asks. I can sense her impatience. She wants to get to Noli. Why are we doing this right now? Also, why didn't I think to mention the fact that I was the one behind Holland's email account?

"You know, the H. Bradley Pro account? Mack was replying to you for me." Holland has the wherewithal to look bashful. "I'm sorry, Poppy, but I was too busy. It looks like it all worked out in the end, though. You two are sort of perfect for each other."

Poppy drops my hand, and the look that she gives me is full of confusion. "You read my emails?"

I nod. "I should have told you. I—"

"Oh, whoa. You didn't know. Oh, gosh. Foot meet mouth." Holland slaps his forehead.

"Poppy, please. I'm sorry."

A myriad of emotions washes over Poppy's face in quick succession. I spy uncertainty, hurt, more confusion, and a flash of anger. "I can't do this right now. I have to go."

I reach for her, but she puts her hands up in a *stop* sign. "No. I-I'm not sure what to think." She meets my gaze, and I hate that my actions are the cause for the pain in her eyes. "I thought I could trust you, Big. But this doesn't feel good. I can't think about it right now." Her voice cracks, and she bites her lip. "I'll...I'll be in touch."

She spins around, and I want to make her stay. Make her stand still until I can convince her that she can trust me. I want to tell her I love her.

But that would be selfish. That would be for me.

What Poppy needs is to get to Noli.

So I do the hardest thing I've ever done. I let her go.

The dust churns up as she drives away.

Holland clears his throat. "My bad."

I barely hear him. I just stare at Poppy's tail lights.

"I'm going to go to Mom and Dad's," he says quietly. "Let me know if there's anything I can do."

You've done enough.

I think the words but don't say them out loud. Sure, it would be easy to blame Holland, but this is my fault. I should have told Poppy about the emails from the beginning. I never should have agreed to deceive her in the first place.

Holland retraces his steps and climbs into his car, and I wait until he's down the road before I let my hands fall to my knees, a renewed wave of grief bowling me over and making it difficult to breathe.

I hurt Poppy, and she's gone.

29

Daddy Issues

Poppy

I use my elbow to knock the door to Noli's room open. She's sitting in her bed, staring out the window. She doesn't look my way.

"I brought you some soup."

She sighs and turns to me. "Pops, I'm not an invalid."

"Soup is a comfort food." I sit down on the edge of the bed. It dips under my weight, and some soup sloshes onto the floor. Dang it. I'll have to scrub that up so we don't leave a stain.

We're staying in a month-to-month, fully furnished rental property. I managed to get a lease agreement signed for us the day I arrived in Florida. Thanks to my former landlord's glowing recommendation (I owe Mack big time) and two months rental payment up front, we were able to move right in here after Noli was discharged from the hospital.

That was two days ago.

It's hard to believe I've been in Pensacola for less than a week. In some ways, it feels like it's been one really, really long day, and in other ways, it feels like I've been here forever.

I shift on the bed, trying to get comfortable. It's a little lumpy, but we've lived in worse places.

I hold out the soup. "Please, eat it. For me."

"Fine." Noli takes the bowl from me and starts stirring it. "I'm still mad at you."

I cross my arms and wait for her to continue.

"You shouldn't be here, taking care of me, looking after me. You have your own life."

I scoff. "As if I'd leave you in the hospital alone. Come on, Noli."

"I know. I know. But I feel so guilty." Her eyes well up with tears. "I should be able to handle myself. I'm a grown woman."

I scoot up on the bed and grab the bowl back from her, setting it on the end table before wrapping her in a giant hug. This is why I'm here. Because my baby sister is going through it right now. Her self-confidence is in the toilet. She broke up with Nelson the second she regained consciousness, but she's still rattled by what happened.

"Even grown women need hugs. And help," I say, gripping her tighter. "It's okay, Noli."

"It doesn't feel okay."

I hold her close before broaching what has become a touchy subject between the two of us. "Are you sure you don't want to press charges?"

She stiffens. "I want to be done with it. I don't want to give him my time or thoughts. I don't ever want to see him again." She's quiet for a second. "It was my own fault for letting it get this far. I'm an idiot."

"Nothing about this was your fault, and you most certainly are not an idiot." My voice is firm.

I think she's embarrassed that it happened to her, a self-proclaimed tough girl. She works in law enforcement. She takes calls dealing with domestic abuse all the time. She feels like she should have seen it coming and prevented it.

I guess when you're in it, it's hard to be thinking or seeing clearly until it's too late.

Nelson shoving her down the stairs was a wake-up call of the worst kind.

Bile tickles the back of my throat at the thought of him. Thank God Noli's injuries turned out to be pretty minor, all things considered. She has bruises on her arms from where he grabbed her, and she ended up with a level-three concussion and stitches near her temple from where she hit her head against the metal railing.

It could have been so, so much worse.

I truly believe Noli could get some closure if she brought Nelson to justice, but she keeps resisting. I can't force her to do anything, and I know she has to deal with this in her own way.

But she's not going to deal with it alone.

I pull back, keeping my hands loosely gripping her arms. "I'm here for you. Always. You know that, right? I'm happy to be here."

Noli nods, biting her lip. "Thanks, Poppy."

I reach for the soup and hand it back to her, knowing full well she's embarrassed and doesn't want to dwell on what she perceives to be her weakness. To need anyone has never been Noli's forte. "Here. Eat."

She slurps up several spoonfuls. I resist the urge to tell her to please not make those noises, because she's a grown-up and she can eat soup how she wants to eat soup. But honestly, it's about as cringy as the turtle's sound effects.

My spirits dip at the thought.

I miss Mack.

I'm mad at Mack.

My feelings are all over the board.

Noli finishes her bowl and sets it on the end table, stirring me from my thoughts. "You always were a soup master. That was good." She rests back on her bed and closes her eyes. "You need to leave," she says.

"Demanding much?" I keep my voice light and reach for the bowl, going to stand. "I'll let you rest."

"No. I mean you need to leave Pensacola." She opens her eyes. "You need to go back to Cashmere Cove."

I take a fortifying breath. "We've been over this, Noli. I'm staying here with you for a while, making sure you get back on your feet."

"I'm already on my feet. I'm fine."

I scowl. *Fine is not having a boyfriend who pushes you down the stairs.* I don't say that out loud.

Noli crosses her arms and gives me an unrelenting look. I remember this stubborn streak of hers well from high school. "I will not be the reason you give up on love."

"Who said I was giving up on love?"

Noli rolls her eyes. "Come on, Pops."

"No, I'm serious! I'm not giving up on anything. Mack and I are fine. We're—we're…"

"You're what? You don't know at this point because you're here with me, and you got into a fight with him that you are dragging your feet to resolve. Don't get me wrong, I'm grateful. I truly am." She sits forward and puts her hand on my arm. "You came when I needed you. You found me this place to live. But you don't need to linger here."

"I'm not lingering. You still need me." My voice comes out a little higher pitched than I'd like. Because being here, with her…this is what I'm good at. I've always been good at being there for my sisters. It's a part of my identity at this point. I'm not sure how to make anything else my focus. I guess you could call this my comfort zone.

Noli's eyes are kind. "Of course I need you, and I know you're always going to be here for me. Right now, I'm being there for you. I'm telling you you're going back to Cashmere Cove. I've already booked your flight."

"What?"

Noli shrugs. "With the help of Rose."

I cock my head, narrowing my gaze. I'm the big sister. I'm supposed to be the one who does the planning, coordinating, and overall logistical work of the Kasper family.

"Don't look at me like that." Noli points her finger at me. "You know best most of the time, Pops, but right now, you're going to sabotage a chance at legitimate happiness. Why?"

I slump down into the bed. "He lied to me."

Noli nods as if she were expecting this. I told my sisters every-thing about the email debacle as soon as we knew Noli wasn't seriously injured.

"He did," she agrees.

"So, that's it."

"That's what?"

"I don't know. I have trust issues, Noli." I throw up my hands.

She nods again, all even-keeled. Meanwhile, I feel like I'm spi-raling.

"Let me ask you a question," she says. "You've known Mack for three months, correct?"

"Give or take."

"And in that time, has he done anything to you that would make you question his intentions or his integrity?"

"Well, no," I admit. "Not until the truth about the emails came out. But how do I know if I can believe him about anything else going forward?"

Noli stares me down. "I think you know the answer to that question," she says quietly.

I swallow against the lump in my throat. Because I *do*. I've known it from the beginning. Mack is a good man. He's honest and hardworking, and he looks out for me. He wants what's best for me. I don't believe he had any ill intentions where the emails were concerned.

I start massaging my temples. "The truth is, now that I left town, I'm terrified of pursuing something with Mack. My feelings for him are so strong they scare me, and what if he leaves me like Dad did?"

I glance over to find Noli watching me with a look I don't recognize in her eyes. I cringe. "I'm sorry. I shouldn't have said that."

Now Noli looks affronted. "Why not?"

I wave my hands around in a circle. "Because. You shouldn't have to worry about my daddy issues."

Noli snorts. "We all share the same daddy issues."

"But I should be able to handle it. I don't need you and Rose to be worried about me."

"Well, newsflash: we care about you like you care about us. We want you to be happy. We certainly don't expect you to be the only one to carry the family's crosses."

I sit back, stunned. "I...well, okay. That's nice of you to say."

Noli shrugs. "It's the truth. We're all in this together. Which is why I'm sending you back to Cashmere Cove where you belong."

"I...how do you know that's where I belong?"

Noli swishes her hand through the air. "It's plain as day, even over video calls, that you are made for each other. Rose confirmed it. She said that when you were together, it was like magic."

I pull in a breath. Mack Bradley is a lot like magic. I feel full of awe and wonder around him.

Noli leans back against the bed. "He's a good man. Don't let your fear or your misplaced sense of duty to me or Rose or whoever stop you from pursuing a future with him."

I open my mouth, not sure what argument I can make against that. Noli stops me before I can get started.

"Is there a chance you'll get hurt? Of course. There's always that chance. But is there a greater chance that this could be something good for you? I'd say so. If I were you, I'd take those odds."

I nod. It's time to put on my metaphorical fancy underwear. "Okay. When's my flight?"

Noli cheers, and it's the happiest and most energetic I've seen her in the days since I've arrived. She pulls me into a hug.

"You're the best big sister a girl could ask for, Pops. Time to go and get your man."

30

HANG THE MOON

Mack

"No, no, no!" Mayor Witmore bellows. I glance up from the lights I'm finagling to see him stalking across the grassy space and over to where a group of volunteers is setting up tables and chairs. "That's where the food trucks will be parked. Haven't you seen the map?" He wields a sheet of paper, waving it in the face of one of the men. "Poppy Kasper left a map. Do follow it, and everything will run smoothly."

It's the eve of Party in the Park, and I'm exhausted. I'm trying to get the lights up at the pavilion and grounds outside the lighthouse, but my heart isn't in it. Everything would be different if Poppy was here.

She's not. So it's just me, and my thoughts, and this endless strand of twinkle lights. The late-August sun is beating down on my back, and I'm trying not to think about how the one woman I want to spend the day with tomorrow is six states away.

And apparently, I'm not the only one missing her.

Mayor Witmore clearly appreciates her map of the day's events. Heather has been stalking around, getting the kids' rides set up. There are signs plastered all over town for the teen scavenger hunt that Poppy coordinated. I heard through the grapevine that they had over thirty kids signed up to participate. My shoulders roll inward. Everything is better when Poppy's around.

And I went and broke her trust.

I want to bash my head into a wall.

"Why are you wasting your time on that?"

I freeze at the sound of Tricia's voice, dripping with its usual disdainful tone.

I straighten my shoulders, take a steadying breath, and turn around. "Pardon me?"

Tricia is standing with her hands on her hips outside the pavilion that I'm currently frosting with enough lights to put the national Christmas tree to shame. She gestures to the roofline. "All the lights. Is it worth it?"

I can't tell if her question is rhetorical or not, so I stay quiet.

She shrugs. "No one cares what the venue looks like as long as there are drinks and good music. Why don't you leave it?"

"I don't mind finishing up." I turn back to the job and continue looping the strand of lights I'm gripping around the nearest rafter.

Tricia scoffs. "Seriously? Why put yourself out like this? You must be miserable. Go home and get some rest, Mack."

I stiffen. I hardly think I'm going to take orders from Tricia. But she is right. I am miserable. This is tedious, back-breaking work. I have so much else I could be doing, but...

"I promised Poppy."

Tricia shoots me a disbelieving look and then makes a dramatic show of looking to her left and right. "I don't see Poppy anywhere around here. I think you're off the hook."

I try to hide my wince. Of course Tricia would know where to poke my open wound.

"I'm almost done," I say, trying to steer the conversation away from the fact that Poppy isn't here, so Tricia is right—my main motivation for creating the proper ambiance for the Promenade is no longer around. Nor does she want anything to do with me at the moment.

Still, I couldn't *not* do it. I promised her.

"You're a sucker for punishment, Mack." Tricia shakes her head. "Why are you letting that woman have such an effect on you? Especially since she up and left."

I grip the lights so hard the wire strand digs into the skin of my palm. That's not what happened. She didn't leave me. She had a good reason for going. I know that.

But it's still hard to believe that Poppy truly ever wanted to be with me. And it's agonizing to think that she doesn't know what to think about me now that I wasn't honest with her.

"I don't see how it's any of your business," I mumble.

"I'm trying to look out for you, that's all. Women like Poppy"—Tricia clicks her tongue—"they breeze into town, make swooping changes, charm the pants off of everyone and their mother, but then they're gone again before the dust settles. I mean, she bounced from Holland to you, right? Didn't you find that odd? She was using you."

I grind my jaw, but it doesn't stop my stomach from lurching. I don't believe that about Poppy. I *refuse* to believe that about Poppy.

Tricia is watching me, and I know she sees my insecurities plastered all across my face. After all, we dated for several years. She knows the complex I have about never being good enough. She reaches out and pats me on the arm. Her contact turns my blood to ice.

"I just don't want to see you get hurt."

With that, she turns on her heel and strides away.

She gets in two steps before I come to my senses, all sorts of thoughts and feelings and emotions cascading to the surface and pressing against my mouth. "Tricia, wait a minute."

She turns and raises a sculpted brow.

"You hurt me," I say.

She opens her mouth, an uncertain glow flickering in her eyes, but I hold up my hand. I need to say this.

"All those years ago, when you cheated on me, you hurt me."

"Please don't." She darts her head around, apparently still terrified that someone will find out her secret.

"I'm not going to out you, but I want you to hear me out. You hurt me when you cheated. You hurt me when you drug my reputation through the mud. When you lied about me to everyone I care about. I never understood why, when all I'd ever done was try to protect you."

Tricia is dangerously close to tears. I hate making women cry, but I can't bring myself to stop now.

"I was hurt. By you. All those years ago. And I let myself keep being hurt because I didn't think I deserved anything better." I steady my breathing. "Until Poppy," I add. "So yeah, I'm going to hang the twinkle lights, and I'm going to make this spot gorgeous because she wanted it like that. You don't have to worry about her hurting me, Tricia. Take those concerns elsewhere. Because Poppy Kasper does the opposite of cause me pain. I'd hang the moon for her if that's what she asked. I'd rearrange every single star in the sky for her."

Tricia is slack-jawed and staring back at me.

My chest heaves.

That felt good.

"That's all," I say. "You can go now."

She blinks. "Um, okay. Right. Whatever."

She stalks off.

I shake my head and am about to get started restringing lights when a slow, golf clap breaks out from the tree line. I squint into the dusky night as a figure approaches.

"Holland?"

"The one and only." He steps in front of me. "Bring it in, man." He pulls me into a bro embrace, slapping me on the back. I wait for him to release me, but he doesn't. Instead, he squishes me firmly into a full-fledged hug. It's a little awkward because I'm holding this string of lights, but I manage to get my arms out and around him and hug him back.

Eventually, he pulls away.

I release the breath I was holding, but I suck it right back in when my eyes catch on Collin.

He steps out of the shadows behind Holland, and from his stunned expression, I know in an instant they both overheard my conversation with Collin's sister.

"Tricia cheated on you?"

"Collin, I—"

"Why didn't you say something?"

I shrug. "It wasn't worth it."

Collin looks exasperated. "Wasn't worth it? Your reputation got shredded, and you don't think the truth was worth it?"

This is so typical of Collin. He's completely by the book. And he's a lot like Holland in terms of his golden-boy status. What he fails to see is that if I would have told the truth about what happened between Tricia and me all those years ago, if people would have believed me, then it would have been her life in shambles.

"I would have hated myself if I'd have driven a wedge into the cornerstone of your family."

Collin flinches, and I can tell he's thinking about his dad. His jaw flexes, and he nods once. "Thank you," he says quietly.

"Don't mention it."

Holland slaps me on the back again. "Well, now that we've aired all our dirty laundry, what's left to do?"

I roll my eyes. Only my brother could manage to diffuse the heavy tension of a situation with his complete lack of awareness at how intense things had gotten.

I shove a strand of lights into Holland's chest. "How do you feel about manual labor? I could use some help."

Holland starts grumbling. "That's not necessarily what I had in—"

"Start stringing this around that pole. When you get to the top, hold the strand in place." I shoo him away.

"I can't go and get electrocuted, Mack. My next tournament is in less than two weeks. My coach will kill me."

I walk away from him, knowing full well he'll do what I asked.

Collin is silent as he takes up a strand of lights I extend in his direction.

"Are we okay?" I ask, letting Holland prattle on in the background about how he can't imagine why I picked the career I picked.

Collin nods. "I feel like I should have known. I should have suspected something. I'm a crappy friend."

"You are not. You're the only one who didn't disown me. I always thought you did know."

Collin tips his head. "I had my suspicions that things weren't as they seemed, but still, Mack. You fell on the sword, and for what? Tricia has been an absolute witch."

I shake my head.

He levels me with a look. "She has. I'm allowed to say so as her brother."

"Fine. You're right. But it's water under the bridge. There's no need for you to confront her about it. Please don't. It's what I've been trying to avoid all these years. And I was fine with it, truly, until..." I trail off, my throat suddenly constricting.

"Until Poppy," Collin fills in.

I offer him a terse nod.

"Have you talked to her?"

I get back to work, talking to the sky instead of meeting his eyes. Together, we get the lights in place. "No." I fill him in on the email situation. "I broke her trust, and I hate myself for it. I think I ruined my chances."

Collin is quiet.

I chance a glance in his direction, and he's staring back at me. I hate the pity in his eyes.

"What do I do?" I ask.

"Have you apologized?"

I shrug. "Barely. She was rushing to get out of town when it all blew up. She's got more to worry about, taking care of Noli, and I know that. I just…I wish she were here."

"Have you told her that?"

"I doubt she wants to come back here now."

"Maybe not, but you owe it to yourself to be honest. And isn't that what she'd want from you too? You don't have anyone to protect in this case, Mack. God knows you deserve to be happy. Tell her the truth about how you feel, and see what happens."

"Yo, guys." Holland waves his free hand, grabbing my attention from where he's standing, dutifully holding the end of the strand of lights above his head, just as I told him to. "I know I have enviable upper body strength, but can we get this show on the road? My rotator cuff hates me, and I kind of need it to be in good condition."

"Coming." I finish tacking up the strand I'm working on and jog across the pavilion to Holland, letting Collin's declaration rattle around my brain.

You deserve to be happy.

It's like it's on a ticker tape running across my brain for the rest of the night as we finish setting up.

I spot Rose when she arrives with Mia. The two of them have put together a storybook walk for the kids, so they're tacking up pages of a picture book all throughout the park.

I don't know where I stand with Poppy's sister. I'm assuming she knows about the emails. She hasn't gone out of her way to avoid me since Poppy left, but she hasn't been chummy either.

I should wait until Rose separates herself from Mia before I try to talk to her about Poppy, because if Mia overhears me, she'll report back to Patrick, who will tell Lou, and then I'll be the laughingstock of my friends, but honestly, I don't care all that much at this point. I'm going to have to man-up here and take my lumps.

I march over. Rose and Mia see me coming. Mia says something and then walks in the opposite direction. Rose stands up straight from where she's tapped a stake into the ground, her expression unreadable.

"Rose." I dip my head. "How's Noli?"

"Noli will be fine. She's tough as nails. She'll recover from this. We'll make sure of it."

I nod. "And Poppy?"

The corners of Rose's mouth lift ever so slightly. "In her element, mothering one of us."

My throat feels like sandpaper. I swallow. How am I supposed to ask if she's contemplating coming back, if she's thought of me, when she's tied up with important things—like making sure her sister has the support she needs in the wake of an abusive relationship. "That's good. Good to hear."

I turn to go, but Rose reaches out a hand.

"Mack, hey, wait."

I pause, hope soaring up from the ground and filling my lungs.

"For what it's worth, I wouldn't hold the emails against you," Rose says.

I meet her gaze. "And Poppy?"

She looks away and shrugs. "She'll have to make her own decision."

My lungs deflate, hope sucked straight out of them and down into the ground like a vacuum. "I understand."

Rose studies me closely before nodding. "See you tomorrow?"

"I'll be here."

· · · · ● · ● · ● · ● · ·

The next day unfolds pretty much like it does every year. Party in the Park is a hot, sticky mess of a good time. Kids are screaming. Adults are laughing. Music blares through speakers throughout the day, and the mingling smell of fried food from all the different food trucks permeates the air like potpourri. There are a bunch of teenagers flitting around this year, and all credit goes to Poppy for that.

I do my best to shove down thoughts of her over the course of the day, but it's nearly impossible when I see her fingerprints on every aspect of the party—not only the scavenger hunt for the teens, but also the wider array of food trucks, the pavilion set up for the Promenade later tonight, and the porta-potties that I helped her coordinate.

Poppy is everywhere except the one place I want her to be—in my arms.

I have lunch with my family and am content to let Holland do most of the talking.

I spot Tricia running the kids' games part of the party later in the afternoon. When her gaze connects with mine, instead of the scowl I've grown accustomed to, she looks wary. I nod at her, and she relaxes, giving me a small nod in response.

It's sort of strange to not be on the receiving end of her ire, but I'll take it.

By the time the Promenade gets under way at eight o'clock, the sky is dimmed to a muted charcoal gray and the air has cooled to a pleasant seventy-five degrees. The lighthouse light is illuminated, casting a warm glow over the grounds of the park, and the lights I've strung up around the pavilion add an extra *oomph* to the scene.

If only Poppy were here to see her vision come to life. I'd like to think I made her proud.

Willow Dunlap is in her element, shoving couples onto the dance floor. Ernest is posted near the speakers, gazing with admiration at his wife. He eventually catches her hand and pulls her in close. They fall into a sweet two-step. My heart clenches, and I have to look away.

When I do, I spy Mia and Patrick, who appear from behind the lighthouse. Mia tugs on the hem of her shirt. Her cheeks are flushed, and she shoots her husband a sly grin. Patrick, for his part, looks besotted.

And this is my cue to leave.

I take off in the direction of my truck, knowing I'll catch flak from everyone for leaving early. But I can't be here without Poppy. It's too much.

"Leaving so soon?"

Piper's voice cuts through the crowd, and I spin back around.

My cousin and her new husband are beaming back at me as they stroll over from the dance floor.

I don't have the energy to muster up a smile in return. "Uh, yeah. I'm tired."

"You'll miss the fireworks," Piper argues.

Since I'm pretty sure no fireworks will ever match the ones from Wool Beach that went off after Poppy and I shared our first kiss, I couldn't care less.

I press my fingers to my temples. "I've got a migraine coming on. The noise would make it worse." I offer up an apologetic shrug, not sorry for my white lie.

Piper's expression turns to one of concern. "Do you need a ride home? I could—"

"No," I cut her off, holding up my hand. "It's fine. I'll be fine. You guys enjoy the night."

I slink off into the night before she can get another word in and mercifully manage to dodge both my parents and anyone else who may have had the intention of halting my progress.

I make the drive back to my place in silence. The Cashmere Cove streets are deserted since everyone is at the park.

Once inside, I flop face-first down on my couch. Maybe I'll sleep here tonight. I don't have the energy to move. I'm emotionally and physically spent, like a wrinkled up dollar bill that someone keeps trying to flatten out and shove back into the vending machine.

I'm in a state of half-sleep, half-wakefulness when I hear the first thud.

I nearly fall off the couch. What in the world was that?

I glance at my phone to check the time, and only twenty-five minutes have passed since I made it home.

Thud.

There it is again. It's coming from the backyard.

I take off through the house, trying to shake off the sleep that was about to overtake me before the walls started shaking.

Thud.

I swing open the back door on my side of the duplex and push the screen door out. What meets my ears is the sweetest string of curse words I ever did hear.

RIGHT BACK

Poppy

"**O**pen up, you worthless piece of—"

A throat clears behind me.

I whirl around to find Mack leaning up against the barrier separating the two sides of the deck off the back of his duplex. He's got his arms crossed. His expression is a mixture of wariness and hope.

"Hi," I say.

"Having trouble?"

"Yes! This stupid door won't open. Again. Didn't you have it fixed? Why does it hate me?"

He takes a step in my direction, but then pulls up short, like he's uncertain how I'd react to him coming any closer. "I don't think anyone or anything could hate you, Poppy."

Before I can say anything, he's speaking again.

"I'm so sorry about the emails. It was stupid of me to go along with Holland in the first place. I should have told you about it, but I sort of got caught up in getting to know you myself, and I swear the emails paled in comparison to what I was learning about you on my own. Then, when everything happened with us, I guess I got my wires crossed and my brain short-circuited, and I spaced on mentioning it."

I fight a smile. "Are you trying to appease me with an electrician joke?"

Mack opens his mouth and then closes it. In the glow of the string lights, I see his lips quirk. "Is it working?"

"Oh yeah. I can't resist you when you talk electrician to me, you know that."

He takes a slow step forward. "Do you really forgive me, Poppy? Truly? I'm so sorry."

"Stop. I forgive you. Do I wish you would have been up front with me? Of course. I felt betrayed, and it was the worst because it was you, and I've come to trust you."

"I know. I hate myself for it."

I give my head a firm shake. "It's over and done with. What's important is that we're honest with each other going forward."

"Going forward?"

I bite my lip. "Dang it. This isn't how any of this was supposed to go. I had grand plans."

"Grand plans?" he echoes, continuing his progression across the deck.

"Yes! I was trying to drop my stuff off quick. Then, I was going to surprise you over at the Party in the Park. But I couldn't get this darn door to open, and it got me all frazzled."

He makes a humming noise and comes to a stop right in front of me.

I pull in a breath, and it's all Mack—mint and leather. I close my eyes and savor it.

"Boo?"

"Mmhmm." I lazily open my eyes, and when I meet Mack's gaze, he's looking at me with such tenderness I swear my bones liquefy.

I fall into him, and he catches me up in his arms, pressing me against his chest in the best hug of my life.

One of his hands is behind my head, coiled up in my hair. His other arm is clamped fully around my waist, and I'm pretty sure I'm going to live here now. I don't want to move again. Ever.

My hands are greedy, and I work them out so I can run them up and down his muscled arms. I reach up and scrape my fingers into the hair along his nape as he drops his head and buries his nose into the skin along my neck column.

"You're here," he whispers, placing featherlight kisses on my jawline, my cheek, behind my ear, the corner of my mouth.

"I'm here."

"Hi," he says, leaning back to look at me.

I grin. "Hi. I missed you."

"That's my fault."

I drop my head. "Not totally. I didn't handle leaving well. I got tunnel vision on Noli and didn't communicate with you how I should have. My sisters say I was self-sabotaging, focusing only on them instead of on myself to prevent anyone else from ever getting close enough to hurt me again like my dad hurt me when he left." I grimace. "Sorry, that's a lot. Probably more than you bargained for. You can tell me to shut up."

Mack shakes his head. "Absolutely not. Listening to you talk is one of my very favorite things."

I wrap my hands fully around his torso and rest my head against his heart. "Thank you."

I feel his cheek come down on the top of my head. "How long can you stay?"

I lean back so I can look at him when I deliver my punchline. "That depends."

A crease appears between his eyes. "On what?"

"On how long you'll have me."

He cocks his head. "Boo..."

"Big..." I parrot.

"What's that supposed to mean?"

"I'm here for good—if that's okay. I mean, I want to move to Cashmere Cove. Mostly to be close to you, but also because I love the job I have here, and Rose loves it here, and Noli is going to move up here for a fresh start, so I hope you'll have me because, otherwise, this is going to be embarrassing, and awkward, and—"

Mack's lips are on mine, effectively giving me the answer I hoped for. And what a relief it is. His kiss is sure and steady, and I wrap my arms around his neck and hold on. He takes his time, and the edges of my reality blur. All thoughts flee except *him* and *us* and *this*.

When we break for air, he gazes into my eyes, reaching up with both hands and using the pads of his finger to trace the lines of my face—around my forehead, down over my cheekbones and chin—like he's taking note of the blueprint of me. His hands are calloused and rough against my skin, but his touch is gentle.

I catch his hands with mine and cradle them to my cheeks, closing my eyes. I could stand here, under the stars and twinkle lights, with him holding me for the rest of my days.

"Boo, I have to tell you something."

I blink to look at him. "What is it?"

"I love you."

Tears spring into my eyes because I know he means those words. I know it down to the core of my being. I trust him enough to believe it.

I open my mouth, about to echo his sentiment, but I see that he's not quite finished.

"In one of your first emails to Holland, you mentioned looking up at the sky, right?"

I nod.

"Then, you told me later that whenever you've felt lost, or drifting, or like you weren't sure what to do or where to turn, you'd look up at the sky and feel grounded."

I cock my head and wait. Where is he going with this?

"You are my sky. When I look at you, I'm grounded. I know exactly where I'm supposed to be. It's with you."

A tear leaks out of the corner of my eye, and he catches it with the pad of his thumb, brushing it softly off my cheek. I never want to forget how absolutely cherished I feel. I don't think I'll have the chance to because I'm certain Mack is going to make me feel this way forever.

I blink my eyes open. "I love you, Mack Bradley. I love you right back."

EPILOGUE

Noli

"Come on. Come on. Come ON." I slam my hand against the steering wheel and crane my neck to the side, trying to peer out the window of my car. What is the holdup?

The map on my phone says I'm only twenty minutes from Poppy and Rose's house, but it may as well be twenty hours at the rate I'm going. I jiggle my knee in the confined space of my driver's seat. I've been on the road for almost a day, making the long trek up from Florida, and I hit major traffic coming through Chicago, which soured my mood to no end.

Now I'm stuck behind a literal tractor, and I can't even.

This is like every country song lyric there ever was. Except, it's not the least bit romantic.

It's pushing seven o'clock. It's mostly dark outside. It's raining. What sort of work could a tractor possibly be doing given the circumstances, anyway?

I swerve my car slightly over the center line to get a better view. There is nothing but open roads ahead. All I need to do is get around this guy.

I accelerate and fly past him, pushing eighty-five miles per hour until I'm sure I'm clear of him, and then I slow my speed.

"Thank goodness." I set the cruise control and hope for no more issues on my way into Cashmere Cove.

I've heard nothing but happy things about this place from Poppy and Rose, and it better be the freaking oasis they've painted it to be after the trip I've made.

I try to relax my shoulders. It's going to be great. This is the fresh start I need. A clean slate. I'm leaving Nelson—the jerk-wad—and all his stupid games in my rearview mirror.

Hey, wait.

Speaking of rearview mirrors, red and blue lights start flashing behind me.

"No, no, no," I chant, angling my car over to the side of the road. "Not now. I'm so close."

I rest my head against my car's headrest before chancing another look in my mirror. A hulking figure emerges from the front seat of the cop car that pulled up behind me. He strides with purpose toward my window, and I roll it down, greeting him with the best smile I can muster given my lack of sleep and complete annoyance at the fact that this dude pulled me over less than twenty miles from my destination.

"Officer," I say respectfully. "Quite the weather we're having." I don't know what compels me to talk like I'm a local, but a little small talk never hurt anyone, and I'd like to get this guy on my side.

"Yes, quite."

He looks at me as rain rivulets trickle down the sides of his clean-shaven face. His jaw is square, and his green eyes are both glistening and unrelenting.

"Do you have any idea why I pulled you over?"

I hold up empty hands in a shrug.

"You were speeding."

"Only to get around the tractor, and then I slowed—"

"And you passed in a no passing zone." He hooks his thumb over his shoulder to the left side of the road where a yellow, triangular sign is barely visible through the sheets of rain that are falling from the sky.

Well, shoot.

I paste on my best-looking innocent smile. "I am so sorry. I'm new to town, and I'm not familiar with the signage around here. I promise it won't happen again."

"Your license and registration papers, please, ma'am."

Oh, come on! He's not going to give me a ticket, is he? I was literally endangering no one.

"Look, Officer. It is miserable out here, and I'm sure you don't want to go through the hassle of jogging back and forth between my car and yours while you write up my citation. Can you let me off with a warning and call it good?"

He's staring at me, nonplussed. I bat my eyelashes for good measure, but all he does is squint against the rain and hold out his hand.

"Please." I'm begging now. "I have somewhere I need to be."

"Then you'd do well to do as I ask so we can get this over with."

I press my lips together and reach for my purse. I produce my license and smack it into his outstretched hand. I have to rummage through my glove compartment, but eventually I find my insurance card and registration paperwork. In the couple minutes it takes me, the cop is getting drenched.

Like it's basically approaching levels of waterboarding torture for him out there.

I can't help but take some smug satisfaction in that.

Serves him right for being such a stick-in-the-mud.

"Here you go."

He takes my documents back to his squad car and leaves me fuming.

Here's the rub. I know cops. I work with them daily. So I know that the minor infraction I committed doesn't merit anything more than a light slap on the wrist...if that.

The rain lets up so I can see out my windows again, and I study him in my rearview mirror. He's got the light on in his squad car, and he's typing something into the computer that's built into his console.

He looks very official, and my best guess is that he does everything by the book.

A classic overachiever.

He's hot too, and I bet he knows it.

I hate this man on principle, and I really hate him because I'm going to be out real, live money when this is all said and done. Not to mention what it'll do to my insurance premium.

All that, and I'm surely missing Poppy's engagement at this point.

Curse this hot cop. Curse him real good.

By the time he strolls back to my window, I can practically feel steam billowing from my ears.

He hands over my license and other documents, along with a brand-spanking-new citation. In spite of my anger, my cheeks burn. I hate being in the wrong, and though I still don't believe I did anything majorly wrong, the ticket says otherwise.

"You'll need to pay this online or in person at the Cashmere Cove Police Department."

"Fine. Yeah. Whatever." I face the windshield. "Are we done here?"

I should respect the police, I know. But I'm over this guy. I'm over his approach. I want to get to my sisters' house.

When the cop doesn't answer me, I swing my gaze to him.

He's staring back at me with a look I can't quite read. "It's my job to keep the community safe, ma'am."

I fight off an eye roll. And it's my job to try to be a good sister and be there for Poppy on the biggest day of her life thus far, but *here I am.* "Of course it is. Can I go?"

He holds out his hand, motioning to the road ahead as if to say, *By all means.*

As I start to roll up my window, he says, "I'm just doing my job."

I cut him with a disdainful look, praying I never see this guy again, and take off.

• • • • ● • ● • • •

I make it to the duplex that Poppy and Mack share in less than fifteen minutes—no speeding required. *Take that, hot cop who I hate!*

Poppy flings the door open and engulfs me in a giant hug. "We're engaged!" she shrieks, and my heart clenches and then expands.

I'm so happy for my big sister. No one deserves to find this sort of joy more.

Mack follows her and opens his arms. I step into them. I've never met him in person, but I feel like I've known him forever.

"Congratulations, you two! Sorry I missed the main event. I got pulled over by this stupid cop on the outskirts of town. He was a complete jerk, and—"

Mack's eyes flit up and over my head.

I turn and follow his gaze. My stomach drops to the floorboards at the sight of Hot Cop, still drenched, still square-jawed, still not smiling, standing inside my sister's entryway.

Poppy loops her arm through mine, looking back and forth between me and the man I'd like to fillet. "Uh, Noli, I guess you've already met Mack's best friend, Collin."

"One of Cashmere Cove's finest police officers and, coincidentally, the newly appointed head of the Emergency Management and Telecommunication Department," Mack puts in.

"Aka, your new boss." Collin extends his hand to me, and when I see the cocky grin slash across his face, I wish I could cut it off.

So much for a clean slate.

• • • • ● • ● • • •

Need more of Noli and Collin? Read *Enemies Don't*, the second book in the Fall In Love series.

ACKNOWLEDGMENTS

All glory to God, now and forever.

Well, I went and wrote a romcom. I wasn't planning on it, and I told myself I probably wouldn't have time to write it for the next three to five years. But the story had other ideas and literally would not leave me alone. And that's how this book ended up in your hands!

Dear reader, thanks for taking a chance on it. If you've been here from the beginning, I'm so grateful you jumped genres with me (again!), and I can't tell you how much your support means. Thanks for every kind word, every message, and every review.

If this is the first time you've read one of my books, I'm so glad you found me! And thank you for reading. I hope this sweet story felt like a warm hug.

Melody Jeffries, thanks for lending your time and talent to the cover. You brought Poppy and Mack to life with your illustration, and it is stunning. I'm so glad our paths crossed.

Once again, thank you to Jenn Lockwood for your keen eye and editing superpowers. You make my books shine.

Thanks, as always, to the librarians, booksellers, bookstagrammers, and readers whom I've had the pleasure of working with. You make the book world go around, and your enthusiasm makes my day.

A massive shout-out to my beta readers, Amanda and Sam, for giving thoughtful feedback and doing a lot of cheerleading in the early days. I wasn't sure if I could hack it as a romcom author, but you made me believe I could.

Thank you to *the* book club for listening to me gush about this idea well before it was a book. Your excitement for it from day one has meant the world, and the way you continue to show up for me blows my mind. I love you all.

To my family, I'm so grateful for your continued love and support. I love you right back.

To my kids, I'm so proud to be your mom, and I'd hang the moon for you.

To Nick, thanks for all of it, especially for telling me all those years ago that we couldn't be just friends. You were right. I love you madly.

ABOUT THE AUTHOR

LEAH DOBRINSKA is the author of the Fall In Love series, the Larkspur Library Mysteries, a cozy mystery series set in the Wisconsin Northwoods, and the Mapleton novels, a series of award-winning standalone small town romances. She earned her degree in English Literature from UW-Madison where she was awarded the Dean's Prize and served as a Writing Fellow. She has since worked as a freelance writer, editor, and content marketer. Leah lives in Wisconsin with her husband and their gaggle of kids. When she's not writing, handing out snacks, or visiting the local library, Leah enjoys reading and running.

www.leahdobrinska.com
Instagram: @whatleahwrote